To TERRI — THANKS!

THE REDEMPTION OF

LONNIE TATE

Book One: The Pentangelo Group

THE
REDEMPTION
OF LONNIE TATE

LOREN GUS
MARSTERS+KOERNIG

Golden Alley Press
Emmaus, Pennsylvania

The Redemption of Lonnie Tate is a work of fiction. References to real people, real places, or historical events are all used fictitiously. Other people, places, and events are the product of the authors' imaginations, and any resemblance to actual places, events, or people, whether living or dead, is purely coincidental.

Golden Alley Press
37 S. Sixth Street
Emmaus, PA 18049

www.goldenalleypress.com

The text of this book is set in Adobe Caslon
Book design by Michael Sayre

Printed in the United States of America

The Redemption of Lonnie Tate / Loren Marsters + Gus Koernig

Library of Congress Control Number: 2018946748

ISBN 978-0-9984429-8-3 print
ISBN 978-0-9984429-9-0 ebook

Golden Alley Press books may be purchased in bulk for educational, business, or sales promotional use. For information please contact the publisher.

Photograph of the authors © Ryne O'Reilly

Cover design by Michael Sayre

10 9 8 7 6 5 4 3 2 1

To Kristina, for your never-ending love.
When I first met you, I knew you would change
my life forever. — Loren

To Glenda, for showing me every day just
how "good" good can be — Gus

MARSTERS + KOERNIG

PROLOGUE

SIMI VALLEY, CALIFORNIA
9 MARCH 1966

Lonnie Tate was a screw-up, and he knew it.

He was the kind of kid who did things—crazy things—without ever thinking about the consequences.

On any given weekday, you could find the eighteen-year-old hanging out in the parking lot of Roy's Café with three or four other guys his age: all smartass, medium-bright, semi-charming, underachieving screw-ups. Unlike the other boys, Lonnie's screw-ups usually ended up with him riding in the back of a police car.

About noon on one particular day, two Ventura County Sheriff's deputies assigned to patrol the Simi Valley-Moorpark area made their usual stop at Roy's to pick up burgers and fries. For some reason, the deputies left the windows on their patrol car rolled down—and the keys in the ignition.

Walking over to the driver's side of the patrol car, Lonnie opened the door and climbed in.

VENTURA COUNTY SUPERIOR COURT, RM. 125
JUDGE HARRISON "MAXIMUM MAC" MACLAMORE PRESIDING
4 DAYS LATER

Judge Mac grabbed his gavel and jabbed the tip at Lonnie.

"This is the tenth time in two years you've stood in front of me, Tate. You're 18 now. You're an adult. Stealing a police car is a felony."

He leaned forward, a Cheshire cat grin creeping across his face. "Here's what you're going to do." He leaned back in his chair, the grin replaced by a joyful smile.

"By the end of the day today, you're going into the military. Or, you're going to be a guest at one of our state facilities, for a term much longer than what you'd serve with Uncle Sam. Maybe that will straighten you out. From what I hear, the stockade makes state time look like a trip to Disneyland."

The walkway from the courthouse to the recruiters' offices was lined with recruiting posters.

The Marine Corps poster stopped Lonnie dead in his tracks. It was the uniform the Marine in the poster wore. The Dress Blues.

So, with no more thought than he devoted to stealing the police car, Lonnie Tate joined the Marine Corps.

RECEIVING BARRACKS MCRD
SAN DIEGO, CALIFORNIA
15 MARCH 1966
2200 HOURS

From the high-and-tight haircut to the toes of his spit-shined shoes, the drill instructor looked just like the Marine in the recruiting poster. Except the Marine in the recruiting poster had a neck.

The rigid brim of his "Smokey" was tilted down on his forehead, partially concealing two carnivorous eyes. His voice and stride were deliberate. His ability to use one specific four-letter word as a noun, a verb, an adverb, and an adjective was almost poetic. His message was clear: for the next eight weeks, they could give their souls to God, because their internal organs and external appendages belonged to him.

Suddenly, the DI's block head bobbed up and down in Lonnie's face, the brim of the Smokey poking him repeatedly in the forehead, the carnivorous eyes piercing deep, the deliberate voice demanding to know why a four-eyed, scum-sucking maggot like Lonnie had joined his beloved Corps.

Lonnie was confused. He'd worn glasses since he was twelve, but he'd never heard the term "four eyes." *Why does this guy think I have four eyes?*

But the DI's grip on Lonnie's throat was making it hard to breathe, let alone speak. That's when recruit Lonnie Tate clearly understood two things: One, *I shouldn't ask him why he thinks I have four eyes.* Two, *I never should have stolen that cop car.*

PART I

1

QUANG TRI PROVINCE
REPUBLIC OF VIETNAM
4 SEPTEMBER 1967

Four days and not a single patrol sighting or wire probe. Not even a sniper.

Shelling from NVA artillery was incessant. Assaults on the hill and its surrounding fire bases were so fierce and frequent, casualties and psychological toll so high, that I-Corps command rotated Marine grunt battalions in and out every 30 days.

Corporals Tate, Pentangelo and Shapiro were into their third rotation on the hill known as "The Meat Grinder." Just a stone's throw from the DMZ, the hill's name in Vietnamese was Con Thien, the "Hill of Angels." The Marines knew it was anything but.

9 SEPTEMBER 1967

Assigned to a Med-Cap, a medical civil action platoon, translators Tate, Pentangelo, and Shapiro stopped in a ville some 100 meters south of the hill. While Pentangelo and Shapiro made the standard courtesy call on the ville's chief, Tate was in a hooch translating for Doc Stitzel, the corpsman.

Doc was examining a very pregnant young woman. Mid-exam, her water broke and Tate found himself assisting in a challenging breech delivery. When it was over, he translated the exhausted mother's teary thanks. Forty-five minutes later, she was out in the paddies harvesting rice, with her newborn in a sling around her chest so the child could nurse.

With 10 months in country and two meritorious combat field promotions each, Corporals Tate, Pentangelo and Shapiro were tough, combat-savvy 0251s—the Marine Corps' MOS for Translator/Interrogator. Or, to quote Tate himself, they were "grunts who could speak Vietnamese."

Not bad, considering Tate and Shapiro weren't old enough to vote, and Pentangelo, the oldest of the three, had missed his chance. The day absentee ballots were handed out, their squad got ambushed and pinned down for two hours while out on patrol.

Life as a 0251 was a gypsy-like existence. The trio had served with two Force Recon teams and almost every grunt unit in I-Corps. Dubbed by various platoon commanders as "The 3 Musketeers," the "Traumatic Trio," and more recently, "The Pep Boys – Manny, Moe and Jack," the three young Marines had become close friends in language school.

"Flunk out or drop," they were told the first day of class, "you're goin' to the grunts. "Graduate in the top five of the class, you'll be assigned to MACV in Saigon."

They graduated the top three in their class. Despite that, as one crusty gunnery sergeant put it, "Yer gonna be more damn useful with the grunts than you will in the rear with the gear."

From a lower-middle class family in Southern California, Cpl. Lonnie Tate was 5' 7", olive-complected, and built like a fire hydrant. A poor student and juvenile delinquent in high school, Lonnie was very much the opposite of his team members.

Cpl. Marcus Pentangelo was a 6' 2" upper class Bostonian.

Growing up, he took some ribbing from family and friends for being the only black kid they knew with an Italian last name. Most of that ribbing came from his mother, who at that time was the only black woman in Boston who was partner at a major law firm. His Italian-American father was a Harvard English lit professor.

Cpl. Brian Shapiro was a street-smart prep school product of Philadelphia's Main Line. A wiry 5' 10", Brian was raised by his German-Jewish grandparents. His grandfather, Hyman Shapiro, was one of the most influential philanthropists on the East Coast.

12 SEPTEMBER 1967

Three more days. Still no activity. Nobody said it, but everybody was thinking it—*something* was wrong. In Quang Tri Province, the past 12 days were a glitch, not the norm.

When "normal" returned, it would more than make up for its hiatus.

13 SEPTEMBER 1967

Lance Corporal Roy Meacham was brushing his teeth when a round from a sniper's rifle ripped through his heart and shattered his left shoulder blade. As his body hit the deck, everyone else around him dropped—weapons locked and loaded, safeties off.

Doc Stitzel saw Meacham go down. One look told him there was no point in checking for vitals.

In the command tent for a briefing, Lieutenant Cortaze, platoon commander, Corporal Murphy, 3rd squad leader, and his radioman, Corporal Mandel, all hit the deck, crawling behind a stack of sandbags that doubled as a wall.

"Sniper! Sniper!" echoed around the hill. The Marines weren't worried about betraying their position. They were in the sniper's back yard. He already knew where all the hiding places were.

Knowing the answer, Lieutenant Cortaze yelled, "Anybody see 'im?" Nobody did, but that didn't mean he wasn't still there. Unlike the Viet Cong, NVA snipers didn't always hit and run. Sometimes they took time to observe a unit. When they hit, they already knew the layout of the CP, the unit's routine, who was in command, and which men were squad leaders.

"Anybody hit?" the platoon commander shouted.

"Meacham—KIA," Doc shouted back.

Cautiously poking his head up from behind the sandbags, Cortaze scanned the surrounding trees, then the thirty or so meters between his position and where the rest of Murphy's squad was hugging the dirt.

Cortaze nodded to Murphy and Mandel. They knew the drill. Keeping ten to fifteen meters between them, Cortaze would venture out first, then Mandel, then Murphy.

As soon as he had crawled maybe two meters...

"Wish you wouldn't do that, Skipper!" Corporal Tate shouted. "You guys get blown away makin' your way over here, we lose a good squad leader and radioman."

Grunt humor: the deeper the pile of crap you stepped in, the quicker it reared its dark, irreverent head.

Cortaze grinned and shook his head. "What about the platoon commander, Tate?" he shouted back.

"Well, ah," Lonnie answered, "him too, I guess...with all due respect."

Murphy and the radioman choked back a snicker.

"Damn, Tate," Cortaze replied, "your...concern is, hell, there just aren't wor—"

The staccato firecracker sound of incoming small-arms fire sent Cortaze slithering back behind the sandbags. A half-second later the ground shook and rumbled.

"RPGs, satchel charges!" the three translators yelled simultaneously.

"In the wire...posts one and three!" shouted another set of voices.

Gut-punch explosions from NVA mortars and the angry air-sucking screams of rocket-propelled grenade fire blended into a deadly chaotic symphony. All hell was breaking loose.

Cortaze, Murphy, and Mandel knew they couldn't stay where they were. If the NVA had mortars, it was a safe bet they had the CP bracketed. The command tent would be hit within the first few rounds.

Another look, then a nod to each other, and they made their move: Cortaze...Mandel...then Murphy.

Trying to run full speed in a crouched position is like trying to pedal uphill on a little kid's tricycle. The thirty meters between their position and Third Squad seemed like three hundred.

As soon as they were out in the open, the jungle erupted, churned, and exploded all around them. Their faces stung and their eyes burned from chunks of foliage, tree splinters, and other jungle debris flying through the air. A lifetime later, they had traversed the thirty meters without getting hit.

Sweat-soaked, out of breath, leg muscles burning, they allowed themselves a few seconds to catch their breath. Then Cortaze, with Mandel on his hip, led Murphy and his squad, including Tate, Pentangelo, and Shapiro, toward the nearest perimeter wire.

Just as they reached two sandbag bunkers and a shallow trench line twenty meters behind the perimeter wire, incoming fire intensified. The NVA were moving closer.

Running, crawling on all fours—profanities flying out of his mouth like an M60 machine gun—Doc Stitzel felt useless. As soon as he got to one wounded man, two more went down.

Cortaze shouted at the top of his lungs into the handset of Mandel's Prc-25.

"Cantilever Charlie, Kilo 3 Actual. Cantilever Charlie, Kilo 3 Actual. Need air and medevac our position now! I say again: Need air and medevac, our position. Now!"

Out of the corner of his eye, Lonnie saw an NVA soldier running toward a bunker off to the right, a satchel charge in his left hand and a second one slung around his neck.

Contrary to what "Hollywood grunts" do, Lonnie fought the adrenalin-driven urge to empty the twenty-round magazine of his M16 toward the target. Real combat experience taught you to take aim and fire—take aim and fire—take aim and fire, especially with a moving target. That way you might actually hit the target. And not waste ammo.

Lonnie took aim and fired until the NVA soldier started doing what the grunts of Kilo Company called "The Spaz"—a macabre death dance of jerks, twists, and contortions, as the human body reacted to the impact of multiple rounds finding their mark. As if the NVA's body finally realized it was dead, it stopped jerking and twisting and crumpled to the ground.

Just as quickly as all hell had broken loose, it fell graveyard quiet. Except for Doc Stitzel's calm, reassuring voice telling a dying young Marine what he told all dying young Marines: "Chopper's on its way. You're gonna be OK. Chopper's on its way. It's gonna be—"

0548 HOURS

Three choppers were approaching. From the sound of their rotor blades, two Hueys and a Chinook. The Hueys were gunships. The Chinook would handle the medevacs.

Pushing himself up onto his knees, Cortaze gave the area another look.

Satisfied the worst was over—for now—he called out, "All

right! Everybody up! Get me a head count."

The radio came alive.

"You shittin' me? Over!" Corporal Mandel shot back into the handset.

19 years old with eight months in country, Mandel was an exceptional radioman. He knew protocol strictly prohibited the use of profanity. He also knew that whoever came up with that rule obviously hadn't spent any time in Quang Tri Province.

Lieutenant Cortaze didn't have to hear the transmission to know what had prompted his radioman's profanity.

"Let me guess. They want a body count...theirs, not ours."

"That's affirm, Skipper."

Cortaze motioned Mandel to hand him the handset. His voice was calm.

"Cantilever Charlie, this is Kilo Three Actual. Be advised—"

Then it wasn't.

"I have to find out if I still have a platoon left! I'll get back to ya. Out!"

"Murphy!" Cortaze shouted to the squad leader closest to him. "You lose anybody?"

"Two so far," Murphy shouted back. "Got a couple of blood trails down here by the wire."

"On our way," Cortaze replied, as he and Mandel headed toward First Squad.

0552 HOURS

"Murph?" Tate said to the squad leader. "Goin' over to check the gook I got. See if he's got any intel on him. Takin' Pentangelo and Shapiro with me."

"Charlie that," Murphy replied.

As the three translators started to move out, Cortaze and Mandel joined up with them

"Goin' out to check the one you got?" Cortaze asked.

Tate nodded. "That's affirm."

Keeping about fifteen meters between them, Tate, Pentangelo, and Shapiro cautiously approached the body to confirm the kill, Tate in the lead. Ten meters away, Pentangelo and Shapiro moved into position, one to the right, the other to the left and rear of Tate so they could shoot the NVA soldier without hitting Tate if the soldier was faking and made an aggressive move.

An arm's distance from the body, Lonnie stopped, then did a slow 360 around the corpse looking for a telltale twitch, eye blink—any sign of life.

Something wasn't right. The guy was definitely dead, but—

It was a woman. A girl, actually. Nothing new about that.

He rolled her over on her back.

Suddenly he couldn't breathe, his vision blurred, and his legs went out from underneath him. The bloody satchel charge hanging around the dead girl's neck revealed itself to be a sling pouch, carrying a dead baby. The same baby Lonnie had helped bring into the world eleven days ago.

Sensing that there was no danger but that something was wrong, Shapiro yelled, "Skipper!" as he and Pentangelo moved toward Tate.

By the time they got to him, Lonnie was gray. Pointing at the body, his lips moved soundlessly. Pentangelo grabbed him, trying to pull him back from the bodies. Lonnie kicked and pushed against him until Shapiro joined the struggle and they wrestled him back. Between sobs and gasps for air, a question clawed its way out of Tate's mouth.

"What's she doin' here? She's got a baby, for Christ's sake. What's...she's—I killed 'em!"

Tearing himself away from Shapiro and Pentangelo, he ran back to her body, kicking it hard. "What the hell's wrong with you?

You're not supposed to be here!" he shouted.

Doc, Lieutenant Cortaze, Mandel, and the remainder of First Squad arrived. Murphy and Doc grabbed Lonnie, trying to contain him.

Violent spasms of chills and nausea drove Tate back down to his knees. Fighting for breath, he sobbed over and over again, "I… didn't…know…I didn't know! What's she doin' here?"

Fighting his own emotions, twenty-four-year-old Second Lieutenant Thomas Cortaze grabbed Tate by the head and pulled him close until they were eye-to-eye. "She was a grunt, Tate. Just like you and me. She was killing us. That's her job. You stopped her. That's your job."

Despite everything, in that instant, the lieutenant's words made perfect sense. Replaying the moment in his mind, Lonnie realized that from her advance on the bunker, the way she moved under heavy fire, she had obviously been trained. She'd done this before.

The stabbing nausea lessened. His breath returned. And for the first time since arriving in country, Corporal Lonnie Tate felt peace.

Doc and Mandel felt the tension leave his body. They watched as he calmly sat up, took a deep breath, and looked at the dead girl and baby.

In his head, a voice not his own asked, *"Corporal Tate. Had you known who she was, would you have done any different?"* It was all so clear. His actions were not only justifiable; they were mandatory.

"No, sir," Tate answered out loud to the voice that nobody else could hear.

Concerned at Tate's behavior, Cortaze asked, "What's the scoop, Doc?"

"Who you talkin' to, Tate?" the corpsman asked.

Lonnie looked at Doc blankly for a moment, then replied, "This place sucks."

"Charlie that," chorused everybody within earshot.

Looking at Cortaze, Lonnie stood up and asked, "Permission to check the body for intel?"

He could feel the platoon commander's eyes boring inside him, trying to discern if he was really okay or if he was a bag of grenades—the pins pulled—just waiting to explode.

After several seconds, Cortaze gave an approving nod. "Carry on, Corporal."

"Aye, sir."

2

VENICE, CALIFORNIA
15 FEBRUARY 1968

The wall-mounted phone rang more than twenty times before Daniel picked it up.

"Yeah?"

The wispy-bearded, overweight twenty-two-year-old liked answering the phone that way. It told whoever was on the other end that he was in charge.

"May I please speak to Ashley?" asked a middle-aged male voice.

"Who?" Daniel didn't know any Ashley. But with the revolving door of people who used the duplex as a crash pad, maybe someone named Ashley was staying there.

"I'm sorry. You probably know her as Shondon. Her family still calls her by her given name. Is she there?"

His politeness irritated Daniel. The phone banged against the floor when he dropped it.

"Shondon—phone!"

"Who is it?" came a muted yell from a back bedroom.

"I don't know. Some old guy." Daniel heard a door open.

"Wish he'd just leave me alone." Shondon said to no one in particular.

Daniel gave her a leering smile when she entered the hallway wearing a man's T-shirt and little else. Her long dark hair framed her unhappy face.

Shondon bent down to pick the phone up off the floor. "What!" she barked into the receiver.

Despite her tone, the man remained pleasant. "How are you doing?"

"What do you want?"

"I'm going to be in Los Angeles on business tomorrow. I apologize for asking on such short notice, but I wonder if you'd have time to join me for dinner or lunch or maybe just a cup of coffee—"

The pitch of her voice raised. "Tomorrow. Tomorrow?"

"I know, and I'm terribly sorry," he said hurriedly. "I just learned I have to be there tomorrow, instead of next week. I wish I could have given you more notice, but it would mean a lot if we could get together. Please?"

He sounded genuinely apologetic, maybe even pitiful.

"Right," she hissed, "it would mean a lot. To you."

"It would," he admitted, "and to a lot of others who care about you."

"OK," she said, slumping against the wall. "Where?"

"How about Denny's, by the airport?"

"Yeah", she sighed, "why not?"

"I know you're probably working, so can you make it at eleven? That way we can get in before—"

"Yeah, fine."

"That's wonderful; I'm really looking forward to seeing you, and—"

She had already hung up.

3

DENNY'S
LOS ANGELES, CALIFORNIA
16 FEBRUARY 1968

Not bothering to stand, he just waved from a corner booth.

"So," he said with his usual threatening smile. "Still working at that nonprofit? Must be interesting work."

She gave him a hard look. "Yes and no. Now why don't you tell me all the really important things you're doing for the world."

Returning her glare, he took another half-minute before speaking.

"Wel-l-l—" a smile drew out the word— "I'm here because the firm has a shipment coming in tomorrow night. Marine supplies. You wouldn't believe how the demand for personal watercraft is growing."

"You're right. I wouldn't."

Ignoring her sarcasm, he continued. "There are close to two hundred units of support products arriving from our suppliers in Asia. Three crates in particular can't go through the usual receiving area, so customs is insisting someone from the firm be present when they arrive. So here I am."

"Yeah," she said without looking at him. "Here you are."

"Our goods are arriving at eight p.m. So I'll probably be gone by ten, eleven at the latest."

Brightening, he said, "Why don't we get together for dinner, Ashley?"

"That isn't my name anymore," she snarled, scooting out of the booth faster than her miniskirt could gracefully handle. Tugging her skirt down, she turned to leave, then shot over her shoulder, "And as far as I'm concerned, we are not family. Got it?"

Ashley was an alias. The terse words on the phone, the scene in Denny's, that's the way they always played it.

He wasn't her father. He was her handler, and he was a creep. She wasn't about to meet him in a private setting. He'd given her an assignment. That was his job. Now she would do hers: tomorrow night, Los Angeles International Airport.

She found a phone booth and dialed the number at the duplex. It rang at least two dozen times before Daniel finally picked up.

Just hearing his voice pissed her off. His asinine "Yeah" pissed her off even more.

"Daniel, it's Shondon. I've gotta make this quick, so pay attention and don't interrupt."

"Uh, yeah, sure, OK."

She could hear the disappointment in his voice. Just like she could feel his excitement when he heard her say, "Daniel, it's Shondon." Like there was something between them.

"Tell Eric: tomorrow night, eight o'clock, airfreight side of the airport. Estimated two hundred John Waynes coming home. You got that?"

No way, he thought. *No military flights coming back from Vietnam ever land at L.A. International. Especially Marines. Coming or going, they always use El Toro, the Marine Corps Air Station in Santa Ana.*

"L.A. International? You sure?"

"No, Daniel," she said. "I made it up because I didn't have anything else to do."

She knew she needed to back off. Weasel or not, now was the time to make Daniel feel important.

"I really need you on this, Daniel. Without you, something that really needs to happen in this city won't happen." Knowing he would find Eric, she hung up.

"Yeah," she said out loud to herself. "Good old Eric. A thug with a peace symbol and STOP THE WAR NOW on his T-shirt."

After their first meeting, she remembered wondering how a 35-year-old drifter from some bend-in-the-river town in the Midwest got to be the leader of the antiwar movement in the greater Los Angeles area.

She knew it was just a matter of time before good ol' Eric and his team of so-called "organizers" would get somebody killed—if they hadn't already.

Shondon had lots of doubts and questions about US foreign policy in Vietnam. But witnessing and sometimes even facilitating the unleashing of raw hatred on a bunch of guys coming home from a war they didn't start certainly wasn't the answer.

4

After sixteen months of a thirteen-month tour of duty, a bout with malaria, two Purple Hearts, and a Silver Star, Sergeant Lonnie Tate, along with Sergeants Brian Shapiro, Marcus Pentangelo, and 184 other marines, cheered as their Pan Am Boeing 707 touched down at L.A. International Airport.

Thirty-six hours earlier, Tate, Pentangelo, and Shapiro were at Khe Sanh, and two weeks into the Tet Offensive.

Returning from a sweep through a ville, and only fifty meters out from their perimeter wire, their squad had walked into an ambush.

Within seconds the point man and the radioman were dead. A new kid who had reported in to the unit earlier that day was seriously wounded.

Thirty-six hours ago and eight thousand miles away.

Lonnie could still hear the platoon commander, Lieutenant Cortaze, on the radio yelling for air support and a medevac; could still smell the cordite from the gunfire; could still feel the blast of air from the medevac chopper's rotor wash as it flared to land.

Thirty-six hours ago and eight thousand miles away.

His body tensed, muscles remembering the strain of hefting the dead weight of the radioman's body over his shoulder, the chopper's rotor wash pushing him backward.

Pentangelo, Shapiro, and Lt. Cortaze had the new guy and the point man. Bullets whizzed past their heads, sounding like bumblebees in flight. Half loading, half throwing the wounded and the dead on the chopper, the platoon commander ordered the three of them to get on as well.

Just minutes before, the radioman had received a transmission: Tate, Shapiro, and Pentangelo were to report back to their parent unit by 0900 hours the next morning "for rotation back to CONUS."

Manny, Moe, and Jack: the Pep Boys—that's what Lieutenant Cortaze had nicknamed them—were finally going home.

"What the—?" The sight of flashing, bright-red lights wrenched Tate back from Khe Sanh to the here and now.

Pentangelo leaned over to take a look. Three airport police units came alongside the aircraft. "Check it out, Tate. They missed ya!"

A Marine sitting at a window seat on the other side of the cabin echoed Lonnie's surprise, as three more police units pulled up on his side of the plane.

Twenty meters away from a large hangar, the 707 and its police escort came to a stop.

More police cars, lights flashing, pulled alongside. Officers climbed out of the cars, some wearing riot helmets and carrying shotguns.

2000 HOURS

Most of the Marines stared straight ahead as they made their way between the barricades separating them from the crowd of war protestors.

The crowd, no longer satisfied with yelling and chanting, started throwing things—including a bag of dog crap. It hit Lonnie, but didn't break open, so his uniform jacket wasn't soiled. But as he walked, he kept taking whiffs just to make sure.

Pentangelo stopped, turned, and faced the crowd.

Calculating the kill zone of one grenade thrown into a crowd that size, he nodded. *Yeah. 'Bout four oughta do it.*

Seeing the defiance on the tall black Marine's face, the crowd became even more agitated. Immediately, two sheriff's deputies jumped the barricades, walked over to Pentangelo and reminded him to keep moving.

Shapiro asked an LAPD officer if he could borrow his shotgun, offering to clean it when he was through.

The officer in charge of processing the returning Marines couldn't figure it out.

"How did they know?" he asked, turning to his executive officer.

"Sir?" the XO asked.

"The airfreight side was specifically chosen to avoid something like this. The entrance is off the main boulevard. We can bus troops over to the commercial side without having to use a main street so we don't attract attention. No flights come in at night. Hell, up 'til this happened, even the press didn't know we were here. How did the longhairs know?"

5

Trans World Airlines Terminal, Gate 24C
2100 HOURS

Boston was home for Pentangelo, Philadelphia for Shapiro. They were both flying military standby through Atlanta, so getting on a flight right away was a question mark.

For all practical purposes, Lonnie was already home. This time of night, L.A. freeway traffic was nothing. His parents could be there in forty-five minutes. No need to call them until Pentangelo's and Shapiro's seats were confirmed.

Picking a spot that kept them within sight of the girls working the check-in desk, the three sergeants plopped their seabags down and sat on them.

An elderly couple pointed over to the three Marines and told the check-in agent their grandson was a Marine.

"Have they just come back from Vietnam?" the couple asked. To her affirmative answer, they insisted they wouldn't at all mind taking a later flight.

"Those boys"—they corrected themselves— "those *men* need to get home to their families."

The grandmother patted the agent's hand. "You just take care of those Marines. We're going to go get a bite to eat, and when we get back, you can take care of us." Off they went, arm in arm.

Checking the standby manifest, habit made the agent grab for the paging microphone. Realizing the three Marines were just a few feet away, she returned the mic to its holder, smiled, and called out, "Sergeant Pentangelo? Sergeant Shapiro? We have a cancellation."

In an instant, they were at the desk, handing her their orders. A quick glance was all she needed, then she handed them back.

"Welcome home, gentlemen, and enjoy your flight."

They couldn't thank her enough.

"Don't thank me. Thank that older couple." She paused and looked around to see if they were still in the area. "There they are. Just over past the water fountains. They said they could take a later flight. Their grandson is a Marine too. Guess all of you just sort of look out for one another, don't you?"

Tate, Pentangelo, and Shapiro grabbed their seabags and ran to thank the older couple, catching up to them just as they were entering a small restaurant not far from the departure gate.

"Excuse us," Pentangelo said.

"Sergeant Pentangelo. So nice to meet you, and welcome home," the grandfather said sincerely, as he offered him and the other two Marines a handshake.

"Sergeant Shapiro. Sergeant Tate, Sergeant Pentangelo." The grandmother nodded as she gave each a kiss on the cheek.

Lonnie, Pentangelo, and Shapiro shared confused looks.

The grandfather smiled. "No need for alarm, gentlemen. We've been waiting for you."

6

"**We would buy you** dinner," the grandmother chimed in, "but we don't want Sergeant Shapiro and Sergeant Pentangelo to miss their plane. Although the flight is going to be delayed for fifteen to twenty minutes."

As if on cue, the announcement came over the terminal paging system: "*Attention: All passengers holding tickets for Trans World Airlines flight 1023 to Atlanta. Boarding will be delayed. Again, all passengers holding tickets for…*"

"We just love the Boston area, Sergeant Pentangelo," said the grandmother. "Spent the first five years we were married living just outside Cambridge."

The grandfather scoffed, "*She* loves the Boston area. I'll take an afternoon at old Connie Mack watching the Phillies any day of the week, right, Sergeant Shapiro?

"Gentlemen," he continued, "yes, we know your names. How? We can't tell you."

"We are here," said the grandmother, "to briefly present an alternative to serving out the remainder of your enlistments. You won't be giving your answers to us. You will probably want to take some time while you're on leave to think about your answers. If you have any questions, we can't answer them, but others will."

The grandfather motioned them inside the restaurant. They hesitated.

"Gentlemen, if you're even a little curious, let's talk. If you're not, just walk away, and you can rest assured that this meeting never happened."

7

Los Angeles, California

She didn't go back to the duplex after the demonstration at the airport. She couldn't. If she went to the duplex she'd have to be Shondon, and she just didn't feel like Shondon anymore. Or Ashley. She didn't know what to feel. So she drove, and drove, and drove around L.A.

By the time she stopped driving, around 4 a.m., she felt like Mary, her real name. And she felt miserable. She shoved a dime into a pay phone and punched zero.

The last 36 hours had been a blur. The only thing she was sure of was that she felt completely hemmed in. Ironic, feeling claustrophobic in the city that invented urban sprawl. Up until last night at the airport, she always thought she could handle it. But not any more. She was through.

"I need to make a collect call."

Unbeknownst to the operator, the call was routed to a secure phone on the seventh floor of CIA headquarters in Langley, Virginia.

"Code name?" said a sterile female voice.

"Thespis."

Hands shaking, she waited while her voice was run through the voice-recognition analyzers.

"Confirmed," said the emotionless voice. "Status?"

"Watermark, watermark, *watermark!*" she said, surprised by her growing panic.

"Stand by."

She heard the click. She was on hold again, but someone was still listening. Someone was always listening.

"Confirm meeting contact?" The voice came back on the line.

"Yes, dammit!"

"Confirm information relay?"

"Affirmative."

Five seconds of silence, then, "We'll begin making arrangements."

"Thank you," she whispered.

It didn't matter. The voice had already hung up.

How did get myself into this?

Three years ago, she had only one identity and one name: Mary Diane Reynolds, a rancher's daughter from Broadus, Montana.

A drama major with phenomenal acting talent, Mary had graduated a year early from Radcliffe in May of 1965. That summer, she reigned at the summer program at ADA—the American Academy of Dramatic Arts. Next stop, Broadway—or so she thought.

8

FACULTY GREEN ROOM
AMERICAN ACADEMY OF DRAMATIC ARTS
NEW YORK CITY
SUMMER 1965

Always the gentleman, he stood as Mary Reynolds approached the table.

"Thank you for meeting with me, Miss Reynolds. I'm Howard Dade. May I call you Mary?"

Mary knew the word courtly, but this was the first time she had observed it in person.

He gestured for her to sit first, then joined her.

"I want to offer you a position that is particularly well-suited to your talents," he said. "It offers substantial financial compensation and an opportunity to serve your country in a very significant capacity."

"I'm sorry," she responded, "but your letter said something about a long-term acting contract?"

Dade nodded. "With the option of being able to leave whenever you want, although I hope you'll want to continue for some time.

"Your compensation will be twenty thousand per year. The money will be deposited in a secure account twice each month. Additionally, the taxes will be paid before the money is deposited—"

"So how much less than twenty thousand would I actually get?" she interrupted.

"You will be paid the full twenty thousand each year. Payment of taxes is part of your compensation."

"And I don't have to take off my clothes?"

Dade laughed. "What you have to do is convince people you are who and what we want you to tell them you are. That you can be trusted, and that they can always rely on you for certain important information."

"What kind of important information?" Mary asked. "And you didn't answer my question about my clothes."

"Information regarding US military personnel returning from Vietnam. Where they will arrive and when," he answered.

She felt a tightness in her chest something like stage fright. Whatever kind of director this Mr. Dade was, Mary knew she was not auditioning for a part in a play.

"Who are these people I'm passing this information to, Mr. Dade?"

"People who disagree with our nation's military policies regarding Southeast Asia," he said evenly.

"Mr. Dade, I may come from—no, I *do* come from one of those small towns that lie between highway signs that read 'Slow Down' and 'Resume Speed,' but please don't think I possess the same hayseed naïveté that—"

Dade politely cut her off. "At last year's ADA summer festival, I saw you in *Fiddler on the Roof.* Your Chava was delightful. The next day you played Martha in *Who's Afraid of Virginia Woolf?* I couldn't believe it was the same person. That is what prompted my interest in you."

She meant to say thank you. Instead she blurted out, "Just exactly what kind of a director are you, Mr. Dade?"

"I'm Director of the Central Intelligence Agency, Mary."

"The what?"

Dade stood up, gesturing for her to do the same. "If you want the part, it's yours," he said, smiling.

"Take a week," he said, handing her a piece of paper. "If the answer is yes, call that number, and you'll be given further instructions. If it's no, there's no need to call. And I will thank you in advance for not saying anything to anyone else about this."

"How do you know I won't?"

"Because rancher's daughters from Broadus, Montana, do not get recruited to work for the CIA—particularly by its director."

Stopping at the door, he turned and gave a slight bow. "But you just did. And you can't think of one person you would tell—who would believe you."

Ten days later, Mary Reynolds reported to the Farm, the CIA training facility at Camp Peary, near Williamsburg, Virginia.

9

If the adage "whate'er thou art, act well thy part" was true, in her past two and a half years with the CIA, Mary Diane Reynolds had turned in Tony Award–winning performances.

Her audience: the leaders of anti war organizations like the SDS (Students for a Democratic Society) and the SNCC (Student Nonviolent Coordinating Committee) that had set up shop on various college campuses.

Keeping track of who she talked to, she passed her communications on to a handler, who reported directly to Howard Dade.

Mary quickly learned that fewer than a handful of those so-called leaders were actually leaders. Most were self-proclaimed know-it-alls who in real life couldn't lead a one-car parade.

Their followers were even more pitiful: a bunch of spoiled rich kids who didn't want to serve their country. Not because of any moral objection, but because it was an inconvenience.

At Berkeley, she was Barbara Francine Shields, a social worker from Somerville, Massachusetts. Her Boston accent was flawless. So were her ID and college transcripts, and the letters of recommendation from professors who themselves had impressive résumés. All of which made it easy for her to land a job with Student Social Services on the campus.

At the University of Michigan, she was Molly Stefanizzi, a student on the work-study program, working in the admissions office.

A few more liberal college campuses—and a few more identities—later, and Mary was off to Chicago and the Black Panthers. She dyed her long blond hair jet black and used radiant blue contact lenses to create what she and the CIA would consider her "role of a lifetime." She became Marsha Hartunian—a violent, political radical on the run, background courtesy of the CIA "Art Department."

When the Panthers checked Marsha out, they found that "the white bitch" had arrest records for assault and arson in four states. She was wanted by the FBI, categorized as "armed and dangerous."

Mary was raised on a ranch. To her, guns were tools used for hunting and scaring off coyotes, mountain lions, and other unwanted predators. Or occasionally, putting down a horse or steer suffering from something that Doc Harder couldn't treat.

With the Panthers, a gun was a necessity for daily survival. On her second day in Chicago she bought a Smith & Wesson .45. She carried it concealed on her person during the day and under her pillow at night.

A month later, at Panther headquarters, she shot and killed a man who made the mistake of trying to force her into a closet to rape her. Then she shot and killed the fool who was watching but ignored her cries for help.

From that point on, the Panthers treaded very lightly around her. Anywhere in the building, within earshot or not, she was referred to as "Ms. Hartunian."

The volatility of the Panther situation so increased the risk of her cover getting blown that CIA operatives, disguised as FBI agents acting on an anonymous tip, staged a raid on the apartment and arrested the ultra-radical political activist Marsha Hartunian.

The Agency next sent her to Los Angeles with a new name and a new cover. She was Ashley Tannehill—idealistic, dedicated to serving the poor, and wholeheartedly convinced that America's war in Southeast Asia was extracting the highest cost from Americans who were least able to pay for anything, even the basics of day-to-day survival. "Ashley" wanted people to know she rejected what she called parental oppression, so she re-named herself. "I claim the right to be who I really want to be, who I really am," she'd tell people, "and my spirit knows I'm Shondon." In truth, it was a part of her cover that she chose on her own, to add to her counterculture credibility.

10

From an acting standpoint, the last two and a half years had been a great gig.

But for Mary Diane Reynolds, "The Ashley-Shondon et al. Show" had reached the end of its run.

The final curtain had fallen at the war protest at LAX, in a moment of nonverbal hate that would freeze-frame itself in her mind for the rest of her life.

As the returning Marines passed in front of the protestors, she watched a tall black Marine stop and face the crowd. The look of defiance on his face equaled the hate of those protesting what he represented.

Responding to his contempt, the protestors pressed toward the barricades.

In turn, the Marine took a step toward them.

Mary knew that if he had had a rifle, he would have opened fire on the crowd and kept firing until everyone—including himself—was dead.

In that moment, she made herself a promise. If she ever saw that Marine again, no matter when or where, she would walk up to him, identify herself, and explain how she recognized him. If he didn't walk away or take a swing at her—or even if he did—she would apologize and beg his forgiveness.

11

CAIRO, EGYPT
AUGUST 1968

The trio could have passed for college students bumming around the Middle East and Europe. Wearing hiking boots, jeans, and faded chambray shirts, they could have been kids whose rich mommies and daddies helped them leave the United States to escape the draft.

Gone were the high-and-tight haircuts. Marcus Pentangelo wore an Afro and Brian Shapiro's sandy-colored hair fell nearly to his shoulders. Lonnie Tate's dark, bushy hair went wherever it wanted.

To the well-trained eye, there was nothing "bumming" about them. The well-trained eye saw three men, probably former military, stalking a target and closing in for the kill.

Tate, Shapiro, Pentangelo, and their target were in a building constructed over what, a thousand years earlier, had been Cairo's most brutal, vermin-infested prison.

Now it was a back-alley nightspot. The music was hot, the booze and food were good and cheap. The owner made the real money in what the "patrons" kicked back for letting them use the club as a place to conduct their "business."

A different species of vermin infested the establishment now: death merchants in the form of arms dealers, mercenaries, and off-the-books contractors who worked for whichever intelligence organization paid the most.

If it needed to be killed, moved from border to border or continent to continent, if it needed to be stolen, forged—hell, if it needed to be anything, the place was to the black ops world of intelligence what Christie's and Sotheby's were to auction houses.

The target: a Fatah operative. Name optional.

Pentangelo's focus: what the target had done. This one had plotted at least a dozen attacks on Israeli buses, shops, and kibbutzim that had served as joint-venture Mossad/CIA store fronts, safe houses, and listening posts. More than seventy deaths, including fifteen CIA assets, could be attributed to his operations.

Shapiro, the analyst, had studied the target's personal habits. Was he a night or day person? Where and what did the target like to eat and drink? Did the target like to eat but wasn't a drinker, or vice versa? What kind of women or men, or both, was the target attracted to?

Lonnie Tate was the "wet boy" of the team—the guy who pulled the trigger, blew the target up, or if time allowed, watched him die after he had poisoned his drink.

Lonnie was the guy who ran him over with a car, preferably on a road or street with little or no traffic or bystanders. That way he could back up and run over him again—just to make sure he was dead.

He would have preferred to "tag" this current target immediately after following him into the bar. But the club had been mostly empty. The team's presence and exit would have been noticed.

An hour had gone by, and now the target was surrounded by friends—all drinking and laughing.

Lonnie was getting impatient. When Lonnie got impatient, he got quiet.

When Lonnie got quiet, something was going to happen—soon.

As the target started shuffling away from his comrades, pointing toward the men's room, Lonnie stood up.

"I gotta take a leak," he mumbled.

Shapiro and Pentangelo looked at each other.

"I'll go get the car," said Shapiro.

Pentangelo nodded. "I'll pay the tab. See ya outside."

Tate moved quickly, but without attracting attention. Timing was everything.

Faking drunkenness, he staggered through the restroom door. The target was at the sink, washing his hands.

Olive-skinned, he was about Lonnie's height, more muscular, and probably ten years older. His hair was black, close-cropped, and curly, almost kinky.

Lonnie's presence was of no consequence to him. Taking a step to his right, the target reached for a hand towel that hung from a rusty nail, turned away, and began drying his hands.

Feeling a sharp pain in his ribs, he stiffened. He felt a hand clamp tightly over his mouth. He felt the blade of a sharp knife puncture his right lung—then he felt nothing.

Wiping the blood off the blade of the knife on the target's jeans, Lonnie slipped it into the sheath that had been custom-sewn into the sleeve of his shirt. He rinsed the blood from his hands, wiped them on his pants, pulled the bathroom door open, and staggered his way to the entrance and out of the club.

Maintaining the ruse of drunkenness, he stumbled toward Pentangelo, who was outside the entrance looking up and down the street.

"Where's Shap?" Lonnie asked, as if he were asking for the time.

Marcus looked calm but didn't sound it. "I dunno."

"Well, Marcus, in about thirty seconds, one of the target's buddies is going to wonder why his friend hasn't come out of the head yet. We don't want to be here when that happens."

12

The pickup point was the narrow street in front of the club. If Shapiro wasn't there, plan B was to meet in an alley two blocks away.

Tradecraft dictated taking an indirect route. But by now, the target's friends had probably discovered his body. One of them was sure to remember seeing a guy stagger into the head just after their friend went in. Two plus two was going to equal four very quickly. Expediency was going to have to trump tradecraft.

The car was there in the street: a gray 1966 Lada sedan, the Soviet Union's interpretation of a Fiat 124. The headlights and dome light were on, the driver's-side door was open, but the engine wasn't running. And there was no Shapiro.

From the small of his back, between his shirt and jeans, Lonnie withdrew his Smith & Wesson .44 Magnum. Even with the four-inch barrel, the Magnum was bulky. Definitely not the sleek, sexy Walther PPK that James Bond carried. Then again, Bond was a fictional character. Equally fictional were the range, Bond's accuracy, and the knockdown power of the Walther PPK.

Without a silencer, the .44 Magnum was a handheld cannon, with a recoil that took some getting used to. As far as knockdown power? If you survived the impact of the round, it was a sure bet you wouldn't be getting up until the paramedics lifted you onto a gurney.

Pentangelo carried a military-issue Smith & Wesson 1911 .45. Like the Magnum, not sexy, and without a silencer, loud as hell. It would definitely knock you down.

Approaching the car, Pentangelo automatically moved to the front, Lonnie toward the rear, stopping by the driver's-side taillight. Once in position, they each paused, gave the car another once-over, then circled the vehicle in opposite directions, making sure not to cross into the other's line of fire.

Lonnie smelled it before Marcus saw it. Blood—lots of it.

Pentangelo leaned in the driver's-side door and saw the Polaroid lying on the dashboard.

Leaning in from the passenger side, Lonnie caught the look on Pentangelo's face, then saw the photo. He instinctively backed out of the car to check the street in both directions, slid back into the front seat, grabbed the photo, and shoved it into his pocket.

"Marcus," he said in a tone of controlled urgency, "we've probably got eyes on us right now. Get in and get us outta here."

Pentangelo slid into the car.

"Shit!"

The seat was positioned for Shapiro's five-foot-ten frame, not Pentangelo's six-foot-two. His knees banged the bottom of the steering wheel as his ribs hit the nine o'clock spot. Fumbling for the lever to slide the seat back, he turned the key to start the car.

13

The four-cylinder engine lit up with a high-pitched growl. Marcus slammed the transmission into gear and floored it, pushing the Lada's engine for all it was worth down a two-lane street that ran alongside a canal.

From out of nowhere, a truck rammed the passenger-side rear door. Metal buckled and ground against metal as the Lada went airborne and into the canal.

Pentangelo's head ricocheted off the ceiling as the car hit the water.

Even with the windows up, the car had little buoyancy. Hissing and bubbling as it sank, the water was already at window level.

With his head throbbing and bleeding and his knees up in his chest, the confines of the interior made it almost impossible for Marcus to move. Though he tried to control it, his panic level was rising.

"Stay cool, Marcus," Lonnie cautioned. "This canal can't be that deep."

So scared he started laughing, Marcus yelled, "How the hell do you know?"

"Because I know stuff," Lonnie shot back.

The Lada hit the bottom of the canal, slamming Pentangelo's head into the ceiling again.

"Told ya," Lonnie said, trying to keep the panic out of his own voice. "On three, we roll down the windows. When the water gets to our necks, the pressure will be equal on both sides of the doors. That's when we take a deep breath, kick open the doors, and swim up to the surface, OK?"

"If you say so."

"OK, one— two—three, now!"

The water was cold, a sharp contrast to the warm evening temperature. Worse than the cold was the water's stench. Lonnie felt like he was being smothered by a smelly, thick, liquid blanket.

A couple of quick, hard kicks on the door and Lonnie wormed his way out. A single stroke and he was at the surface.

Marcus had to wrestle his way out. Flailing more than swimming to the surface, he was gasping, coughing, and spitting as his head broke the water.

Lonnie grabbed Marcus's arm up under the shoulder and yanked him over to the center of the canal. Still holding Marcus's arm, Lonnie straightened his legs and dropped below the surface until his feet touched the top of the car. Guessing he was just four inches or so under the water, one scissor-kick and his head broke the surface.

"Marcus—you—can stand on the car—'til—you catch your breath! You'll—be fine. Then let's find a place to get outta this water."

"Whatta you mean... 'find a place!'" Pentangelo said between gasps for air.

Lonnie scanned the concrete sides of the canal as he treaded water.

"OK, yeah. The sides are—smooth here. So—we'll float downstream a little."

Still gasping for air, Pentangelo gave Lonnie a skeptical look. "Sure. Why not."

"Calm down, Marcus. We're out of the car. Control your breathing. You're gonna hyperventilate."

"No, no—way, man!" Marcus coughed back. "I'll probably drown first."

"For cryin' out loud, Marcus, just point your feet downstream. Move your hands back and forth to keep your head up. Didn't anybody teach you how to swim?!"

"Of course they did, asshole!" Pentangelo answered. "In a pool!"

Half-an-hour of floating later, they spotted rebar handholds on the canal wall.

Figuring they had to be somewhere near the extraction point at the east end of Qasr-al-Nil Bridge, Lonnie guessed they had about a half-hour walk ahead of them. Marcus bet it was closer to an hour.

Forty-five minutes later, they were on a plane heading back to Langley. They called the bet even.

14

OFFICE OF HOWARD DADE, DIRECTOR, CIA
LANGLEY, VIRGINIA
LATE AUGUST, 1968

The Phoenix Protocol—FEEPRO—had been operational for six months. Of the thirty-six FEEPRO agents, six had been killed and three were missing.

What started as a threat-elimination ops group had become a contract service much like Murder, Inc. to the entire intelligence community.

The only upside: the exceptional team performance of agents Lonnie Tate, Brian Shapiro, and Marcus Pentangelo.

Brian Shapiro was an analytical genius. Another six months and he would have been transferred to the Middle East Analyst Desk. Within two years the young Marine would have been its number-two man.

Dade had always looked at Marcus Pentangelo as a lifer. Maybe not with CIA, but the young black man with an Italian last name had definitely found his niche.

As for Lonnie Tate, after the completion of their first op, there was no doubt in Dade's mind that Tate would be a perfect fit for another outside-the-charter unit he had developed and implemented.

Cairo changed everything.

Shapiro was dead. That, coupled with the death of a man all sources had confirmed to be a terrorist, only to find he was actually an agent working deep cover for another intelligence agency, made the Cairo operation a disaster.

And from the look on the face of the young man now sitting across the desk from DCI Howard Dade—Cairo was about to claim another casualty.

"My value," Agent Lonnie Tate began, "has been compromised. I'm a risk you can't afford to take anymore."

Dade exhaled deeply, came around from behind his desk and sat next to Lonnie.

"It's only been a week since the incident. Four days since the debriefing. It's still very present in your mind. Shapiro wasn't just a team member. He was a man with whom you had already been to death's door a number of times before you came to work for us. It's understandable you feel that way."

Lonnie gave the director a hard look, "You left out the part about me killing the wrong guy."

Dade nodded. "The sad and foolish reality of what happens when two agencies can't or won't communicate with each other."

Lonnie shook his head and looked down at the floor. "Who was he? I gotta know."

"Mossad, working deep cover," Dade replied.

Lonnie felt even worse. They liked working with the Mossad agents and considered them brothers.

"What happened?" Lonnie asked.

"The deputy director seems to think it was—"

"The Russians," Lonnie interrupted. "The deputy director doesn't know his ass from a can of C-Rations about the KGB—not the field guys, anyway."

Dade suppressed a smile. Lonnie's opinion of the deputy director matched his own. Just the same, appearances demanded some semblance of a defense for the DDCI.

"May I remind you, Mr. Tate, the deputy director was a very good field agent? It's where he got his start."

Lonnie laughed.

"Sir, taking Shapiro's body? Leaving a Polaroid? Crashing us into a canal, figuring we'd drown?

"Ivan," Lonnie went on, using the CIA's nickname for the KGB, "doesn't screw around like that. He tags Shap, leaves his body in the car, waits for us to find the car—then tags us."

Dade was impressed. Tate, a rookie agent, had learned the ways of his enemy faster than many of the agency's veteran agents.

"With that said, Mr. Tate; the point here is that it's not your value that's been compromised. It's your commitment."

"Yes, sir," Lonnie replied without hesitation. "I don't think what the unit does is wrong. I just can't do it anymore."

"So what am I supposed do with you?"

"Send me back to the Corps, sir."

"Consider it done." The director got up to return to his chair. "You'll have orders in three days."

That wasn't the response Lonnie was expecting. Three days? After the access he'd been given and what he'd done? They were just going to let him go diddy-boppin' back to the Corps?

Yeah, right.

The events of a night six months earlier played back in his mind.

One-hundred-eighty-seven Marine grunts touch down at Los Angeles International Airport.

The flashing lights of police cars. A large group of war protestors yelling and throwing things.

An elderly grandma and grandpa type. The grandpa's reassuring words, "No need for alarm, gentlemen. We've been waiting for you—"

The grandma, "We are here to briefly present an alternative to serving out the remainder of your enlistments—"

The announcement, "Attention: all passengers holding tickets—"

"You seem to be at a loss for words, Mr. Tate," said Dade. "Definitely uncharted territory for you."

Lonnie nodded and leaned back in his chair, "One-hundred-eighty-seven guys return home from Vietnam. They step off the plane and the first thing they run into is a war protest."

15

"**Considering the antiwar climate,** I don't find that at all surprising," Dade replied. He pulled what looked like two SRBs, military service record books, from a desk drawer.

"Except—" Lonnie steepled his fingers— "we landed on the airfreight side of L.A. International. There's no gates, no terminals. Public access is restricted."

Dade had always known Lonnie would eventually figure things out.

"You think the protest was staged, Mr. Tate?"

Lonnie snickered. "I think the protest was a front for a recruiting op."

The director grinned.

"You graduated number four eighty-three out of a high-school senior class of four-hundred-eighty-five, Mr. Tate. Exhibiting an even higher degree of underachievement, you dropped out of junior college to avoid flunking out. One of the classes you were flunking was a foreign-language class.

"Ironic, considering you go into the Marine Corps, become a Class-A Vietnamese interpreter/translator—who also becomes proficient enough in Hebrew, Russian, and Arabic to get around the streets of Jerusalem, Moscow, and Cairo without having any trouble ordering a meal or asking where the bathrooms are.

"Put that well-hidden intelligence together with that of a Shapiro and a Pentangelo—"

As if on cue, the director's office door opened.

Lonnie turned to see an Asian man, probably Japanese, late thirties, about five feet nine. His face revealed a life that had taken him around more than a couple of blocks, more than a couple of times.

Dade continued as if the man weren't there. "I have three outstanding combat-experienced Marines, with a strong sense of purpose. I wasn't going to pass that up. I just needed to get your attention."

Dade stood and offered the Asian man a warm smile.

"Cyrus. Good to see you. How was your flight?"

Returning the smile, the man replied, "What flight? I'm not here."

Taking the chair the director had vacated, the Asian man offered Lonnie a handshake.

"You must be Tate. Read your dossier and SRB. Impressive."

Gesturing to the director, Cyrus continued, "Just so you know, the conversation you two were having before I came in, the one we're having now, and the one we're gonna have after he leaves—"

"Yeah, they never happened," Lonnie interjected. "I get it... deniability."

"Hot damn, Tate," the man named Cyrus exclaimed. "You did learn something at that spy school, didn't ya?"

"Yeah," Lonnie paused, "best school I never went to."

Dade buttoned his suit coat and made his way to the door, "The man who isn't here is Cyrus Watanabe, Mr. Tate," Dade said. "Good seeing you again, Cyrus. Mr. Tate is a good man. He and you are a lot alike."

Stopping at the door, he turned to Lonnie. "Mr. Tate, thank you for your service to this agency and your country. I mean that sincerely." He left, closing the door behind him.

Cyrus, broke the silence. "Ya got that look in your eye, Sergeant."

Lonnie was irritated he was showing any expression at all.

"What look, Cy-rus?"

Cyrus grinned. "That look that says you were played and it sucks. But part of you thinks it was a pretty damn slick piece of work.

"You did good, Tate. You did better than good, otherwise I wouldn't be here. The director likes you, didn't want to lose you, but he knew you were right. You gotta go."

Lonnie slumped in his chair. "Yeah, well. Speaking of that, where am I going?"

Cyrus gave Lonnie's shoulder a brotherly squeeze, "First things first, Sergeant. You have to know where you've been before you can go where you're going."

PART II

16

Morgenthaler & Trent Advertising Agency
Sherman Oaks, California

Back in 2000, Steve Morgenthaler was looking for a creative director for his agency. He needed someone who could manage what most agencies consider the psych ward of their operation: the creative department.

The answer to his problem appeared when he was judging ads for that year's Southern California Ad Club Awards.

After three hours of reviewing television commercials, they were all were beginning to look and sound the same. Standing to take a stretch break, he noticed a box of DVDs with REJECT scrawled on it. He grabbed a random DVD out of the box and put it in the player. A blue screen came up slating the contents: NATVET.ORG: 4–30 second spots.

NATVET.ORG was a well-known, not-for-profit veterans advocacy and support group.

Morgenthaler watched the DVD twice. The writing, music, and voice over talent were exceptional. He couldn't understand why the commercials had been rejected.

The next day he called NATVET.ORG to find out the name of the agency that did the work. Turned out they didn't use an agency. A freelancer named Lonnie Tate had written and directed all their television and radio spots. He had also designed their new print campaign which was about to break in *Time* and *Newsweek*.

Morgenthaler hit a newsstand a couple of days later and picked up copies of both magazines and thumbed through until he found the full-page ads. Being equally impressed with the print work, he called this Lonnie Tate to set up a meeting.

"Thanks, Mr. Morgenthaler, but there's a reason I'm a freelancer."

"Why is that, Mr. Tate?"

"Call me Lonnie, OK? And I'll call you Steve?"

"Works for me, Lonnie."

"Cool. See, Steve, everybody likes my work. They love my work. It's me they can't stand."

"Why is that?"

"I'm a pain in the ass. Don't play well with others. The list goes on. I could email it to you, save you the trouble of calling other agencies I've done work for."

Normally Tate's attitude would have put Morgenthaler off, but in this case he felt just the opposite.

"Let's do this, Lonnie. Lunch...on me...you name the place. If we both like the conversation, we can go from there. You good with that?"

Lonnie never passed up free food. "You're paying. You name the time and day."

"One-thirty tomorrow?"

"I'm there. Place is called Bud's."

"I know it well, Lonnie."

Five minutes into the meeting, both men knew they could work together.

17

By 2005, Lonnie had turned a creative department originally comprised of throwaways from other ad agencies into a tightly-knit department of writers, graphic artists, and illustrators.

Even more impressive: although Lonnie's crew was less than one-third the size of the creative departments found at L.A.'s Top 10 ad agencies, it produced twice the award-winning work.

Mid-2008, with the economy starting to take a nosedive, Lonnie saw the signs of impending bad times for ad agencies in L.A. He warned Morgenthaler.

Morgenthaler shared Lonnie's observation with Jason Beck, CFO and VP of Human Resources. But the odds of Lonnie Tate and Jason Beck ever agreeing on anything were equal to a politician passing a lie detector test.

Not only opposites in opinions, Tate and Beck were opposites physically. Beck was blond-haired, six-foot-four, lanky, and eternally tan. Lonnie was olive-skinned, built like a fire hydrant, and had bushy, salt-and-pepper gray hair with eyebrows to match.

Beck described Lonnie as "a bull who carried around his own China shop." He never said that to Lonnie's face, though. There was something about Lonnie that made him very uneasy. Truth be told, Steve Morgenthaler wasn't so sure that Lonnie wouldn't throw Jason Beck out of a window one day.

As far as Lonnie was concerned, Jason Beck was "a proctologist's dream—a perfect asshole." As to doing any kind of bodily harm to him, Lonnie assured Morgenthaler, "Relax, Steve. There's a law against child beating in the state of California."

By late 2009, the time had come to start letting people go. Beck planned to give notices to the creative department first.

Lonnie wouldn't have it. "I hired them. I'll fire them, Jason. They're my kids, and I take care of my own."

And that he did.

Over that year, Lonnie called around, setting up interviews for his people with other agencies. Despite the ad agency community's widespread dislike for Lonnie—a hangover from his freelancer days—every creative director at every major agency in L.A. knew Lonnie's people were good. They were more than willing to review portfolios and demo reels. All but one of his "kids" had been placed, and she had an interview that afternoon.

Chomping at the bit to tell Lonnie he wouldn't be missed, Beck tapped on Lonnie's office window and mouthed, "May I come in?" then came in anyway.

"Jason Beck," Lonnie announced. "Morgenthaler and Trent's resident angel of death. Shouldn't you be out contesting somebody's unemployment claim?"

Hating that Lonnie got in the first insult, Jason picked up a framed photo sitting on Lonnie's desk, "So this is you...in your gung-ho days?"

From behind him came the voice of Steve Morgenthaler. "Vietnam: Christmas 1967."

Lonnie smiled and nodded. "Khe Sanh. A couple of months before I came home."

"Your team," Morgenthaler said, taking the picture from Beck.

Lonnie never talked much about his time in the Marine Corps or Vietnam. The photograph on his desk and a cross-stitched wall hanging in his office, something his daughter had done for him for a birthday present many years ago, said it all: "Ain't no such thing as an EX-Marine."

The photograph showed three war-weathered Marines. Two of them were leaning against an equally war-weathered sandbag bunker. The third was sitting on his haunches between them, flipping off the camera.

The three sweat-soaked, mud-crusted faces, which looked older than they actually were, wore grins that said "Screw you!"—a look Steve Morgenthaler had become very familiar with over the years.

The Marine on his haunches, flipping the bird, was nineteen-year-old Sergeant Lonnie Tate. The tall black Marine standing to his left was twenty-year-old Sergeant Marcus Pentangelo. The skinny white Marine to the right was Sergeant Brian Shapiro, also twenty.

Morgenthaler laughed, as he did every time he looked at the picture.

"Gotta love the caption."

Photoshopped over the bottom third of the image were the words "My award-winning creative team."

Taking the picture from Beck and setting it back down on the desk, Morgenthaler said, "Lonnie...Lunch, on me. You name the place."

Lonnie smiled. "Bud's."

Whether Morgenthaler & Trent celebrated or mourned, Bud's was always the venue of choice.

18

BUD'S
SAN FERNANDO VALLEY, CALIFORNIA
AUGUST 2010

Ask anybody who had ever eaten at the fast-food grease pit in Southern California's San Fernando Valley. Bud's made the best chili burgers and chili-cheese fries in the world. A reputation it had proudly maintained for more than six decades.

Old publicity photos and newspaper clippings hanging on the walls since its 1946 opening showed a funky little hamburger stand sitting on a one-acre dirt lot. People ate inside their cars or leaning on them.

In 1961, remodeling turned it into a funky little hamburger stand with seating for fifteen people and a paved parking lot. Paper towels replaced the regular napkins that couldn't hold up to Bud's thick-as-sludge chili.

Not much had changed since then. A roll of paper towels still sat at each table and hung from makeshift holders on the walls. Picnic tables provided outside seating for twenty to thirty people, but most people still ate inside their cars or leaning on them.

Day or night, hookers, gangbangers, cops, corporate executives, high-school kids, even senior citizens living on pensions—everybody ate, and nobody or nothing looked out of place at Bud's. It was the perfect spot for those who wanted, or needed, to hide in plain sight.

Dabbing a glob chili off his chin, Steve Morgenthaler commented, "The last time I ate here, my cholesterol went to DEFCON One. By the way, there's something that's bothered me ever since it happened. You've blown me off every time I've asked about it. But not this time."

"I owe you that," Lonnie nodded.

Stabbing up a forkful of fries, Morgenthaler said, "Four and a half years ago. The—"

"The trip to Tel Aviv."

"Yeah," Morgenthaler's eyes narrowed, "the trip to Tel Aviv."

Lonnie took a long sip of his soft drink. "The guys from the State Department."

"The guys from the State Department," Steve said, mimicking him. "You say that like they were a couple of UPS guys dropping off a package."

Lonnie snickered. "You sure you want me to go into this? It's—"

"Complicated? Imagine my surprise. For the record, I was fine until they started talking about the travel restriction."

"I told you, the Marines sent me to Israel after I got back from 'Nam."

"You left out the part about Israel not wanting you back."

"I didn't know. When I left, me and Israel were still on speaking terms."

Morgenthaler shook his head. "Only you could tick off an entire country, Lonnie."

"Israel is a state, Steve. And I was a military courier...a messenger boy in a uniform."

No doubt there was more to the story, but Morgenthaler knew he wasn't going to hear it today—or ever.

"So what's next for you?"

Lonnie shrugged. "I'm sixty-two. You were the only one crazy enough or desperate enough to hire me. And we both know there were days when you wished you hadn't."

"What about consultant work?"

Lonnie laughed. "Consultant. Isn't that just a fancy name for freelancer?"

19

MAIN GATE
ROARING ROLLER COASTERS AMUSEMENT PARK
VALENCIA, CALIFORNIA
JUNE 2014

He wasn't hard to spot. The bushy, silver-gray hair and eyebrows to match were a dead giveaway.

Adjusting the tote bag hanging on her shoulder as she approached the metal detector, she flashed the security guard a killer smile.

When the alarm went off, she said she was sorry, flashed another smile, and pulled up the right leg of her jeans. Revealing a titanium prosthesis from just below her knee down.

"Enjoy your day at the park, ma'am." Lonnie smiled. "And thank you for your service."

"Thank you, Sergeant Tate," she said. "How did you know?"

"You're welcome," Lonnie answered. "I, ah, volunteer at a vets center. Young gal your age with a prosthetic like that, more likely the result of an IED."

"Wow, Lonnie, you're good. The boss was right. You got some game."

"Mind if I look in your bag?" he asked. "Park policy, no glass containers, no drugs."

"Can't you just take my word for it?" she laughed.

"I could. But checking your bag allows me the time to ask you what branch of service you were in. And who your boss is, which might give me some idea as to how you know my name."

"You're cute, Lonnie, for an old guy," she smiled, slipping the tote off her shoulder and handing it to him. "In answer to your first question...Semper Fi, Sergeant Tate."

Lonnie continued inspecting the contents of her tote.

"I even know your service number. Go ahead, ask me."

"Oorah," Lonnie responded. "What's your name, Jarhead?"

"Connie Patino, but you can call me Patino."

He closed the bag and handed it back to her.

"As far as who my boss is? I'm supposed to mention something about a night in 1968. And something about a...and I quote, 'hole-in-the-wall dive' in Cairo, Egypt."

Connie looked in vain for a twitch, a blink, anything to betray the gut shot Lonnie had just taken.

Memories of that night, many nights and days, from his life more than forty years ago began flooding his mind, as if they had happened just yesterday. They always did.

"He'd like to meet you tomorrow night. Seven-thirty at Bud's." Her voice shook him back to the present.

"He says you go there a lot. Said to tell you he's buying."

20

Car Club Night
Bud's

Deuce coupes, roadsters, Mustangs, Corvette Stingrays—any American-made car that rolled off the assembly line no later than 1968—one could find it proudly displayed in Bud's parking lot on Car Club Night.

Bud's owner, Bud Janic, always laughed at the fact that on one night every month the paint jobs on the cars filling his lot cost triple what he had paid for the whole property back in 1946.

Of all the car club regulars, the 55 Bel Air group was the smallest. In the thirty-five-plus years of its existence, it had amassed a grand total of six members. Tonight they sat in camping chairs between a cherry red four-door sedan and a salmon-pink-and-gray two-door coupe.

Anyone stopping by the three parking spaces they occupied— two for the cars, one for the club members—would receive a friendly greeting and a cup of coffee, hot cocoa, or soft drink, depending on the season.

A few years back, one of the other clubs had complained, "Two cars taking up three parking spaces for the whole night? Why can't they do like the rest of us...roll in, stay for a while, then let somebody else roll in and park? What makes them so special?"

Bud Janic made them special. Yes, there was a backstory, but neither Bud nor the 55 Bel Airs were talking.

Being a place where no one looked out of place, Bud's was the last spot anyone would think to look for the head of a small, shadowy, but very profitable high-tech arms and munitions export company blandly named the Pentangelo Group. Yet, on almost every Car Club Night there he sat: Marcus Pentangelo, the president of the 55 Bel Airs.

Sitting to Marcus's left was the club's "secretary," Darcy McManus. To his right sat the Pentangelo Group's "computer guy," Russell Branco. Next to him, the group's logistics chief, Doyle Stackhouse.

Connie Patino, former Marine and Iraq/Afghanistan War vet, sat next to another former active duty Marine: 84-year old Korean War vet Cyrus Watanabe.

Regardless of the years and an observation point some seventy feet away, Lonnie Tate recognized Marcus Pentangelo immediately.

Looks like a college professor, Lonnie laughed to himself, recalling the words of an instructor at the Farm on their first day of training. "Ladies and gentlemen, boys and girls," he had said. "In the intelligence world, most bureau chiefs look like DMV employees; most field operatives look like car mechanics, librarians, secretaries, or sales clerks. And nobody looks like Sean Connery."

"Your boy is late," Russell Branco said in his usual abrasive tone. Pentangelo knew better.

"He's here, Russell. Probably been here for some time. Reconning the area. Making sure it's me he's meeting, instead of a mob."

"You're a mob all by yourself, Pentangelo." Lonnie appeared as if out of nowhere, a half smile on his face.

Everyone but Pentangelo jumped with surprise.

"Get used to that," Marcus said. "He does it a lot."

Neither man knew what to say next.

21

Each man studied the face of the other. Physically, the years had been good to both of them. Their eyes told a different story. Each saw in the other how hard some of the intervening years had been.

"Patino said dinner was on you," Lonnie said.

"Still a smartass," Pentangelo replied with a knowing shake of his head. "Some things never change." He walked around to the passenger's side of the coupe. "Let's take a ride."

Lonnie smiled. "The last time we went for a ride, we ended up in a canal."

Marcus looked over to Darcy. "All right if we borrow your car?"

Retrieving her keys from her jacket pocket, she tossed them to Marcus who, in turn, tossed the keys to Lonnie. "This time you drive," he said, getting in the car.

Opening the door and sliding in, Lonnie turned the key. The 262-cubic-inch V8 came to life.

"Don't make 'em like this anymore, ya know?" Lonnie said, backing the car out of the parking space and heading onto the street.

Darcy and the rest of the Pentangelo Group watched as the car moved east toward the freeway.

"Haven't seen each other in over forty years," growled Russell Branco. "And not even a handshake? Your boys are hard-core, Darce."

22

"**Stay on the Five.** Head toward Dodger Stadium," Pentangelo directed. That was fifteen minutes ago. He hadn't said a word since, so Lonnie broke the silence.

"I recall a conversation back in '68. I was going back to the Corps, and you were going to who-the-hell-knows-where.

"We agreed that just living on the same continent could pose a threat to our future life expectancies. So getting together later on in life to compare pictures of the grandkids probably wouldn't be a good idea. What's changed?"

Marcus remained silent.

"I'm not a mind reader, Marcus. But I couldn't help but notice that all your club members are packing, what—Desert Eagle Glocks?"

Impressed but not surprised, this confirmed to Marcus that regardless of the years, his old friend's observation skills were still sharp.

"I mean, hey," Lonnie expounded, "even veteran cops sit, stand, and walk differently when they're carrying something that bulky."

"I need you to come to work with us, Lonnie." It sounded like a reluctant confession.

"Since when does a car club need an ad consultant?"

Marcus's jaw twitched. He'd forgotten how irritating the smart-ass in Lonnie could be.

"I'm an arms dealer, Lonnie."

"Since when does an arms dealer need an ad consultant?"

Marcus ignored the sarcasm. "Most of our clients are small one-time buyers, but we have one client that accounts for ninety percent of our business."

"And that client is?"

Pentangelo paused.

"Israel."

"Why would Israel need anything from you?"

"Being surrounded and outnumbered sixty to one gives them an appetite for some exotic and sophisticated gear, Lonnie. And before you ask, no, I don't sell 'em nukes. They make their own.

"I need...to expand my client base," Marcus continued. "In a particularly uncomfortable direction."

"Why would you do that?"

Pulling over to the emergency shoulder, Lonnie kept the car idling, but switched on the interior light. He needed to look into Pentangelo's eyes when he asked the question.

"What's goin' on, Marcus?"

After an uneasy pause, he answered. "There's a potential client I once turned down. I can't turn them down again."

23

Lonnie waited for more, but Marcus went quiet again.

Switching off the interior light and putting the car in gear, Lonnie merged back into freeway traffic.

"You're gonna have to give me a little more here, Marcus."

"It's complicated."

"I'm sure it is," Lonnie shot back. "I'm taking the next off-ramp and heading back to Bud's. If by the time we get back I don't know any more than I do now, I'll buy my own burger and call it a night."

Lonnie took the next off-ramp, made a left, drove under the overpass, accelerated up the on-ramp, and merged onto the freeway going the opposite direction.

"1989. This group approaches us." Pentangelo spoke as if each word had a bitter taste. "They've heard we have access to a wide variety of products, we deliver promptly, are discreet, yada, yada, yada. Would we be interested in doing business?

"One of my people, Darcy McManus, her BS detector goes off. Meaning these guys aren't what they say they are. Meaning A), CIA, NSA, et al., are probing us...again. Or B), they represent a buyer, or buyers, that plan on using what they want to buy from us against Israel. Either way, it's a lose-lose for us. But we don't tell them that. We tell them we'll get back to them.

"Over the next two weeks, Darcy does some intense digging. Imagine our surprise when she learns these guys are fronting for a man called 'The Engineer.'

"She discovers that The Engineer—that's what the guy liked to call himself—was a Saudi. Bankrolled and fought with the Mujahideen against the Soviets in Afghanistan."

Lonnie's was starting to connect the dots.

"This Engineer guy—you say he *was* a Saudi? He's not a Saudi anymore?"

Pentangelo grinned. "He's dead."

Lonnie gave a wistful nod. "Dead happens. Financing the Mujahideen? Interesting. Where did the dead Saudi get that kind of money? Wait. Lemme guess. Inherited, right?"

"Family was in construction. Father was tight with the royal family, built their palaces and most of their government buildings... made billions.

"Anyway, Darcy keeps digging and finds out that the year previous, Mr. Engineer is hiding out in the Arabian Desert founding a new group of sociopaths called al-Qaeda."

Outwardly, Lonnie gave a subtle nod. Inwardly, his gut tightened. *Osama bin Laden.*

"We set up a second meeting," Pentangelo went on, replaying it in his mind. "As soon as we sit down, I say, 'Who's the Engineer?' You should have seen the looks on their faces. I ask them what they need, which is our way of saying, 'Cut to the chase. You don't get to be stupid twice.'

"They hand me a list. I look at it, shake my head, tell them that at best it's iffy, but give us twenty-four hours.

"Twenty-four hours later, we sit back down. I tell them we can't deliver what they need as fast as they need it without attracting a lot of attention.

"They don't like being told no, but like anyone affiliated with this business, they understand not attracting attention."

"No fallout?"

"Strictly business. When a client can't get what it wants from one supplier, they move on. There are plenty of people who do what I do."

"I'm still not getting it, Marcus."

The arms dealer massaged his forehead. "You remember those stories about the guys in Room 319?"

"A CIA within the CIA? Come on, Marcus." Lonnie gave Pentangelo a skeptical look.

"Need I remind you who we worked for?"

Lonnie's loyalty to Howard Dade had been unwavering, but he was a realist. If Dade had deemed the creation of the Phoenix Protocol necessary back in 1968, he could also have created the Room 319 group: a group rumored to have been so specialized and stealthy it could "walk between the raindrops in a monsoon."

Lonnie grinned. "I'll admit; Dade had us working so far outside the agency charter those LSD experiments in the '50s looked like part of the agency's health-care plan.

"But it's not any screwier than you telling me that twenty-five years ago you turned down cutting a deal with some guys fronting for bin Laden."

They exited the freeway. Bud's red-and-white sign was visible a mile down the street.

"There's the rub," Marcus said in a hollow voice. "They weren't fronting for him. They were using the deal as a way to get inside his organization."

"And you know this how?"

"They paid me a visit last week."

Lonnie made the turn into the Bud's parking lot.

"So from out of nowhere, Marcus, these Room 319 guys just come diddy-boppin' into your office and say, 'Hey! Remember us?' I'm assuming you guys do have an office?"

Marcus gestured to the parking lot.

"Too upscale? You think we should tone it down?"

Lonnie chuckled.

"These are different guys," Marcus sighed. "The unit doesn't have a name. But they are definitely Room 319."

He shifted in his seat to face Lonnie.

"Things are going to get ugly with these people, Lonnie."

Lonnie maneuvered the '55 Chevy into its parking space and put it in park. "I've been out of the game a long time, Marcus."

"You still know the beast," Pentangelo countered. "You still speak its language. Point of fact, old friend, had things gone differently in Cairo, you never would have left the agency."

Turning off the ignition, Lonnie waved to Darcy, Patino, and the others.

"OK, Marcus, I'm in. But at some point, you're gonna have to tell me what you aren't telling me now. You know that, right?"

24

Darcy watched the two men get out of her car. She tossed Marcus a subtle look that asked, Well?

"Yeah, I'm in," Lonnie said to her. "Do I get a cool jacket like the other kids?"

"Maybe," she grinned. "Let me introduce you to everybody." She turned to the others. "You've already met Patino. She wants to take you home to meet her mother. She thinks you two would make a cute couple. Not her and you...you and her mother."

Lonnie liked McManus. She had sass.

"The sour-looking guy," Darcy continued, "who you will discover has a personality to match, is Russell Branco. Next to him, Doyle Stackhouse. Last, but most certainly far from least, the elder statesman of the group—"

"Cy Watanabe" Lonnie interrupted. Smiling, he offered the one-time colleague a warm handshake. "Semper Fi, my brother."

Watanabe returned the handshake, adding a bear hug. "Do or die, Slick."

Marcus was as surprised as everyone else. "Cyrus? You two know—?"

"I can neither confirm nor deny how or where," Watanabe smiled. "But yes, Marcus. Lonnie and I know each other."

Lonnie had parked in the parking lot of the brewery across the street from Bud's. As he approached his car, he felt a twitch in his back.

Somebody was watching.

From out of nowhere, a kid—eighteen, maybe nineteen—was in his face.

"Money, old man...right now."

An inch or so shorter than Lonnie, and weighing half as much, he had a knife pressed firmly against Lonnie's stomach.

"No problem." Lonnie's voice was relaxed, almost soothing.

The kid was borderline panicky. That told Lonnie he wasn't a pro, which made things worse. Nervous, panicky amateurs—especially punk kids with knives—do nervous, panicky things.

"My wallet is in the inside pocket of my jacket."

Lonnie slowly raised both of his hands, one straight up in the air, the other to the inside of his jacket.

The kid's eyes widened, he slapped down the arm reaching for the wallet, and pressed the knife firmer against Lonnie's stomach

"Get that hand up, or I'll gut you, old man."

Lonnie slowly raised the hand. "Alright, alright. Relax. No need for this to get any more intense than it already is."

The kid reached his free hand into Lonnie's jacket to retrieve the wallet. He never saw Lonnie's arms move. Never felt Lonnie's cupped hands slam against his ears.

But he did feel an explosion in his head, immediately followed by a combination of roaring and ringing so loud and painful he almost vomited. Which was followed by a painful loss of sight, as Lonnie gouged his fingers into the kid's eyes.

Choking on an agonizing scream that wouldn't come out, the kid buckled to his knees...then puked.

Now in possession of the knife, Lonnie stood over him.

"There was a time," Lonnie said in the same relaxed voice, "I would have slit your throat."

He paused to unlock his car door.

"But, as Bob Dylan once said, 'I was so much older then...I'm younger than that now.'"

Dropping the knife to the ground, Lonnie scanned the parking lot. Somebody else was watching.

Come out; come out, wherever you are. Nothing.

Calmly getting in the car, Lonnie started the engine and drove away.

A man wearing a yellow windbreaker approached the kid, who was having trouble getting back up on his feet.

His head still ringing, the kid mumbled, "That old guy is crazy."

"Hardly," the man scolded. "You let his age and girth make a fool of you. You were stupid."

25

ENCINO, CALIFORNIA

Four turns after getting off "the Boulevard"—Ventura Boulevard to non-San Fernando Valley residents—Lonnie pulled into the driveway of a house much like the others in the wooded hillside area just below the Encino Reservoir.

Parking next to a new pearlescent-white Silverado pickup with a hard cover over the box, he wondered. *Marcus driving a pickup?*

Unlike the Silverado, the house matched Marcus Pentangelo's persona: upscale but understated. This had to be a storefront. Longevity as an arms dealer relied on never mixing your professional life with your personal life.

As Lonnie reached to ring the bell, the door swung open. Connie Patino welcomed him with the same smile she had the first time they met.

"Hey, Lonnie."

"Semper Fi, Ms. Patino. OK to park in the driveway?"

"I'll open the garage so you can pull in," she replied. "Follow me." She led him through the large kitchen toward a door he assumed opened to the garage.

Walking behind her, Lonnie's attention was drawn to her attractive rear end. He found moral redemption in the fact that he noticed this because of something even more impressive—her walk.

Just losing a toe threw off a person's balance so much it required learning a new way to walk. Although she had a prosthesis from her knee down, Connie walked with the grace of an athlete. *How many hours of exhausting physical therapy did this kid put in to pull that off?*

Connie opened the door that did in fact lead to the garage, and smacked a button on the wall. As she closed the door, Lonnie heard the garage door going up.

Taking his arm, she led him through what had at one time been a living room, then back out to the driveway. Her smile got even bigger when she saw his gleaming silver 1999 5-Series BMW.

"A vintage Five-Series Bimmer? Class and a half, Lonnie." She ran her fingers along the roofline.

"You're lucky I like you, Ms. Patino," Lonnie growled.

"You don't like people touching the car, I know," she smiled again. "Marcus said you get mental about that kind of stuff."

"I might get more mental about you describing a car built after I turned fifty as vintage."

Connie folded her hands in front of her as she walked toward the front door.

"BMW broke the mold when they rolled that model off the line. You knew that when you bought her. In fact, I bet that's why you bought her.

"If you think I'm sharp," she added with a wink, "wait 'til you meet my mom. Pull in and park. We'll see you back inside."

Lonnie couldn't help but smile. And he couldn't help but notice that there were no cars parked in the two-car garage. And that where the back wall should have been, there was a second open garage door.

He climbed in his car and twisted the key.

26

As soon as Lonnie drove in, the garage door lowered behind him. Pulling through the open back wall, he found four angled parking spaces sheltered by an opaque canopy.

Lonnie pulled his BMW in beside a late-model black Corvette just as the rear door descended.

A pair of open French doors led into a tastefully appointed conference room. There to greet him were Marcus and his wife, Mary. Although they had never met, Lonnie recognized her from the family pictures included in the Christmas cards the Pentangelos had been sending him for more than thirty years, always to his current address, no matter how recently he'd moved.

"Morning, Marcus. I'm guessing the attractive woman you have your arm around is your wife?"

"Lonnie Tate." Mary Pentangelo smiled as she stuck out her right hand. "You wouldn't believe how much I've heard about you over the years."

Lonnie glanced at Marcus as he shook her hand. "Any of it good?"

Releasing Lonnie's hand, she slipped her arm into her husband's. "All of it."

"Yes, well, Marcus is at the age where the memory starts to go." Mary's laugh sounded like music, loud music.

Marcus spoke for the first time. "Told you he's a smartass."

"Well, this should be fun," Mary teased. "God knows nobody else around here is like that."

She's smart, and she has a story, thought Lonnie. *No doubt she keeps him on his toes.*

"You're driving a pickup now, Marcus?" Lonnie asked. "How... *everyman* of you."

Marcus shook his head. "That's hers. I've been trying for more than forty years to get her to—"

"I was raised on a ranch," Mary explained. "You can take the girl out of Montana...." She grinned at Marcus, then kissed him on the cheek. "I've gotta run, and you have work to do."

Marcus pointed to a mug of coffee on the counter as they stepped through the kitchen. "That's yours. Follow me."

Marcus's office was bigger than the others. *Must have been the master bedroom.*

"Yeah," Marcus said, reading Lonnie's mind as he sat down behind his glass-and-steel desk, "this was the master. We bought the place a few years after we moved out from Boston. Raised the kids here. After they both went off to school, we moved out to Agoura Hills."

"See 'em much?" Lonnie asked, lowering himself into a chair facing Marcus.

"Oh, yeah. Half a dozen times a year." Marcus folded his hands behind his head and leaned back. "And we all meet up someplace for the holidays. Speaking of kids, rumor has it there's an attorney in Phoenix, I believe. Seems she's making quite a name for herself."

"Yep. Best damn lawyer that scum-sucking, bottom-dwelling, shyster law firm ever had. By the way, the Christmas cards over the years? Nice touch."

Marcus nodded. "You weren't that hard for Darcy to keep tabs on, old friend. The few times you went off the grid, she just started keeping tabs on your daughter. Eventually you showed up."

"Don't know what hurts the most, my daughter leading you to me, or my daughter being a lawyer," he laughed. "Gotta tell you, Marcus. South of the Boulevard, San Fernando Valley lifestyle? This 'Masters of War' thing has worked out well for you."

"Get your cryptic, not to mention cliché, description of my profession straight. I'm a Death Merchant. I sell 'em. I don't build 'em...most of the time."

After a few seconds of silence, Marcus said, "You obviously have questions."

Lonnie nodded.

"Shoot."

"These Room 319 guys who don't have a name. You said they didn't like being told no the first time. Guys like that don't usually knock on the door a second time if they think they're going to get the same answer."

Lonnie's tone softened. "Marcus...what do they have on you?"

The arms dealer frowned, looking off into the distance. Lonnie was putting the pieces together faster than he had anticipated.

"Suffice it to say," Marcus sighed, "you and I aren't the only people who did work we don't want anyone else to know about."

Lonnie gave a knowing nod. "Mary."

Marcus shook his head and looked away. "I'd rather not—"

"I don't need to know anything else, Marcus."

"Yes, you do. But I can't right now."

27

Walking back into the conference room, Marcus took his usual seat at the head of the table. He motioned for Lonnie to take the empty chair at the opposite end.

Lonnie made eye contact with each member of the group as he sat. His gut told him Russell Branco didn't like him. Which was confirmed my Branco's opening question.

"Marcus? What did you get us into that we need this—whoever or whatever the hell he is?"

Russell Branco was a Vietnam vet. After discharge from the army, he evolved into a Steve Jobs–type genius for computer program development—minus the Jobs high profile. Which was OK with Russell. A high profile tended to attract wannabes and the press. Among those in the world he classified as "scabs on the ass of humanity," which included almost everyone, wannabes and the press were tied for first place.

Appreciating Branco's Jobs-esque genius meant tolerating his John Gotti–type temperament. Consequently, Russell got fired a lot.

Doyle Stackhouse brought Branco to Marcus. The circumstances surrounding how Stackhouse and Branco met remained a mystery to Marcus and the rest of the group.

Doyle Stackhouse came to the Pentangelo Group in 1980 through a chance meeting at Bud's and a conversation with Marcus that lasted all night. Also a Vietnam vet, Stackhouse was an Air Force F-4 Phantom mechanic. The day after his discharge in 1971, he hitchhiked from Andrews Air Force Base near Washington, D.C., to Florida to attend NASCAR's Daytona 500. Once inside the raceway, he talked his way into the pit area, where he approached a pit-crew chief and talked his way into a job.

By 1979, Stackhouse was the logistics crew chief for a well-known Formula 1 racing team. He was also the NASCAR and Formula 1 racing world's go-to guy when it came to acquiring, warehousing, or delivering anything having to do with a race car anywhere in the world within twenty-four hours—without leaving a paper trail.

Connie Patino was in rehab learning to walk again when Darcy McManus found the young Iraq/Afghanistan War vet. Observing Patino tough her way through the pain of rehab, and learning from contacts at Headquarters, Marine Corps, that Corporal Patino had been awarded the Silver Star for bravery, Darcy went to Marcus.

"This kid can do something for us, Marcus."

"OK, what?" Pentangelo challenged.

"That's what we have to figure out."

"We?"

"Yes, Marcus...you and me. We are going to make a place for her, and you are going to be glad we did."

Darcy was right. When it came to designing, building, defusing or disposing of a high-tech explosive device, Connie Patino was one of the best Marcus had ever worked with.

As for Darcy McManus, she, her late husband, Aaron, and Marcus were the original Pentangelo Group. Marcus and Aaron set up and ran the everyday workings of the organization. Darcy was the palace guard—the reason the CIA, NSA, and the rest of the global intelligence community couldn't find and infiltrate the group.

"She can spot a phony and smell a lie from across the continent," Marcus would always say. Even as a child, Darcy had an uncanny ability to read people. Teachers and friends found it a little unnerving.

Her parents and two older brothers found it downright creepy.

In Vietnam, she spent three years as a U.S. Navy trauma nurse with 1st Hospitals Company in Chu Lai. In civilian life she would eventually become the head nurse of a regional trauma center in Southern California before retiring.

Now a doting grandmother, Darcy was also Marcus Pentangelo's consigliere, the job her husband held until he was killed as the result of an aerial-surveillance analyst at NSA "misreading" three photographs and having the military SMART-bomb the wrong target.

Then there was former active duty Marine, Cy Watanabe. Marcus likened the 84-year old Korean War vet to a more sophisticated version of Lonnie Tate.

As with Lonnie, if you looked closely, you could see death in Watanabe's eyes. And it had nothing to do with his ability to rebuild and make more lethal any sidearm, rifle, or automatic weapon made since World War I.

Though Marcus had no firsthand knowledge, he was quite sure a few people had died after coming face-to-face with Cyrus Watanabe. Certainly that was why and how Cy and Lonnie knew each other.

28

Marcus knew Branco wouldn't like the answer.

"Well, as to what I got us into, Russell, and why we need the talents of my longtime friend, Lonnie, here...suffice it to say, we're going to be doing business with some very bad people."

"How bad?"

From the expressions on the others' faces, they were wondering the same thing.

"I'm not happy about it either, guys."

Branco slumped down in his chair like a sullen teenage boy. "That's a non-answer answer, Marcus. Which begs two more questions. Why the hell are we doing it? And what about our client in Tel Aviv? Our main and most revenue-producing client, I might add. What are they gonna say when—not if—but when they find out?"

"Russell, I'm not sure whether to tell Tel Aviv right away or wait until I see what kinds of safeguards we can create so it won't come back and bite them."

"Or us," Branco countered.

Lonnie had to give Branco his props. The cyber geek wasn't afraid to play devil's advocate. It made Marcus crazy, but he was thankful for it as well. From the group's beginnings, Marcus knew he didn't know everything, nor could he do everything. That's why he never had a problem asking, as he did now, "Any ideas?"

Stackhouse spoke first.

"What, specifically do they want and how much of it do they need? Where will it be going? That's going to have a lot to do with what you tell these guys."

"How so?"

"What, how much, and where determines how it's sent. Small lots in containers means sea transport. Are we gonna haul it over the road, or will they pick it up at the dock? There could be a lotta moving parts just in the delivery. As far as assurances to Tel Aviv, I'm guessing the best assurance would be giving them the information to interrupt the supply chain, right?"

"Something like that." Marcus nodded.

Cy Watanabe frowned. "They requesting modifications?"

"I don't know yet, Cy. They phoned me three days ago. Told me in vague terms that they wanted to do business. That I'd find it 'mutually rewarding.' They said they'd give us a few days to check them out, then one of their 'associates' would meet with someone from our team and present a list of what they require."

Branco sneered. "They think one of us is gonna sit there and check boxes on an order sheet?"

Marcus gave him a tired smile. "The guy who called said they'd give us a flash drive with—"

"No." Branco interrupted. Leaning forward, he jabbed the table with his finger. "Don't take anything digital from these guys. That gives them access to our system. No tellin' how many files they'll corrupt or steal. Tell 'em to put it on paper."

Now it was Patino's turn. "Marcus, you still haven't answered the question. Why are you doing this?"

Marcus looked up at Lonnie and then turned to the twenty-eight-year-old veteran.

"I'm being coerced by, for lack of a better term, an agency of our government. This agency surreptitiously tried to get me to do business with Osama bin Laden in the late '80s. I turned them down."

Marcus paused. No one said anything.

"It's been made very clear to me that this time I don't have a choice. This is going to get ugly. That's why Lonnie is here."

"How soon do they want to meet?" Stackhouse asked. "The sooner we know what they want, the sooner we can start mitigating the damage."

"I got another call this morning. They want to meet in Tampa this week." He looked at Lonnie. "Let me rephrase that. They want to meet with you in Tampa this week."

Before anyone could respond, Darcy's cell phone rang. She spun her chair so she was facing away from the table. It didn't matter; everyone was listening.

"Hey, Peg. What's up?"

Her daughter, Patino mouthed to Lonnie.

"Oh, no! Anyone hurt? Uh-huh. OK. How are Brittany and Nathan? Uh-huh. Yeah, I'll bet. You're leaving now? Let's do this: I'll pick up some Happy Meals for the kids and meet you at your place. Sound good? OK. See you in about a half-hour."

"What's up, Darce?" Branco asked, something like genuine concern in his voice. He showed more civility to Darcy than to anyone else.

"Minor catastrophe. I've gotta make an emergency run over to Thousand Oaks," she said, closing her notebook and putting her phone in her purse. "Peggy's kids' school bus was in an accident. No one's hurt, but the kids are a little shaken up. Actually, I think the kids are fine, but their mother is pretty shaken up."

Marcus smiled and nodded.

"Come to think of it," Darcy grinned, "Peggy must really be freaking out. She didn't tell me no when I said I'd bring fast food for her kids." She stood up. "I'll be back this afternoon, Marcus."

"No need," Marcus said as he stood. "We're just about done here, and there's nothing that needs your attention today."

"You sure?" Darcy asked.

"Absolutely. Go take care of your grandchildren, and their mom."

"Thanks, Marcus." She glanced around the table. "Don't worry, people. We're going to take care of this thing." With that bit of reassurance, the former combat trauma nurse let herself out through the French doors.

"I don't like this new guy Tate."

Branco and Stackhouse were in Doyle's Chevy Suburban.

"You don't like anybody, Russell," Stackhouse replied. "That's why you can't get along with anyone."

"I get along with you," Branco protested.

"Doesn't count," Stackhouse countered, turning into Branco's driveway. "I get along with everybody."

"I'm bettin' those guys don't just want computers, Doyle," Branco said as the Suburban came to a stop. He looked straight at Stackhouse, concern replacing the low-grade anger he usually nursed. "High-end weapons systems interface with computers. And computers can be weaponized."

29

As soon as Branco walked in, he saw it. "The Cat" hung unevenly. That alone was enough to send him to the edge of rage.

The original oil painting of a mountain lion stalking over snow-covered ground was his favorite—the first piece he'd bought. When he saw it in a Jackson Hole art gallery, he didn't know it would begin a valuable collection of more than a dozen works by contemporary artists.

Branco retrieved a small level from a drawer in the kitchen. After doing some naked-eye straightening, he used the level to complete the job. Then panic hit him. *My computers.*

Hurrying through each room of his immaculate home, he was relieved to discover that nothing was missing or even slightly out of place. His computers were still there.

He checked the front and back doors. Neither had been forced or jimmied. It was all very odd. *Who would break into a house just to make a painting hang crooked?*

Doyle Stackhouse saw the dog biscuits as soon as the remote-controlled gate opened. Someone had tried to get onto the property. They'd done enough homework to know he had dogs and had probably tainted the treats to sedate or kill them.

What they didn't know was that Stackhouse had trained his two Rottweilers, Donnie and Marie, never to accept food from anyone but him.

A minivan was parked in Patino's space. She paid an extra hundred bucks a month for that space at the end of a row in the gated garage. It was her spot—and everybody in the complex knew it. It didn't matter that it was a longer walk from the stairs and elevator. Snugging her 'Vette close to the wall made it impossible for anyone to open the door on the passenger's side and get into her car.

Patino noticed a small car-rental sticker on the minivan's rear bumper. Driving around to the leasing office, she parked, went inside, and talked to the leasing manager. He called a towing company. Half an hour later, the minivan was gone.

The minute Lonnie saw his front door slightly ajar, the Magnum was in his hand.

He checked the kitchen first, then the dining area and living room. *Nobody.*

Entering his bedroom, he saw that the closet door was open and the light was on. Swinging the door open with his left foot, he planted and pointed the Magnum into the walk-in. *No one.*

He hurried back to the living room. The drapes over the sliding glass door were in the same position he had left them. Regardless, he went out onto the balcony and opened the door to the storage closet. *Empty.*

Holstering the Magnum, he stepped back inside.

Front door slightly open. Nothing taken, but things were moved. Things I would notice...like the closet light.

Lonnie knew what this was. He just didn't know who did it or why. Normally he would have brooded over it. But not tonight.

30

Beverly Hills, California

Driving through Beverly Hills reaffirmed to Lonnie that he could never live there. Even though now, with his new job, he could afford it.

Tonight, he could tolerate this designer-label-infested enclave, where pet dogs and cats looked every bit as arrogant as their owners.

Tonight, he was having dinner with the only female he had ever known how to talk to. It had been that way from the time she was a little girl. His daughter, Donna.

"We're celebrating, and I'm buying," she'd insisted when she called him to make the date. That's why he was wearing his "grown-up clothes," an expensive suit, classy tie, and spit-shined shoes.

Getting out of his car, Lonnie handed the valet the keys. "No jacking around with my ride, son. She's old, but she's like a daughter to me, OK?"

"Dude, you're kidding, right?"

"Dude?" Lonnie answered. "Young man, being young entitles you to be stupid, not to call me 'dude.' Yet, seeing as how 'dude' may be one of the more eloquent words in your vocabulary, you can address me as Mr. Dude. That way I won't get back in my car and run over you."

"You'll have to excuse my father, Jason," said a woman's voice from behind the valet. "He's a sixty-six-year-old man with an attitude ten times his age."

"Ms. Tate?" The valet recognized her voice. "Wow! Cool deal. How's things in, ah, Arizona, right?"

Wearing a tailored gray knit dress that complemented her figure, Donna Tate's blond hair, deep green eyes, and Arizona-tanned face made it hard for Lonnie to picture her as the little girl she once was.

"Yes, Jason. Arizona is great, and things are going well, thank you. Be nice to my father. He will run over you." She said, smiling at Lonnie.

"Dad, this is Jason. Despite his talent for making lousy first impressions, he really is a bright kid."

Lonnie offered a handshake.

"Jason, Lonnie Tate. But like I said, Mr. Dude will work."

In heels, Donna was half a head taller than her father. Without a hint of self-consciousness, she wrapped her arms around his neck and pressed her cheek against his.

"Hey, kid, how ya doin'?" Lonnie whispered.

When she held the embrace, he knew something was wrong.

31

Donna leaned back and looked at her father. "Let's go inside. We've got some serious celebrating to do."

Escorting him past the smiling maître d', Donna slid into their booth. Lonnie beamed. In a room full of beauty, he was sitting with the most elegant woman in the place.

"What's the special occasion?"

She glanced down, then looked up and shot him the smile she had perfected by the time she was five years old.

"Well, you know I've been living in that apartment I found when I first moved to Phoenix because it's close to the office. But the building is old and has...issues."

Lonnie smiled. *Issues, hell. The place was a hazmat dump site disguised as an apartment building.*

"So, while grousing about said issues at work one day, one of the other lawyers asks why I don't just buy a place. He reaches into his shirt pocket and pulls out a business card. It's a real-estate agent who helped him and his boyfriend find their place. He said she was knowledgeable and wasn't pushy, so I should call her.

"Well, I did. We met at a Starbucks to talk about what I need, what I can afford. The next day she calls with three places to check out, and they're all within five minutes' drive of my office.

"Long story short," she grinned, "one of them is on the same block as the law offices, so I took it."

Lonnie's eyes widened. "That neighborhood's like...like here."

"I know. It's half again more than I was paying, but half again bigger because...there's a nice-sized guest room. And I can walk to work, even in the summer. It's beautiful. I can't wait for you to see it."

"Congratulations, kid. I'm happy for you."

"Now, before I tell you the second reason we're celebrating"—she pretended to be serious— "you have to promise not to go into your speech about my 'butthead, bottom-dwelling attorney bosses finally pulling their heads out of their collective asses," she said, mimicking him perfectly.

"I'll do my best."

Pausing slightly for dramatic effect, she said, "I made partner."

"'Bout damn time." Lonnie exclaimed loud enough to be heard throughout the restaurant.

The proud father shrugged his shoulders apologetically. "Counsel should acknowledge that despite the outburst, not one comment about your butthead, bottom-dwelling attorney bosses has escaped my lips."

"Counsel acknowledges, but stipulates that the night is still young. You do realize," she laughed, "making partner officially makes me one of those butthead, bottom-dwelling attorneys you hold in such low regard."

He reached across the table for her hand. "You making partner brings an element of class to that firm that did not exist until they had the good sense to hire you."

She glanced down. "Thank you, Dad," she whispered.

When she looked up, there were tears in her eyes.

He waited for her to tip her head back slightly and sniffle, her way of regaining her composure.

"You want to leave?"

Arching her eyebrows, she folded her arms and leaned forward on the table.

"No, let's stay. And order something ridiculously expensive. I'm a partner now, so this goes on the firm's expense account."

He gave her the "whenever you're ready" look she needed to see. Then halfway through dinner, she came back back around to the subject.

"Last Friday, the day I made partner, a bunch of us went out for drinks after work to celebrate. I don't ever have more than a glass or two of wine. That's all I had on Friday. That's why I'm sure... someone drugged me."

Lonnie flinched.

"I woke up Saturday morning in a suite at the Biltmore, near the office. But I don't remember going there or—" Her eyes welled with tears again.

"I looked around the room for my clothes, but all I saw was a hotel bathrobe lying on a chair a few feet from the bed. I'm thinking, Great. Now I'm a statistic.

"There are sliding doors that close off the bedroom from the rest of the suite. I get up, put on the robe, open the doors, and there's this woman from the firm."

"Your firm?" Lonnie asked.

"She showed up when we were having drinks...says she is with the San Diego office, even gave me her card. She tells me she was at Berkeley when I was. Says we had some of the same professors. We laugh about some of 'em, their tics and idiosyncrasies." She paused, as if not knowing what to say next.

"Keep talking, hon," Lonnie encouraged.

"She asks what year I graduated from law school. I tell her. She says, 'Me too.' I tell her I don't remember her from any classes. She asks if I was at Boalt, and I say, 'No, Hastings,' and she says, 'Oh, well that explains it.' She did law at Boalt. And that's the last thing I remember about our conversation."

Donna fell quiet again. Reaching for her water glass, she

knocked it over, then robotically mopped it up using the cloth napkin from her lap.

"My only thought is to get dressed and get out of that hotel room. I ask her what she's done with my clothes. She's sitting on them. I can't believe it.

"I walk over and reach for my clothes...she pulls them away and holds them back over the couch and says, 'Not so fast.'"

"She tells me to...take off the...the robe. Then she...hands me one item of clothing at a time. Like I was a whore."

Donna looked at her father. "Dad...I'm not...I've never been attracted to other—"

"And if you were," Lonnie gently interrupted, "no judgment here. You know that, right?"

Sniffling, she nodded and smiled. "Yeah. I just needed to hear it."

"Did you report this to the police?" He already knew the answer.

"And tell them what? There was no evidence of a crime."

It was good to see her temper flare, trying to move herself out of victim mode.

"Yeah," Lonnie sighed, "and she knew you wouldn't say anything to anyone at the firm."

"But I checked her out when I went back to work on Monday, Dad."

"What came up?"

Donna's voice became calm and analytical. "Berkeley and Boalt have no record of anyone with her name. The State Bar of California has no record of anyone with her name ever being a member, or taking the exam.

"But there's something else. I got an email at home Sunday night, no return path. 'Have a nice weekend?' on the subject line. And there was an attachment. They're photos. Photos of her and me—"

"Photoshopped?" her father asked.

Donna shook her head. "No. I noticed I had bruises when I

got home Saturday morning. The pictures explain the bruises. Dad, I'm a partner at a firm with some very conservative clients. If those pictures ever—"

"Don't worry about those pictures."

"How can I not worry about them?"

"Well," he began, "this is going to sound strange—"

"Strange?" Donna interrupted with nervous laughter. "Based on this conversation, I have to ask, as compared to what?"

"Point taken, sweetheart. So I'm just gonna say it. Send me that email."

"Right. Just what every girl wants to email her dad. Pictures of—"

"I know a guy. He's a computer geek; one of those guys they keep locked away in a room all by himself. I'm going to show him that email...don't worry; he won't open the attachment. He'll know how to track this back to whoever sent it. And he'll fix it so it doesn't happen again."

Lonnie watched Jason climb out of his daughter's Lexus, hold the door open, then close it when she slid in.

Seeing Lonnie, the valet gave him a nod. "I'll get yours next, Mr. Dude."

"Thank you, Jason." He looked at his daughter. "I might start liking that kid."

"He's a smartass, like you," Donna replied. "With time and the right guidance, he might even become as good at it as you—Nah, I take that back."

"The only person that even comes close to being as much of a smartass as I am, is you. Makes me proud. And don't worry about a thing," he reassured her. "Like I said, I know a guy."

Other than the large outlines of his time in the Marine Corps, Vietnam, and his ad-agency days, Donna Tate knew very little about her father. She had wanted to know more, but whenever he said things like "I know a guy," a little voice warned: Be careful what you wish for.

"How come I can tell my dad anything because he knows everything about me, but I know very little about him?

"You started a new job today," she said before he could respond. "You didn't say a word about it at dinner."

"Because you are more important than my new job. But in the interest of partial disclosure, I'm working for an old friend. A guy I was with in Vietnam. The job is great, and so is the pay. As to your other concern, there are things you never need to know about me, kiddo. Yeah, I know. To quote one of the guys I work with now, 'That's a non-answer answer.' But it's the most truthful answer I can give you. You get what I'm sayin'?"

"Yeah, I get what you're sayin'...for now. Love you, Dad."

Putting her car in gear, she drove away.

32

Lonnie's brain wouldn't turn off.

His daughter's assailant had done some homework. She knew studying law at Berkeley meant graduating from Boalt or Hastings. Granted, a Google search would tell you that. But a Google search wouldn't give you an individual student's professors and said professors' idiosyncrasies. Gathering that kind of intel required gaining access to the student's personal records and class schedule, then observing the professors' behavior by sitting in their classes. Which meant Donna's assailant was a pro.

A week ago, he was a security guard at an amusement park. Then an Iraq/Afghanistan War vet sets off a metal detector coming through a turnstile.

The next night he is reunited with a guy he hasn't seen since they served together in the CIA. The guy offers him a job paying ten times per week what he makes in a month as a security guard. The job's only downside? He could get killed.

Topping off the evening, some jerk kid tries to mug him on his way back to his car.

Then today, his first day on his new job. His buddy tells him that because of something having to do with the buddy's wife, the buddy is being blackmailed.

The school-bus accident with Darcy's grandkids.

The break-in at his apartment.

In a life lived a long time ago, Lonnie had learned that when so many of those kinds of "events" happen within such a short time frame...it's never a coincidence.

33

Russell Branco didn't recognize the number on his cell phone. It was after midnight. That was reason enough to ignore the call. But he picked it up anyway.

"Who's this?" he barked.

"Hey, Russ, it's Lonnie Tate. Marcus gave me your number."

Branco didn't know whether to be more irritated at Tate for calling or Marcus for giving Tate his number.

"Whatta you want? It's after midnight."

"I hate to be a pain in the butt, Russ, but I need you to track the source of an unsolicited email. It's got something to do with the op."

Branco's defenses shot up. "What kind of something?" Unsolicited contact with anybody at this time of night meant nothing but trouble.

"If I knew that, I wouldn't need your expertise, now would I? Look, Russ. I know there's no way you want me to send you this email. I know you don't want me pokin' around stuff at your place and maybe touching something I shouldn't. So could you stop by my place in the morning, on your way into the office? You can look at the email on my computer, and we'll go from there. I'm sure I don't live too far from you."

"How the hell do you know where I live?" Branco's irritation returned.

"I don't, but when we met at Bud's I realized I see you sometimes at the Ralph's store over on Coldwater and Ventura."

"You what—?"

"Relax, Russ, I notice everybody. Old habits, ya know? Look. I wouldn't bother you if it wasn't important." Lonnie set the hook. "I'm giving you a chance to screw with people who really have it coming, who damn sure won't expect it, and who probably don't know half as much as you do."

The quiet on Branco's end said it all. Lonnie had him.

34

Hunched over Lonnie's laptop the next morning, Branco's fingers flew over the keyboard.

"Who sent you this?"

"I had my daughter forward it to me."

Branco looked up. "You said it has something to do with the op. You're importing corrupted emails? And what the hell is your daughter doing on this op?"

Lonnie let the questions hang in the air for a moment. Once again, the computer genius was asking the right questions.

"My daughter isn't doing anything on the op," Lonnie said. "Someone sent the email to her. It has an attachment with compromising photos, and—"

"You imported an email with an attachment? Because, what? Your daughter took pictures with her boyfriend?"

Lonnie took a deep breath. "My daughter didn't take the pictures, Russ. She was drugged and has no memory of what's in them.

"Whoever set this up," Lonnie continued, "did it to get at me, at us. Maybe so we'll back off...maybe so we'll speed up. I'm not sure yet."

"Whattaya want me to do?" Branco looked away. Lonnie made him nervous.

"I want you to find out where the email came from. And block any more transmissions from that source to my daughter's email. This is her personal account. If I give you her work account, can you block transmissions there too?"

"Hell, yeah."

"Good. Because I want you to mess with the sender's account, cripple it...permanently if possible. Can you do that?"

"I can block any account from anything, once I find where it's coming from. As far as screwing up the sender's account...temporarily? I can have it done in about forty-five minutes. Permanently? I'd need more time."

Lonnie thought for a moment.

"It's probably better if it isn't permanent. Let whoever's on the other end think temporary is the best you can do. Let them underestimate you. Make 'em more vulnerable, right?"

A rare smile, then Branco turned back to Lonnie's laptop and went to work.

Forty-five minutes later, mission accomplished.

"It came from a source in the federal government," Branco explained. "It was buried...deep. But not deep enough, arrogant bastards."

"Thanks, Russ. I appreciate it, and I'll return the favor."

"How? What the hell can you do for me?"

"Who knows?" Lonnie replied. "Something'll come up. It always does."

Branco studied Tate, running all sorts of scenarios. Nothing fit.

"Uh, yeah. OK." He stood and made his way to the door of the apartment. "I'll see ya, Tate."

Walking to his car, Russell Branco couldn't remember ever feeling more relieved to get away from someone.

35

LOS ANGELES, CALIFORNIA

The caller told Marcus he wanted to meet with him and Lonnie at 10:00 a.m. Could they come to his office? He apologized for any inconvenience. *Right*, thought Marcus.

The skyscraper screamed success, stretching up thirty-six stories midway between the Harbor Freeway and Staples Center. Getting off the elevator on a middle floor, Marcus and Lonnie turned left and entered a suite of offices identified only by a number.

The receptionist escorted them down a short hallway and into a conference room, where they found a large polished-mahogany table and ten executive chairs. Three walls were paneled with dark wood. The fourth was filled by north-facing windows overlooking Griffith Park and the "Hollywood" sign.

Marcus took a chair at one end of the table; Lonnie sat beside him.

After two minutes of silence, the door opened and a man carrying a manila folder walked in. Marcus had never seen him before. Lonnie had...four years earlier.

The smug smile on Jason Beck's face matched the double-breasted dark suit, muted tie, and starched white shirt ensemble he'd worn every day at Morgenthaler & Trent.

Jason's smile melted away when Lonnie returned it with a look of boredom. This annoyed Beck, who was relying on the element of surprise to establish who would be in charge of the meeting.

Placing the folder on the table, Beck sat down next to Tate. "Good seeing you again, Lonnie," he said. "How long has it been?"

Lonnie didn't answer, an immediate indication to Marcus that whoever Jason Beck was, this meeting was a bad idea.

"You're not going to introduce me to your new boss?" Beck asked.

Giving Beck a cold smile, Lonnie addressed Marcus.

"Marcus, this asshole is Jason Beck, from my advertising days at Morgenthaler and Trent. Look up the word weasel in the dictionary, and you'll find an eight-by-ten glossy of him."

"What do you want, Mr. Beck?" Marcus asked, brushing an imaginary piece of lint off the pant leg of his $4,000 suit.

Beck opened the manila folder, casually thumbed through the pages inside, then set it down again.

"We need a progress report, Marcus."

Marcus had been around men like Jason Beck all his life. At the university where his father taught and which he later attended. At the social gatherings he had to tolerate. They all looked the same: generic square-jawed, country-club-handsome face; fitness-center physique; outsized family connections; oversized ego; contempt or jealousy for everyone they met. All talk and no walk.

"It's been less than two weeks, Mr. Beck. Your concern is premature."

"You're a lot like your pal Lonnie." Beck glanced at Tate. "No sense of urgency about anything unless you decide it's urgent, right? Let me give you a little...incentive."

Opening the folder again, Beck spread a dozen large photos on the table. The pictures, obviously surveillance shots, showed two women, attractive...and naked.

Marcus recognized Lonnie's daughter in the photos and immediately knew what was going to happen next.

Beck looked up from the photos briefly and glanced at Lonnie. "Your little girl takes a nice picture, Lon—"

Suddenly Jason Beck was unable to speak. Or breathe. His eyes bulged wildly; his face turned bright red.

Lonnie, much quicker than a man his age and bulk should be, had clamped his right hand around Beck's throat, his fingers and thumb digging deep into Beck's windpipe. His trachea giving way, Beck's face turned from red to blue. His hands flailed as he tried to grab Lonnie's wrist. Marcus could only watch.

Nobody heard the door open, but Marcus's head snapped around when he heard a distantly familiar voice shouting in a language he hadn't heard in more than forty-five years.

"Dung lai, dung lai!"

Keeping his eyes on Beck, Lonnie slightly loosened his grip. Something was out of sync. The language...it was Vietnamese. He still understood it, and he recognized that command. He was being told *Stop...don't do it!* But the voice—.

A hand gently squeezed Lonnie's forearm. "Lonnie, please," Brian Shapiro said, his voice relaxed yet firm. "Let him go."

36

The face was drawn and gaunt, the eyes dull and nearly lifeless. Brian Shapiro could have passed for being ten years Lonnie's and Marcus's senior. The only thing time hadn't stolen was his unmistakable Philly accent.

In disbelief, Lonnie and Marcus instantly flashed back to 1968. Cairo, Egypt. A car in an alley. On the dashboard, a Polaroid of Brian Shapiro's bloody, battered corpse lying half in, half out of the car.

"Mr. Beck," Brian Shapiro said evenly, "I ask you to make a phone call to set up a meeting...." His voice trailed off as the photos on the table caught his attention.

"What is this, Mr. Beck?" Shapiro pointed at the pictures. "My first rule: families are always off-limits."

A discernment that had lain dormant in Lonnie for more than four decades was instantly reawakened. *Families?* he thought. *He knows one of those women is my daughter.*

"Lonnie, I have well over forty years that need to be accounted for to you and Marcus," Shapiro said. "I don't care what you do to Beck, but you can't do it now. If it would advance the course of what needs to happen, I'd do it for you. But it won't. So please, if for nothing else than our time in Vietnam, hear me out."

Advancing what course? What needs to happen? Instinct forced Lonnie to dial back his rage.

Gasping and rubbing his throat, a sputtering Jason Beck tried to find words to justify his actions.

"There is no defense for this, Mr. Beck. Get out." Shapiro again pointed to the pictures. "Take that filth with you. And as soon as time and circumstances permit, I will inform Mr. Tate of your whereabouts and assist him in getting to you. And you can be assured, he will kill you."

Panic-stricken and cowering, Beck grabbed the pictures and ran from the room.

Shapiro allowed a few seconds of silence to clear air. He turned to Pentangelo. "The years have been good to you, Marcus."

With a hint of a nod, Pentangelo acknowledged their resurrected friend. "Don't take this the wrong way, Brian, but why aren't you still dead?"

"You realize," Shapiro said, gesturing to Lonnie, "that that's something he would say. He must be rubbing off on you."

Lonnie was quiet, his face expressionless.

Remembering that a quiet, poker-faced Lonnie Tate was usually the precursor to somebody getting seriously hurt...or worse, Shapiro answered, "I assure you. None of this...is what I wanted."

Pentangelo nodded encouragement.

Shapiro took a moment to reflect on the contrast between his two former comrades-in-arms.

Lonnie Tate: An instinctive master at tactical superiority. The best he had ever seen at dealing with right now. As good as they were, Shapiro's superiors could learn from Lonnie Tate.

Marcus Pentangelo: An astounding ability to envision the most advantageous of all possible options. Marcus would be the one asking him all the questions.

As if on cue, Marcus leaned forward. "Maybe we should talk about Cairo."

Shapiro exhaled, shrugged, shook his head. "The first thing I remember after leaving the bar, I wake up in a hospital room...been unconscious for a week. Fractured skull, cracked ribs, internal injuries.

I can't stand or even sit up by myself for another two or three weeks.

"An older gentleman—an American—comes in to talk to me. 'We've been very impressed with your work for some time, Sergeant Shapiro,' he says. As drugged and beat up as I was, something told me he was—"

"From Langley," Lonnie finally spoke up.

Shapiro continued, his voice flat. "He shows me a Polaroid. It's a guy, face beat all to hell, blood everywhere. Took me a minute to realize it was me.

"The guy pulls up a chair and tells me I should consider our meeting a 'change-of-assignment briefing.'" Shapiro went quiet and stared straight ahead, grinding his back teeth.

"Why the interest in you specifically?" Marcus asked. The question brought Shapiro back to the here and now.

"They, ah, had something on me," he laughed bitterly.

Shapiro turned to Lonnie. "By the way, the Bob Dylan quote in the parking lot across the street from Bud's? That was good."

Neither Marcus nor Lonnie reacted, just as Shapiro had anticipated. But he wanted them to know that he knew. That would keep them listening.

Mimicking the soothing voice he had used in the parking lot, Lonnie quipped, "Never liked Dylan. Just seemed like the thing to say at the time." His tone changed.

"The guy was from Langley, Shap. Most likely seventh floor. Nobody would have pulled something like that without..." He forced himself to finish the sentence. "*Nobody* would have done something like that without Howard Dade's approval. But what could that guy have possibly had on you, the fresh-faced, clean-cut kid from the Main Line?"

Staring straight ahead, Shapiro replied, "My grandfather."

"Holy Hyman?" Lonnie challenged.

37

Holy Hyman

A brilliant attorney at age twenty-one, by the time Hyman Shapiro turned thirty in 1920, he had become one of the wealthiest men in Europe.

That same year Hyman captured the heart of the woman of his dreams: Leah Pearlman, a beautiful, sassy, and brilliant accountant. At her suggestion, Hyman quietly began refocusing his investing outside of Europe.

By 1925, the Shapiros were the proud parents of two small boys, David, born in 1923, and Ezra, born in 1925.

The Shapiros loved Germany. But in November of 1923, a psychotic young megalomaniac tried to seize control of the government. Despite his political party's defeat, Hyman and Leah feared Germany hadn't heard the last of Adolf Hitler. After reading *Mein Kampf*, they knew that their—and all Jews'—days in Germany were numbered.

On January 1, 1927, Hyman, Leah, and their sons boarded a train bound for Switzerland. As the train pulled out of the station, the boys sat quietly while Hyman and Leah wept. They knew they would never see Germany again.

Their financial fortunes grew rapidly in Zurich. Leah continually wrote to her parents, begging them to accept Hyman's offer to buy them a home and pay for their move. Her father refused. "We're Germans. Why should we leave?"

Hyman frequently telephoned his brother, Isaac. "You're highly skilled. You'll do well here."

"I'm a tailor, Hyman, not a watchmaker," Isaac told his younger brother.

Everything changed the night of November 9, 1938. Kristallnacht: The Night of Broken Glass. The night Nazi propaganda minister Joseph Goebbels set off a free-for-all against the Jews. Leah's parents and her two sisters were killed. Isaac's home and tailor shop were among the seven thousand Jewish homes and businesses looted, burned, or destroyed.

Hyman and Leah knew that they were Isaac and his family's only hope of getting out of Germany. To save their lives, Hyman had to make a deal with the devil.

In 1940, Hyman and Leah Immigrated to the United States and made Philadelphia their home. There, Hyman's legal skills, business acumen, and the couple's unpretentious social prowess placed them among the most prominent movers and shakers on the East Coast. An invitation to the White House soon followed. Leah and First Lady Eleanor Roosevelt became close friends, and FDR insisted that Hyman become a member of the president's tight-knit intellectual circle. Historians would later credit Hyman's influence when FDR became serious about what Hitler was doing to the Jews.

It was sadly ironic that the same man who awakened America to the plight of the Jews in Europe would spend the rest of his life atoning for the betrayal of countless German Jews in exchange for the freedom of his brother and family.

On April 6, 1947, Hyman and Leah Shapiro, with tears in their eyes, held their first-born grandson in their arms, thanking God for the child's birth.

They could not have foreseen that the pact Hyman made in 1938 would one day ruin that child's life.

PHILADELPHIA INTERNATIONAL AIRPORT
TWA GATE 12
FEBRUARY 1968

Now a widower, bent with age and with tears in his eyes, Hyman Shapiro once again held his first-born grandson in his arms.

And once again he thanked God as he kissed Marine Sergeant Brian Shapiro's cheek, welcoming him home from Vietnam.

38

Shapiro began slowly rocking back and forth.

"Grandfather represented and socialized with some of the most prominent Jewish businessmen in Europe. Men in finance, industry, the government...you name it." His voice went hollow. "Sometime in 1938, a man from Himmler's SS came to his office."

He stopped rocking and took a deep, labored breath.

"In exchange for safe passage for his brother and his family across the Swiss border, Hyman had to give up the names of all the prominent Jewish businessmen he knew in Germany."

Marcus gave a thoughtful nod. "And he did."

Lonnie nodded in agreement. "He had no choice."

Shapiro shook his head. "You guys don't understand Jewish culture."

"Under extreme pressure, the man had to make a terrible decision," Lonnie challenged.

Shapiro gave him an appreciative smile. "In your eyes, yes. In the eyes of his generation...he was a sellout."

"You're right, Shap," Lonnie answered softly. "I don't understand. Tell you something else I don't understand." He turned to Marcus. "Sixteen months in 'Nam. Another, what...six months working for Langley? Dead Guy here talked about Hyman so much that, if he was a category on Jeopardy, we could have aced it."

Turning back to Shapiro, Lonnie continued. "So how come this is the first we've heard of this uncle?"

Shapiro shook his head, his silence answering Lonnie's question. "You never knew the man. The SS guy didn't make good on the deal, did he?"

"No. They strung my grandfather along until they were sure he'd given up everyone. Then they killed Isaac's daughters and raped his wife, in front of him. Then they killed her. Then they butchered him. They filmed it...sent a reel to my grandfather through the mail. I've seen it."

Marcus stood up. "Which made Hyman feel like it was all for nothing." Pacing a few steps, he turned to Shapiro.

"The foundation Hyman started after your parents were killed... plane crash, right? You and your brother were just little kids?"

"Yeah, I was seven; Josh was five. Hyman named it after our mother and father."

Marcus nodded. "The Deborah and David Shapiro Foundation. According to my people, a hundred-million dollars from the foundation went to build and pay for two-dozen schools, community centers, and clinics in Israel."

Shapiro was impressed. "Ms. McManus is to be congratulated. That information is extremely hard to come by. Even those in Israel responsible for distribution of the funds didn't know Grandfather created the foundation."

Dots weren't connecting for Lonnie, "I still don't see the tie-in between you and him."

Marcus explained. "If our formerly dead friend here doesn't play ball, Hyman's dealings with the Nazis...minus the part about trying to save his brother, of course...conveniently get leaked to the JDL, and every other major Zionist advocate group."

Doing a quick take to Shapiro, Marcus asked, "Your brother doesn't know about any of this, right?"

"Hyman never would have told him," Shapiro replied. "He came out of retirement to teach Josh how to run the organization when our Uncle Ezra died. Over time, Josh became the face of the organization. It would kill Josh if he knew!"

Lonnie gave a knowing nod. "The guys you work for would have killed him if he knew." He looked at Marcus, "That's it. That's what these guys have on him."

Marcus spoke as if Shapiro wasn't in the room, "His brother, the foundation, its legacy, along with the reputations of anyone and everyone who donated…hell, maybe even those who accepted money from the foundation—everything Hyman worked for would be destroyed."

"If I was the bad guys, that's what I'd do," Lonnie mused. He turned to Shapiro. "No offense, Shap."

Shapiro smiled. *Shap.* That's what they had called him in Vietnam. His eyes welled with tears.

The three men sat in silence as if they had run out of things to say, though a million things remained unsaid.

"Well, OK then," Lonnie broke the silence. "So besides the fact that you're not dead anymore…what else has been goin' on in your life since '68, Shap?"

Shapiro laughed. "An op here, an op there. You know how it is," he said, casually waving his hand.

Marcus smiled, then his eyes narrowed. "Brian, there is nothing that we're into that competes with or represents a threat to these people you work for. Why come after us?"

"Pentangelo Group's very existence makes it a threat, Marcus. It goes places and does things nobody else in the global intelligence community can get near. Case in point, we're looking at a terrorist group that's deliberately keeping a low profile."

"But you know about them," Marcus said.

"Only because an asset accidently stumbled across them, Marcus."

"And most of those thugs are media whores," Lonnie interjected. "You come across a bunch that doesn't want to be all over the news, they stand out. Makes you worry a little, right?"

"Yes," Shapiro confirmed. "However, I suspect the honchos aren't so much worried as they are curious."

"These, ah, thugs. They have a name?" Marcus asked.

"Yes." Shapiro sighed, knowing what was coming. "The S.O.C.— Soldiers of the Caliphate. Their aim is total world domination."

Marcus stifled a laugh. Lonnie rolled his eyes.

"I know," Shapiro conceded. "Not exactly an original mission statement. But these guys have taken the time to study what the other groups and cells have done"—Shapiro allowed himself a small smile— "and got caught and killed doing it. What they've learned is that they don't want to recruit the lone wolves who publicly blow up a few people before getting blown away themselves."

Marcus nodded. "Bad PR."

"They also know that taking over parts of countries in the Middle East, or even an entire country, isn't a winning strategy either."

Marcus went into analyst mode. "Because eventually, the other nation-states in the region, along with the big world powers, will start taking them seriously. Then they'll start grinding them down and wiping them out."

"Excellent analysis," quipped Shapiro. "Ever thought of going into the clandestine services?"

"OK," Lonnie weighed in, "so in the short term, what's the goal?"

Shapiro sat back, his expression serious.

"We don't know. But in order for them to reach their goal," he looked directly at Marcus, "they have to partner with an arms broker that can design, build, and deliver some extraordinarily sophisticated hardware and software."

Marcus's tone was matter-of-fact. "We're the bait."

"Marcus, your organization is the best- and worst-kept secret in the arms-brokering business and international intelligence community. You know how many years and dollars they had me spend in staff and high-end surveillance equipment, just to find out you operate out of a hamburger stand in the San Fernando Valley?"

Marcus enjoyed imagining how embarrassed Shapiro's bosses must have felt when he shared that discovery.

Shapiro leaned forward. "No one has ever been able to hide from us...but you."

39

The three friends sat quietly for a moment, reflecting on the past, and on the present circumstances that had brought them back together.

Lonnie laughed to himself. He was the teenage screw-up who accidently discovered he was smart. But not nearly as smart as the two men he considered his best friends. Shoving has hands in his pockets, he decided it was his turn to pace back and forth.

"I don't get it," he said to Shapiro. "You...dean's list at Penn. Granddad's connections. You held all the cards. And you dropped out to join the Corps?"

"You should have seen my grandfather. It was like telling him I wanted to be a Catholic."

The friends shared a laugh.

"I wanted to be somebody," Shapiro said earnestly, "other than the grandson of Hyman Shapiro. The rich Jewish kids from the well-connected professional families didn't like me because their families weren't as rich and well-connected as mine."

An unspoken memory triggered a bitter chuckle. "To the rich Goy kids, I was the rich Jew-boy living on the Main Line."

Shapiro's tired, drawn face suddenly got younger. He had missed their camaraderie. Getting it back was bringing him back to life. It was bringing all three of them back to a life that, as miserable as it was, they all missed.

"One day Hyman has me drive him to city hall. He's got some business to take care of. He gets out, says he'll be done in an hour, and goes inside. I'm sitting in traffic, and I see a Marine Corps recruiting poster. I see that guy in his dress blues—"

"The dress blues" Lonnie interrupted, laughing. "That's how they get ya every time. Damn sure how they got me"

"Bullshit. A judge got you, old friend," Shapiro chuckled.

"Hey, dress blues as opposed jailhouse stripes?" Lonnie shot back.

"No contest," Marcus interjected.

"That's when it hit me," Shapiro said. "The Corps doesn't care who my grandfather is. I join...I'm not the rich Jewish kid who doesn't fit."

"Yeah," Lonnie said. "You're just like everybody else...a scum-sucking maggot."

"Exactly," said Shapiro. "You have no idea how comforting that was."

40

Walking out of the building at Eighth and Figueroa, Lonnie and Marcus had a better picture of what they had been dragged into. Yet Marcus knew something was eating at Lonnie.

"What's wrong?"

"Something's telling me these SOC guys aren't the only targets of this op," Lonnie said.

"Go on."

"He mentioned Darcy. So he's gotta know about Stackhouse and Patino."

"And Cy and Branco," Marcus added.

"And we're not concerned?"

Marcus shook his head. "I think Brian and his masters are more worried about what they don't know about us than what they do know. You know what I'm sayin'?"

Lonnie smiled as they got into Marcus's car. "They think there's more than just the seven of us."

The drive back to the office was quiet as they mentally focused on their next moves. Marcus would tell Darcy about the resurrection of Brian Shapiro, then meet with him again. Lonnie would meet with the representative of the Soldiers of the Caliphate in Tampa.

Soldiers of the Caliphate? They couldn't could say the name without wanting to laugh, throw up, or kill somebody.

41

TAMPA, FLORIDA

The contact suggested picking up Lonnie at the airport.

Lonnie knew better than to get into a car with someone he'd never seen or talked to before. No, Lonnie and Mr. Kadar—undoubtedly not his real name—would meet in a chain restaurant at the intersection of two busy streets, near more than a half-dozen hotels. That way the men Kadar brought with him to surveil Lonnie couldn't be sure of where he was staying.

To make things even more confusing, Lonnie had made reservations at four different hotels. He wouldn't be staying at any of them. He was flying back to LA right after the meeting.

Kadar was easy to spot. Trim and of indeterminate age, as young as thirty or as old as fifty. Olive complexion, dark hair combed straight back. He wore a dark-blue open-collar shirt under a light-gray sport jacket. Lonnie guessed him to be about five feet eight.

"Welcome to Tampa, Mr. Tate," said Kadar, with a smile that was without warmth. "Did you have a good flight?"

"Mr. Kadar," Lonnie replied, returning the same smile and ignoring the question.

They sat at a small table near a far corner of the restaurant, away from the windows. Kadar had a cup of coffee in front of him. He raised his hand and snapped his fingers for the server.

"Please, order lunch," Kadar said, maintaining that same cold smile. "My treat."

"Not hungry," Lonnie growled, looking at him through narrowed eyes.

Lonnie gave the server a warm smile. "Don't mind him, miss," he said. "He thinks you're a servant, not a server."

The tightness in her shoulders relaxed.

"I'll have a Diet Dr. Pepper, easy on the ice, please," Lonnie said, returning her smile.

"You bet," she said cheerfully. "I'll be right back, sir."

"It was not necessary to say that," the younger man said.

"Yes, it was," Lonnie replied evenly. "Look, Kadar, which I doubt is your real name. Why am I here? Your boss has already talked with my boss. He's the one who can get what your people want."

"We know of the excellent work done in Cairo, with the Zionist spy, back in 1968," he said with forced calm. "We need to know if you are that man, and if you still have the same passion for such work."

Lonnie was silent.

"I can understand why you would want to do meaningful work," the terrorist continued, "especially after so many years in ridiculous pursuits. But why now," he smiled, "at your age?"

The server returned with Lonnie's soft drink. "The change is yours," he said, handing her a ten-dollar bill.

Lonnie took a long sip of his drink.

"You're right, Mr. Whatever-your-name-is," Lonnie said. "Getting back into"—he waved both hands and glanced absently around the restaurant— "into this...doesn't make much sense for a man my age. But there's unfinished business. And that makes sense at any age."

"What sort of unfinished business?" Kadar tried to sound offhand.

"The guy in Cairo," Lonnie said, pausing for another sip. "He wasn't the last guy to do that kind of work, ya know?"

"Indeed not." Kadar said. Lonnie noticed his eyes were shining, his breathing shallower.

Kadar leaned forward, dropping his voice to a whisper. "What I want to know, Mr. Tate, is how eager you are to finish such business. And"—he arched an eyebrow— "that you're capable of finishing it. I should like to see that you aren't merely a bitter old man who speaks of great deeds but can't perform them."

"Here?" Lonnie asked. "Now?"

"Why not?" he said in a conspiratorial tone. "This place is filled with old Jews. What your military people would call...a target-rich environment, right?"

"No," Lonnie replied, "This room would have to be filled with people like you. Then my military people would call it a target-rich environment."

He studied Kadar for a moment. "Do you know what a mortal lock is?"

"I'm not familiar with this term." Kadar leaned back, shifting his eyes away from this unpleasant American.

"It's a gambling term," Lonnie explained. "A sure thing. A bet you can't possibly lose."

"Let's say"—Lonnie paused to take another long sip— "Let's say I decided to start shooting up the place. If I could get out of the restaurant, my chances of getting away go way up, because I look like a thousand other guys on the street. I blend in. It's getting out of here that's tricky," he clarified. "First, I'd have to get past your guy sitting in the booth behind the cashier stand."

Kadar's color faded.

"It's possible," Lonnie mused. "The yelling, the screaming, people running for the door...possible, but iffy.

"Escape option number two," Lonnie pointed over Kadar's shoulder, "the back door through the kitchen. But I'd have to get past your two guys sitting in the booth right by the doors into the kitchen. Which I might be able to do if your guy in the suit, sitting at the table by the window, over your left shoulder, doesn't see me make my move."

Kadar's agitation increased.

"So"—Lonnie continued, sounding like a high-school science teacher— "as you can see, my chances for success vary, based on the chosen escape route, right?"

Kadar nodded. "But the mortal lock...the can't-miss bet?"

Lonnie looked Kadar squarely in the eyes.

"Killing you. Right here." Lonnie tapped the table. "Right now. Guaranteed one hundred percent chance of success."

Kadar's eyes widened. Lonnie smiled.

"No running, no jumping over tables. Definitely some screaming and yelling, people running for the door. But other than that, just one dead body. Yours."

Kadar started coughing so violently that the server came to the table. "Is he OK?" she asked Lonnie.

"It's a swallowing thing. He'll be fine." Lonnie leaned over and slapped Kadar on the back. "Right, Kadar, old buddy?"

"You"—he struggled to get the words out between the final spasms of choking— "are an extremely...unpleasant...man."

"Yeah," Lonnie said casually, finishing the last of his soft drink. "It's a gift. By the way, you got a list for me, right?"

Kadar reached into a briefcase on the floor beside his chair and pulled out a large manila envelope. He passed it across the table.

Lonnie took it and stood up.

Kadar's eyes widened in panic. "You can't just carry that...unsecured." He clutched at Lonnie's forearm. "That's proprietary infor—"

"You really think I'm going to take this proprietary information to the FedEx next door and give it to a kid making twelve bucks an hour part-time, so he can make sure it goes out to our office in California?"

Tucking the big envelope under his arm, Lonnie picked up his briefcase and backpack. Strolling past the cashier, he nodded at Kadar's bodyguard, who glared back.

Knowing he was being watched, Lonnie shifted his briefcase to the hand holding his backpack and waved the envelope to hail a cab. Once inside the cab, he tucked the envelope safely into his briefcase.

Two hours later, he was on a plane heading back to L.A.

42

ENCINO, CALIFORNIA

Marcus looked up from a stack of papers to see Lonnie standing in his office. He gestured to the steaming cup of coffee waiting for him.

"You'll need to start getting up to speed on this stuff."

Taking a sip of coffee as he sat down, Lonnie studied Marcus as his attention returned to the papers. Even reading them upside down, Lonnie could tell that each category of weapons, explosives, and computer hardware and software ran to as many as a dozen pages.

Twenty minutes later Marcus sat back, pushed his reading glasses up on his forehead and rubbed his eyes.

"That bad, huh?" Lonnie asked.

Shaking his head, Marcus tossed the papers back down on his desk. "My God, if this stuff actually gets delivered."

He stood up and began pacing the room, looking everywhere except at Lonnie. "If Israel can't intercept this—"

"What?" Lonnie asked quietly.

Marcus gestured to the stack. "The stuff on this list? It could disable a moderately-sized military. Every branch of its operations."

"C'mon, Marcus. They'd need an air force for that. We don't have a jet-fighter division, do we?"

Marcus shrugged. "I wouldn't call it a division. But the weaponry and explosives and computers they're asking for—" He shook his head and sat back down. "Just the software could take down a country's military central command-and-control apparatus. Not us, or another big power like Russia, China, or Britain, but a smaller military, say Jordan?"

"How?" Lonnie asked.

Marcus was on his feet again. "Jordan's a country with a high degree of technical sophistication, which translates to a high degree of technical vulnerability."

"But they have safeguards, right? Firewalls?"

Marcus exhaled and looked out the window before turning back to Lonnie. "I'd have to double-check it with Russell, but as near as I can tell, the SOC wants software that can override the safeguards and breach the firewalls."

Looking up at the ceiling, Lonnie pictured a map of the Middle East. "Who else's military in that part of the world is vulnerable to this?"

"Lebanon, Qatar, Yemen, and the UAE for sure. Almost certainly Iraq and Syria, maybe the Saudis, maybe Egypt, maybe Iran."

"What about Israel?"

The arms dealer folded his arms across his chest, raised one hand to his mouth, and shook his head.

"I don't know."

43

ONE WEEK LATER

Unlike most staff meetings, the quick-witted banter was replaced by a quiet, uneasy feeling.

Over the past week, Patino, Branco, and Watanabe hadn't slept more than a couple of hours a night, double and triple-checking the accessibility of each item on the lists relevant to their areas of expertise.

Russell Branco's sullen crotchetiness had increased by a factor of ten.

Stackhouse felt like he was juggling chainsaws, trying to figure out how to acquire components, get them to where Patino and Watanabe would assemble and customize them, and then get the weapons, ordnance, and computers delivered to more than two-dozen locations around the Middle East.

By choice, Lonnie had limited his knowledge of the specific content of the list. His intuition would direct his contributions to the op.

Stackhouse spoke first, trying not to sound as tired as he was.

"OK, looks like Connie and Cy are gonna need the usual stuff, just a helluva lot more of it, which changes where it gets assembled."

"Why?" Marcus asked.

"I have to find warehouses with more space."

"The places you usually use can't hold this?" Marcus tapped on the papers in front of him.

"Yeah. As long as Connie and Cy don't need room to move around. Besides, we want make it easy to get the stuff loaded."

"So Australia's out this time?" Patino asked.

"No," Stackhouse replied, "but there's racing at Eastern Creek in August, so teams will be in and out for testing. That's gonna put all the garage space we usually use off-limits."

"How far off the beaten path are you sending me, Doyle?" Watanabe asked, hoping to lighten the mood. "No place too remote, I hope."

Stackhouse held a particular liking for Watanabe, in no small part because the octogenarian tolerated, if not encouraged, the logistics man's sense of humor.

He grinned. "Been to Vietnam recently, Cy?"

Watanabe grinned back. "I can neither confirm nor deny."

"Moving on," Marcus said. "Darcy?"

Her customary sense of confidence was conspicuously missing.

"I don't have much to tell you," she began. "This group that wants to take over the world? So far I count a couple thousand at most. But they could be even less than a thousand."

Watanabe held up his hand and leaned forward. "Excuse me, Darce. You know I have the deepest respect for your intelligence gathering..."

She nodded as Cy paused.

"These guys are buying enough weapons to arm ten thousand men. Patino is saying it will take hundreds just to deploy the explosives we're selling them." The old Marine shook his head. "I'm doin' the math, and two plus two don't equal anything close to four."

Darcy agreed. "You're right, Cy. On paper, they barely have enough people to unload this stuff off the trucks."

"Where are they operating out of?" Patino asked.

Darcy's answer made the air in the room even thicker.

"I don't know. I can't find a base."

They could hear the frustration in her voice "There's a few dozen cells in North and South America, Europe, and Africa. They have a few...very few...people who drift in and out of the Middle East. Failed state areas mostly. But no one's based there."

"No hint as to who the deep pockets are? And how they're getting the money?" Patino asked no one in particular. "There has to be a money trail, right?"

"That's even more unsettling," Darcy replied. "Until these guys came along..." she pointed to Stackhouse, "Doyle was the only guy in the game that could cover his tracks like that."

"You know," Watanabe began, like he was telling a story, "Hitler had relatively few people with him when he started."

"But he was visible, Cy," Darcy countered.

"Ain't no way Darcy McManus can't find anybody, or anything," Watanabe shot back. "I love ya, doll. But I think you might be missing something. Hell, I think we're all missing something."

Darcy knew why Cy was needling her, but she was still defensive.

Marcus's silence and the looks on the faces of the others told Lonnie he was witnessing something that didn't happen often.

"For God's sake, Cyrus. You think I haven't looked and looked—."

"Darcy, my angel," the weapons master interrupted. "I think you're so damn focused on what you can't find that you can't see what you're missing."

"What the hell is that supposed to mean, Cyrus?"

Everyone—except for Marcus and Lonnie—was asking themselves the same question.

"The last thing I need right now is one of your inscrutable Cy-isms," Darcy added.

Lonnie knew how she felt. Over the years he had learned that

"Cy-isms" were just part of the "Old Corps" Marine's style of candor. But they could really piss you off just the same.

Marcus remained conspicuously silent. There were two reasons for this.

Reason number one: This is what Watanabe did so well. He needled and poked you. It made you want to kill him. But it also made you take a step back and think.

Reason number two: Ever since Darcy's husband died, Cy was the only person who could push her out of her own way and live to talk about it.

Watanabe gave Darcy a playful smile. "Based on what you said about Stackhouse being the only game in town until now, I gotta ask myself...are these Caliphate yay-hoos really that smart? What if they're nothing more than a distraction? Like I said Darce, there's something we're all missing. And by the way, woman," he winked, "I, by God, love it when you call me Cyrus."

44

Russell Branco carefully closed the door to Marcus's office behind him, then slammed the list down on Marcus's desk.

"Do you know how much damage this stuff can do?" he hissed.

Marcus looked at the brilliant computer expert. Though they were nearly the same age, Marcus always felt like he was dealing with someone much younger.

Branco rapped his knuckles on the small stack of papers. "This is how these guys are gonna take over the world, Marcus. I've been telling you for years not to play around with this kind of technology. But you just don't get it, do ya?"

"Then help me get it, Russell," Marcus fired back.

"This technology? It has offensive applications that go way beyond the military. This software gives these guys the capability to hack into energy systems, financial systems, traffic signals, air-traffic control systems. Everything. We're talking a global fire sale here, Marcus."

Marcus knew that in the world of cyber technology, fire sale meant a worldwide computer-systems crash. Every country—every municipality—their infrastructures completely obliterated. The full force of Branco's words began to sink in.

"Don't ask me to do this, Marcus. Please."

Marcus leaned back in his chair and closed his eyes, his head throbbing. He hated what he had to say next.

"Russell, I'm not asking."

"What?"

"I am telling you. I need you to do the best work you've ever done, and that's saying something."

Branco stood up. "You want me," he shouted, "to give these crazies the means to destroy everything?"

"Russell." Now Marcus was on his feet. "Again, you need...to do the best...the very best...work you've ever done. Do you understand what I just said to you?"

Branco nodded slightly before storming out, yanking the doorknob so hard that the door slammed against the wall.

45

FOUR DAYS LATER

The one and only blind date Lonnie ever experienced had ended in disaster—they got married. Eight months later, she was the fourth ex-Mrs. Tate. Which is why Lonnie had sworn off blind dates forever—until Patino talked him into trying one more time.

Linda Patino, Connie's mother, had gone on three blind dates as an adult. After the third she vowed that, barring a personal witness from the Father, Son, and Holy Ghost, she would never do it again—until her daughter talked her into trying just once more.

This time, much to Lonnie and Linda's surprise and relief, everything was going well.

The restaurant Lonnie chose had a classic down-home ambiance and a menu that never disappointed.

Linda Patino was smart, funny, easygoing, and easy to look at. She found Lonnie a little edgy, but his straightforwardness was refreshing and she loved his wit.

Without a lull, their conversation ran the gamut from work and life to music, movies, and travel. The wait staff had been enjoying watching them from across the room. After a while, their server approached the table.

"I'm sorry for being nosy," the young woman smiled, "but we're trying to guess how long you two have been together."

Lonnie looked at his watch. "About two hours."

As the server's smile started to fade, Lonnie said, "You gotta forgive me. I'm a hopeless smart...smart aleck," Lonnie edited himself. "Seriously, we just met. Linda's daughter and I work together."

The server's smile returned. "Well, you guys seem to be a real match."

46

LINDA'S HOUSE
COSTA MESA, CALIFORNIA

Dinner had gone so well that when Linda invited him in, Lonnie surprised himself by accepting the invitation.

Glancing around the living room as they walked in, Lonnie thought the decor reflected his dinner date's personality—comfortable, but not cluttered.

Pictures hanging on the walls hinted at what was important to her. He saw a picture of someone Lonnie figured was Jesus Christ. Underneath it, a large framed photo of a church building so beautiful that even Lonnie, who was not religious at all, found it appealing.

Most of his attention, however, was drawn to the three largest pictures. Not because of their size, but because of their subject matter.

In the first picture, he saw Connie in her Marine Corps dress blues, a full bird colonel standing in front of her, awarding her the Silver Star.

The second, a graduation photo, showed Connie receiving some kind of diploma or degree.

Lonnie was most curious about the third picture. It showed Connie and another girl, both of them about twenty-one, smiling and standing back-to-back in a Charlie's Angels pose. In the background, a beautiful harbor filled with small boats. The girls' pose looked comically out of character, considering they were dressed modestly in high-necked blouses and skirts with below-the-knee hemlines.

Sensing his interest, Linda smiled and answered his unasked question. "Australia. A little seaside town called Ulladulla. Connie served a mission for our church after she graduated from UC Irvine. Spent most of her time in Ulladulla."

Lonnie looked puzzled.

"We're Mormons, Lonnie. Mormon missionaries work in pairs. Connie calls it the Mormon version of the Marine Corps buddy system."

Seeing Connie Patino before her Marine Corps days struck a slight emotional chord in Lonnie. She didn't look all that different. The smile was the same now as it was then, yet something was different...her eyes. The innocence was gone. Taken away—more like blown away—by an IED in some hellhole in another part of the world.

"My, my, my. Lonnie Tate lost for words?" Linda said gently. "According to Connie, that never happens."

Still taking in the picture, Lonnie gave an embarrassed chuckle. "Some people would tell you it should happen more often."

"We could sit down if you'd like. That's one of the reasons I bought the couch."

Lonnie laughed as he sat. In her own way, Linda Patino was every bit the smartass he was. He liked that.

"You can be who you are with me, Lonnie. I know about Marines. Between Connie's time at Camp Pendleton waiting to deploy, and her time in rehab for her leg, I've had a few jarheads in my home." She paused. "Seems I raised one, without intending to."

"You did one heck of a job, dear lady," he said, motioning to the pictures.

"Thank you," she replied, propping her feet up on the coffee table.

Lonnie leaned forward. "Because I'm one of those guys who asks questions that are none of his business," Lonnie said, "I'm going to ask a question that's none of my business."

"OK," Linda said with a touch of wariness.

"Connie's father?"

"Dead," she replied. The lack of regret in her voice wasn't lost on Lonnie. "He was killed in a car accident when Connie was thirteen."

"I'm sorry. That must have been tough."

"It was a relief," she said, looking away. Then she paused, embarrassed that she had nearly violated her first rule of single adult dating: never bad-mouth the ex.

"Sorry." Kicking off her shoes, she sat up and tucked her feet under her. "Tommy Patino is the Pandora's box in my life."

Lonnie didn't picture Linda Patino as the type to play the vulnerability card for dramatic effect. This was real...and accidental.

"You don't see me bolting for the door, do you?" he answered.

"No. Thank you."

A few seconds of embarrassed silence later, she smiled. "Well. Courtesy of me, we just had our first awkward moment of the evening, didn't we?"

Lonnie liked that she made him laugh...again.

"So Linda, what do you do for a living?" he asked, trying to lighten the mood.

"I'm a life coach."

"English translation?"

She laughed. "I help people get out of their own way."

"This is Southern California. Talk about ground zero."

She had to agree. But despite the prime location, the majority of her client base was spread out over three dozen states, as well as Canada, Australia, New Zealand, and Europe.

She did volunteer work as well and was the leader of the women's organization at her church. "More like a mother or big sister to half the congregation" is how she described it.

Now it was Linda's turn to grill him.

"Not much to tell," he said easily.

She'd heard that same answer...many times...from Connie while she was in the Marine Corps. And even more so after she started working for the Pentangelo Group.

"So why not tell me what kind of work you used to do, with more details than that generic stuff you spouted at the restaurant." Linda arched an eyebrow and waited.

He gave her a very edited version of his successful yet stormy advertising career.

"You and my daughter," she said, shaking her head.

"What about me and your daughter?"

"The shorter the story, the more story there is. She didn't used to be that way. Is that a Marine thing?"

Note to self, Lonnie thought, *nothing gets past her*.

"What about marriage?" she asked tentatively.

"Gosh, Linda, we just met."

She playfully slapped him on the arm. "You know what I meant."

"Well, you have one Pandora's box in your life," he laughed. "When it comes to marriage, I have five."

Her eyes widened. "Dare I ask about kids?"

"One. Her name is Donna. And she is absolutely, positively the greatest achievement of my checkered life. She's an attorney with a big firm in Phoenix. They have an office in LA, so she's here 'on business' about once a month, checking up on her crazy father."

Linda gave him the kindest smile he'd ever seen. "And I bet he spoils the daylights out of her."

"Every chance he gets."

47

Neither one of them was the kiss-on-the-first-date type.

It seemed so complicated. Standing on the doorstep, looking at each other. She's hoping you will...or praying that you won't. You're hoping she wants you to...or praying that she doesn't.

But this time, there was no hesitation. It was perfectly natural. This surprised Lonnie, who had come to consider romance and himself as direct opposites, not naturals.

The kiss was nice. And he would have enjoyed it even more had he not felt the slight twitch in the small of his back. The one that warned him when somebody was watching.

Whoever you are, your timing sucks.

"Thank you for a very nice evening, Lonnie. Call me again really soon, OK?"

He needed to get her back inside her house...just in case. He also wanted to say a really witty kind of yes to calling her again. What came out was, "Ah, well, ah...I mean, yeah."

Embarrassed, he asked, "Did that sound as dumb as I'm pretty sure it did?"

"Yes, but don't worry about it. Good night, Lonnie Tate," she whispered, closing the door quietly.

Turning and walking down the walkway to the curb, he looked at his watch. 2:45 a.m.

As he approached his Bimmer, Lonnie retrieved the small flashlight he always carried in his front pants pocket. Once at the car, he shined the light into the back seat and floorboard, making sure he didn't have an unwelcome passenger.

First rule in spotting surveillance, especially at 2:45 in the morning in a residential neighborhood: look for something that looks so commonplace, it looks out of place.

He checked up and down the street before unlocking the driver's-side door. Satisfied there weren't any cars on the street that weren't there when he pulled up in front of her house, he got in, put the key in the ignition, and started the car.

Good. The car didn't blow up.

His senses bristling, Lonnie put the car in gear, eased out the clutch, and pulled away from the curb.

Come out, come out, wherever you are, he silently sang as he drove.

About half a block before the stoplight that would take him out onto a main street, he saw the brand-new Cadillac CTS sitting at a gas station on the corner.

As the light turned yellow, a voice inside Lonnie's head said, *Run it.*

Immediately downshifting, he put the accelerator to the floor.

In that same instant, the Cadillac shot out of the gas station, swerved in front of him, and stopped as the light turned red.

Lonnie hit the brakes. His car stopped about a half car-length behind the Cadillac.

Headlights from another car appeared in his rearview mirror. *Thump-thud.* The BMW bounced forward with the impact.

Seeing the driver's-side door of the car behind him swing open, Lonnie cranked the steering wheel to the left to maneuver around the Cadillac. But the Cadillac was backing up.

Bump.

The driver of the Cadillac was out of the car—gun drawn— heading for the passenger side of Lonnie's car.

The driver of the car behind Lonnie was already on his side

of the BMW, keeping a deliberate distance clear of the door's opening radius.

Both men had Glock 9mms with silencers pointed at him. The man on Lonnie's left quickly repositioned himself to face Lonnie. The man on his right positioned himself just off Lonnie's right shoulder—both out of each other's line of fire. That told Lonnie these guys knew what they were doing.

The man on the left looked to be just a couple of inches taller than Lonnie and was built like a Ken doll on steroids. Lonnie nicknamed him "Steroid Ken."

The Cadillac driver—Lonnie tagged him as "Cadillac Guy"—was about six feet three and looked a little less juiced. Both were dark featured, their hair black and close-cropped.

If push came to shove, Lonnie figured he'd end up with some ugly bruises, a split lip, and a black eye. But he could probably incapacitate both of them and escape. They weren't going to kill him...not here, anyway.

Steroid Ken motioned for Lonnie to get out of the car.

Lonnie slowly slid out, hands in the air. He noticed a slight bunching at the bottom of Steroid Ken's right pant leg, which meant he was carrying a second piece in an ankle holster.

Despite both men being armed, they kept their distance.

"The Magnum," ordered Steroid Ken.

The accent, Lonnie wondered, *Turkish...Central Asian?*

"Put it on ground. Then move four steps toward middle of street...slow."

Cadillac Guy mirrored Lonnie's steps, while Steroid Ken walked to where the Magnum lay and kicked it toward the Cadillac.

A faint metallic sound drew Lonnie's attention. Out of the corner of his eye, he saw the Cadillac's trunk lid rising. He turned and looked at the open trunk, then at Cadillac Guy.

"You aren't serious," Lonnie said.

A hint of a smile lifted the corners of Cadillac Guy's mouth. He nodded.

"Get in," Steroid Ken hissed.

Lonnie didn't have to fake making it look hard to get into the trunk. There wasn't an inch between the Cadillac and the BMW, so he had to climb up onto the BMW's fender, spin on his rear end to put his feet into the trunk, then twist his body so he could lie down.

Keeping the Glock pointed at Lonnie, Steroid Ken smirked down at him. "Can't believe you drive this old piece of shit."

Lonnie gave him an unsettling grin.

Cadillac Guy held out his right hand. "Phone," he commanded.

Fishing his cell phone out of his sports jacket, Lonnie handed it to Cadillac Guy, who slammed the trunk shut.

48

The trunk was well insulated, making it difficult to hear them talking to each other. But not so difficult that Lonnie couldn't tell they were arguing.

Apparently Steroid Ken lost. Lonnie heard him bite off a four-letter word that sounds the same in any language.

The next thing he heard was the BMW's engine starting up.

Pushing the button on the bezel of his watch, the face lit up. 2:57 a.m.

He knew if he didn't keep moving, his arms and legs would get numb. The trick was not making noise. Otherwise Cadillac Guy might decide to just pull over and tag him right there on the spot.

3:14 A.M.

Been on the freeway about twelve minutes. Lonnie corrected himself. *Make that freeways.*

Less than five minutes after pulling onto what he guessed was the Costa Mesa Freeway, the Cadillac slowed and turned to the right, then resumed cruising speed.

Gotta be on what, the 405...going south? To where? The San Diego freeway, maybe? Why not. Lots of open spaces in North County to leave a '99 BMW with a dead man behind the wheel.

3:19 A.M.

The Cadillac slowed and banked right again.

Yeah...we're on the Five.

If San Diego was the destination, they'd be on Interstate 5 for another twenty-five minutes, maybe longer.

3:46 A.M.

The Cadillac slowed to nearly a crawl, and the road surface changed again. Then they stopped. A half minute later, they were rolling again.

Where does the Five run this close to city streets?

Coast Highway. Oceanside?

3:58 A.M.

The right-turn signal lit up the inside of the trunk as the Cadillac slowed to a crawl. After making the turn, they straightened out for a few car lengths, then turned left onto a dirt road.

Within a minute, the car stopped. Lonnie heard the door open, the trunk latch clicked, and the lid popped.

Gauging by how well he could hear the ocean, he guessed they were a hundred yards or so from the beach. The first thing he saw when he stuck his head up was the barrel of the Glock glinting in the dark.

"That old piece of shit don't drive too bad," Steroid Ken motioned with his head to the BMW. "Standard transmission...I'm impressed. I thought all old men drive automatic." His neutral expression hardened. "Get out."

Painfully pushing himself up to lean on the edge of the trunk, Lonnie calculated that Steroid Ken was about five feet from the Cadillac's rear bumper. Cadillac Guy looked to be about ten feet to his right.

"Damn!" Lonnie groaned. "I got no feeling in my legs."

"Pull yourself out with hands!" Steroid Ken barked. Cadillac Guy stage-whispered something Lonnie was sure translated to "Quiet! The neighbors will hear you."

Lowering his voice, Steroid Ken ordered, "Get your fat ass out that car, old man. Now!"

Lonnie groaned. "Gimme a minute, will ya? Gotta rub some feeling back into my legs. Unless you want to have to drag my fat ass over to wherever you plan on burying me."

The constant chatter was irritating Steroid Ken. Exactly what Lonnie wanted.

Reaching down into the trunk, Steroid Ken grabbed Lonnie to lift him out. "Get out of car!"

That's when Lonnie lifted his rear end onto the edge of the trunk and swung his right leg as hard as he could at Steroid Ken's head.

From ten feet away, Cadillac Guy heard a distinctive crack.

The initial impact of the kick broke Steroid Ken's nose. Lonnie felt bone give way as the full extension of the kick fractured Ken's eye socket.

A silent scream. Then shock. Then pain so intense Steroid Ken dropped the Glock. His hands clawed at his face.

Grabbing Ken to use him as a shield, Lonnie dropped to the ground.

Pulling the gun—*A snub-nose .357?*—from Steroid Ken's ankle holster, *Who the hell carries a .357 in an ankle holster?*—Lonnie fired two rounds, center mass, leaving a hole, more like a cavern, where part of Cadillac Guy's rib cage, heart, and some of the left lung had been.

Calmly picking up the Glock, Lonnie asked, "My Magnum? Please tell me you didn't throw it away on the way out here."

Steroid Ken was in too much pain to answer.

"What's a matter? Cat got your tongue?" Lonnie asked. "Look, I'm running out of time here, ya know?" He paused. "Well, wait a minute. Actually you're the one who's running out of time here.

Check that. You are out of time."

Lonnie fired two rounds point-blank into Steroid Ken's head.

3:59 A.M.

Checking the interior of the Cadillac, he found his phone and the Magnum on the passenger's seat. Flicking off the dome light, Lonnie left the driver's-side door wide open, dragged Cadillac Guy over, and propped him in the driver's seat. Then he opened one of the back doors and let down the seat back before closing the door.

Feeling every bit of his sixty-six years, Lonnie grabbed Steroid Ken's body by the ankles and dragged it the few feet to the Cadillac. Now came the really hard part—getting the body in the trunk.

It was damned hard, and he was pretty sure he broke a couple of Steroid Ken's bones cramming him in the tight space.

Looking down at the body, Lonnie gave it the same smile Ken had given its former occupant. *It's not nice to abuse a senior citizen, asshole!*

49

Going back to the driver's side door, Lonnie reached in and released the gas-filler door. He pulled Cadillac guy's shirt off his body and tore it in half, then walked to the rear of the car, unscrewed the gas cap, and fed half of the shirt down into the gas tank as far as it would go. Pulling it back out, he had a two-foot-long strip of cotton soaked in gasoline.

Putting the shirt in the trunk with Steroid Ken, Lonnie muttered "*Asshole!*" once more, pulled one of Ken's feet out and slammed the trunk lid on it, leaving the trunk slightly open. He furled the other half of the shirt like a flag, then shoved it down into the gas tank, leaving the tail hanging down onto the ground.

Once lit, it would take a few minutes for the shirt tail to burn into the gas tank. When the fumes ignited, the tank would explode, setting fire to the gas-soaked cloth in the trunk. The open front door would draw flames into the interior, setting fire to everything in the car, which would take care of the bodies.

Lonnie retrieved a lighter from the console of the Bimmer, then went back and lit the end of the shirt hanging out of the Cadillac's gas tank. He ran back to the BMW, jumped in, fired up the engine, and drove away.

Turning right off the PCH and heading back toward Interstate 5, he saw a fiery orange glow above the buildings in his rearview mirror.

On the I-5 North heading back to LA, Lonnie tried to make sense of the attempt on his life. It didn't give Shapiro's people additional leverage over the Pentangelo Group. What they had on Mary Pentangelo was all the leverage they needed. This was personal. Payback. But for what? And by who?

The list of for whats and the names attached to them was long. Discounting five ex-wives, who despite intense desire had neither the connections nor the finances, only one other name came to mind.

The bigger problem: Steroid Ken and Cadillac Guy had known where Lonnie would be tonight. How did they know?

Eventually, and there always was an "eventually," whoever sent them would send somebody after Linda Patino to get to him. Lonnie didn't want that. He really liked Linda. And if he could keep from getting her killed, they just might be able to keep seeing each other.

It was a few minutes before six when Lonnie finally turned into the driveway of Pentangelo Group HQ. As he punched in the code to open the garage door, it didn't surprise him that the house and the hidden parking pad were empty.

He didn't move after switching off the BMW's engine, not right away. Letting all his mental circuits reset, he closed his eyes just for a second. When he opened them, Patino's Corvette was parked next to him. Marcus's Lexus and Darcy's Mercedes sat in the spaces across from the 'Vette and his Bimmer. Lonnie squinted at the digital clock below the speedometer.

8:47 A.M.

Opening the door to climb out, he almost fell to the ground. His legs were still asleep. He took a moment to rub some feeling back into them and eased himself out of the car.

50

Entering through the French doors into the kitchen, Lonnie eyed a steaming mug of coffee on the counter. Assuming it was for him, he grabbed it and headed back to Marcus's office.

Darcy and Patino were seated on the couch opposite Marcus's desk. Both gave Lonnie big smiles when he stopped in the doorway.

"Late night?" Patino asked.

Lonnie took the chair by Marcus's desk, took a sip of coffee, and set the mug on the desk before turning toward the women.

"Best evening I've had in a long, long time."

Patino smiled. "She called me this morning. She's looking forward to seeing you again."

"Wait a minute," Marcus said. Looking at Lonnie, he asked, "You went out? On a...ah, date?" He looked over at Patino. "With your mother."

Patino raised her eyebrows and gave Marcus a theatrical smile.

"Great lady. Only glitch," Lonnie said into his coffee, "was the two guys that tried to kill me after I left her house."

Marcus leaned forward in his chair. Darcy and Patino's faces fell.

"Pinned me in a few blocks from the freeway, put me in the back of a Caddy—I'm sure it was a rental—and drove down to Oceanside."

"Where are they now?" Marcus asked.

"Probably the morgue."

"Did they say anything to you?" Darcy asked.

"Other than, 'Get in trunk,' very little. When they talked to each other, it sounded like Turkish. Or maybe some Central Asian dialect."

Patino asked the question Darcy and Marcus were asking themselves. "Who would want you dead…and why?"

"Other than my ex-wives, only one other person hates me enough to try something like this."

Marcus shook his head and grinned. "The ex-wives—you just couldn't help yourself, could ya?"

"Didn't even try."

"This isn't funny, you guys," Patino reprimanded. "All kidding aside, please. If not the exes, then who?"

"A guy named Jason Beck," Lonnie replied.

"Who's he?" Patino asked.

"The poster child for birth control," Lonnie quipped.

Darcy glanced at Patino. "A guy who spied on Lonnie during his ad-agency days."

Lonnie looked from Marcus to Darcy.

"What?" Darcy said. "You think I didn't know about that?"

"What did this Beck guy do at your ad agency?" Patino asked.

"CFO," Lonnie answered, "and general pain in the butt. Not a spy."

Patino wrinkled her forehead. "A black-ops group using a bean counter to do a hitter's job?"

"I'm sure they didn't," Darcy said. "I think your resurrected friend, Brian Shapiro, did."

Marcus shook his head. "That's a real reach, Darce."

"Think about it." she challenged. "Shapiro's been keeping tabs on you two for more than forty years." She looked at Lonnie. "He knows he could never pull that off using experienced field personnel. You would have picked up on it."

Marcus smiled at Lonnie. "She's right. Nobody would ever mistake your buddy Beck for someone who knew what he was doing."

"That's true. But factor in me trying to kill him at the meeting—"

"You tried to kill Beck...why?" Darcy asked.

Lonnie looked over at Marcus, then took a deep breath.

"He set my daughter up. A compromising situation with pictures to match. Did it the day she made partner at her law firm. Those pictures show up at the firm, she's got no job, maybe no career."

"You've seen the photos." Patino stated.

"We both have," Marcus replied. "Beck showed them to us at the meeting."

The room went quiet, then Marcus chuckled.

"That's what you get for pissing off an accountant with spy-master-wannabe issues."

"Yeah. It truly is a gift, ya know?"

Darcy just shook her head at the two sixty-something teenagers.

51

"No. No way," It was Patino's turn to shake her head. "We're not looking at this right. Neither your friend Shapiro nor the accountant had anything to do with this."

"Go on," said Marcus.

Patino got up off the couch. Perching herself on the corner of Marcus's desk, she leaned toward Lonnie.

"Everybody agrees the attempted hit was not tactical. Darcy's right, Shapiro is the first person to look at as far as knowing Lonnie's whereabouts. But as Lonnie pointed out, this was payback."

They weren't with her yet, so she continued.

"Lonnie. Your conversation with Kadar in Florida. You insulted... no...you humiliated him. We're talking about a man who is a product of four thousand years of tribal mindset and tradition. Men with that in their DNA can't let insult slide. And the kind of guys that came after you are the kind of guys he would send."

"There was no surveillance on us while we were at dinner, Jarhead," Lonnie reminded her. "And I made sure nobody tailed us on the way back to her house."

Patino nodded. "I have no doubt, Lonnie. And admittedly this is a long shot, but—" She plucked an imaginary piece of lint off Lonnie's sport jacket. "Let me ask you, were you wearing this when you met with Kadar?"

"Yeah. So?"

"At any time did he touch your jacket? Maybe he grabbed your forearm when you guys shook hands?"

Dismissing her suggestion at first, Lonnie replayed the scene in his head. Then he remembered.

"He grabbed my arm when I got up to leave. I gave him a dirty look, and he let go."

Patino's smile widened.

"Wait right here." Pushing herself off Marcus's desk, she ran out of the room and into her office. Ten seconds later she returned with an electronic wand in one hand and a small tool case in the other.

"Show me which arm he grabbed." Lonnie held out his left arm. The wand emitted a tone that increased in pitch as she moved it over the area between the cuff and Lonnie's elbow.

When the high-pitched tone was steady, Patino asked, "Darce? Hold the wand right here, please?"

Darcy held the wand in position while Patino opened the tool case and took out a pair of magnifying goggles. She put them on, then then retrieved a pair of surgical clamps from the case.

Bending close to Lonnie's sleeve, she carefully closed the clamp over a tiny, nearly-transparent square. Closer examination revealed faint lines across its surface, with hooks at two corners and pegs at the other two. Patino brought the clamp up close to her goggles and grinned. "Oorah."

Removing the goggles and handing them to Lonnie, she held up the clamp so he could get a look.

"What am I looking at, Jarhead?"

"A GPS transmitter. This is how Kadar's guys knew how to find you. He put it on your jacket when he grabbed your arm."

She looked over at Marcus. "Got an envelope?"

Marcus pulled one out of his desk drawer and handed it to Patino. Lonnie passed him the goggles.

Patino held the clamp over the opened envelope. Marcus looked at the technology that had almost cost Lonnie his life. Patino followed him to the couch, where he handed the goggles to Darcy.

Impressed, Darcy said, "Good job. Now we know what our clients used to track Lonnie. And us."

THE REDEMPTION OF LONNIE TATE

"**This is the transmitter,**" Patino declared, releasing it into the envelope. "The guys that went after Lonnie had the receiver. That told 'em when Lonnie was wearing his jacket and where he was going."

"So where's the receiver?" Darcy pressed.

"Burned up," Lonnie answered.

Darcy sighed. "But isn't Kadar going to start missing the men he sent after Lonnie?"

"They were contract hitters, Darcy," Patino explained. "He wanted Lonnie dead, but he didn't want anything coming back on him. Whoever hired them wouldn't hear back until the job was completed. It could be several more weeks before whoever gave them the assignment wonders why it hasn't been carried out."

Lonnie was in awe.

"How does a nice kid like you know about stuff like this?"

"After boot camp and Motor-T School, the Corps sent me to Dam Neck, Virginia, for four months...then to Iraq."

Lonnie smiled. "Office of Naval Intelligence?"

"How ya like me now, Sergeant Tate?" Patino laughed.

"Better all the time, Jarhead. Better all the time."

"Connie," Darcy spoke up, "is there any possibility there's a backup team out there?"

"It's not unheard of, but highly unlikely. Why?"

"Well—" Darcy looked at Lonnie, who immediately saw where

she was going. "Two really bad people with eyes on your mother's home in the past twelve hours? The lady is going to need protection."

Marcus nodded agreement. "The question is, how much do we tell her?"

"Whoever tells her," Patino cut in, "better be wearing a helmet and flak jacket when they do. She's going to be less than pleased."

Lonnie looked at Marcus, then Patino, then back to Marcus, then back to Patino.

"Yeah, OK," Lonnie sighed. "I got her into this. I'm the one that needs to start painting the picture for her."

Patino and Marcus shared a collective sigh, but it wasn't relief.

"But you guys," Lonnie added, "are going to do the finish and the touch-up. 'Cause we all know she's going to have some questions I can't answer."

53

The drive from Linda's to Pentangelo Group headquarters was pleasant—until Lonnie mentioned that two men had tried to kill him. Which led Linda to ask why. Which led to answers that left her incredulous, stunned, confused...and angry.

Turning to look out at the traffic ahead of them, she waited another minute before she spoke.

"My daughter said you were a complicated man. And she has become a more complicated person. She wasn't like that before she went in the Marines. Who and what are you, Lonnie Tate? And why is my daughter a part of this?"

Lonnie had nothing to say. He had already resigned himself to the idea that if they all survived this—whatever *this* was—Linda Patino probably wouldn't want to have anything more to do with him.

What he hadn't resigned himself to was the sense of loss he was feeling for a woman he hardly knew.

Entering Marcus's office, the first person Linda saw was Darcy McManus. They had met while Connie was going through rehab. Of all the staff and volunteers, she remembered Darcy as Connie's biggest cheerleader and sternest taskmaster. Linda had spent many a late night on the phone with Darcy, seeking her advice, or her strength...sometimes both. Linda always wondered why she and Darcy had lost contact after Connie completed her treatment. Suddenly she realized that maybe this was the reason. The moment was awkward for Darcy as well. She could sense Linda's feelings of confusion, maybe even betrayal.

Lonnie and Linda seated themselves on the couch across from Marcus's desk. Darcy sat in a chair, while Connie leaned against the wall on the opposite side of the room. Marcus was sitting on the corner of his desk.

"I'm guessing you have some questions," Marcus said to Linda, as though asking if she wanted fish or veal.

Giving Lonnie half a glance, Linda asked, "Do all Marines have this gift"—she shot a hard stare at Marcus and her daughter— "for exquisite understatement?"

Connie fought a smile. Growing up, she had been the target of her mother's prosecutorial side on more than one occasion. Marcus had no idea what he was in for.

"What has Lonnie told you?" he asked, more earnestly than he had intended.

Linda took a breath. "That two men tried to kill him after he left my house the night before last. That you two served in Vietnam together, and on the night you came home, you were recruited by the CIA. Which has something to do with why he works for you now.

"What he didn't tell me was what you do. Apparently, whatever it is has something to do with the attempt on his life." She glanced over at Lonnie. "Do I have that right?"

Lonnie nodded. "Yeah, pretty much."

"So, Marcus, forgive my curiosity," Linda challenged, "but what does the Pentangelo Group do that makes people want to kill its employees?"

Ducking his head and rubbing the back of his neck, Marcus tried to play things down. "Linda. That's really not a fair—"

"Night before last," she cut in, "I went on a blind date, and before sunrise the next morning, my life, which was busy enough already, has turned into something out of a Tom Clancy novel."

Focusing on the floor, Marcus took a deep breath and exhaled slowly, then looked up at her.

"Linda, before I go further, I have to know you won't say anything to anyone else regarding this conversation."

Looking at her daughter, she asked, "What does he think I'm going to do, put it in the church bulletin?"

Lonnie smiled. Connie swallowed a laugh before she spoke. "Marcus, our secret is safe with her."

"The Pentangelo Group sells arms." Marcus stated.

"So my daughter's an arms dealer."

"No, Mom" Connie interjected, "Your daughter's an explosives expert."

Mother and daughter glared at each other.

Marcus leaned forward. "Linda, rest assured Connie has never broken the law, nor would I ever ask her to."

Now in full professor mode, Marcus continued. "More than ninety-percent of our business is with the State of Israel. We also sell to law-enforcement agencies in the United States and some foreign countries as well."

The silence in the room was thunderous.

"This is an awful lot to take in. You want to take a minute?"

She took a deep, angry breath. "No, please, let's just keep going. You said you run guns for the Israeli government—"

"That's not what we do, Mom," Patino countered.

Lonnie and Darcy stifled grins. It was entertaining to see what had been passed down from mother to daughter.

Linda sat back, then looked at her daughter.

"Well, I can certainly see why you never talk about work."

Trying to dial mother and daughter back a little, Marcus continued. "Let me clarify something, Linda. Just because a client or potential client wants something, doesn't mean they always get it."

With a skeptical smile, Linda asked, "What...or...who

determines who gets and who doesn't?"

It was dawning on Marcus that Linda Patino was much smarter than what her daughter had warned.

"I make the call after consulting with the people who work with me,"

"And besides my daughter, Lonnie, and Darcy, how many other people work with you?"

Marcus hesitated and then answered.

"Three."

"You expect me to believe you carry on an international arms trade with a staff of six?"

Lonnie grinned. "Pretty impressive, huh?"

Marcus relaxed. "It's why our corporate profile doesn't rise to a level that would invite attention that could impede our operations."

"So, regarding this current...situation and client," Linda argued, "after what I'm sure was a soul-searching consultation with your staff, all of you thought it would be good business to do business with people who want to kill at least one of you?"

Touché, thought Marcus.

Damn, I really did want to see her again, thought Lonnie.

"That one's on me, Linda," said Marcus. "I couldn't turn them down."

Then he explained why.

54

Leaning forward to bring herself away from the wall, Connie knew it was time for her and her mother to have a talk.

"No disrespect, Marcus, but things might be better served if my mom and I have the room for couple minutes. Please?"

Lonnie tried to lighten the mood. "Don't worry, Marcus. I'm sure they'll pay for anything they break. Right, ladies?"

Standing up, Marcus joined in. "In that case, feel free. There are some things in here I've been looking to replace for quite some time." Retrieving a pad and pencil off his desk—which he didn't need, but he thought it played well—Marcus glanced at Darcy and Lonnie. "The ladies need the room, folks."

With the room clear and the door closed, Linda did what she'd done when her daughter was a teenager. She yelled.

"Consuelo Maria Patino!" The last time she felt this hurt and angry was when Connie enlisted in the Marine Corps.

In response, Connie calmly sat down beside her mother, wrapping her arms around her tenderly.

Linda tried to push her away. But the harder she pushed, the tighter Connie held on. Linda was amazed at her daughter's physical strength.

Both women's eyes welled with tears. After a few seconds of muffled sniffles, Connie was the first to speak.

"I know you have a lot to say. I won't interrupt. Then it's my turn. Same rules...no interruptions."

Linda nodded. Connie released the viselike hug and gave her mother's shoulders a gentle rub.

"You have no idea what the past five years have been like for me."

Connie nodded. She knew that would be her mother's lead.

"I was so proud when you graduated from UCI. I was proud when you left on your mission. I worried. You were seven-thousand miles away, and if anything had happened to you—" She stopped herself. "Then you came home.

"Three weeks later...you enlisted in the Marines. Eight months after that, you're in Iraq for a year. You come home for six months, then they send you to Afghanistan. Eight months after that, I get a call: You're on a hospital flight to Ramstein, Germany. 'She'll be getting the best medical care in the world, Ms. Patino.'"

Tears rolled down Linda's cheeks.

"When they wheeled you off that plane...your sunken eyes. You couldn't have weighed more than a hundred pounds."

Linda paused.

"I won't even go into your time in rehab," she continued. "And now this? These people you work for?"

Her eyes welled up again. "I almost lost you once. Excuse my selfishness, but this life you have, these people you work with...this is not what I wanted for my daughter."

Linda reached into her purse and retrieved a small packet of Kleenex. Pulling out two tissues, she handed one to Connie and dabbed her own eyes with the other.

"Your turn. I'm through...for now."

"For now?"

"I'm the mom. I get to be through more than once."

Connie took both her mother's hands in hers. "I know what you wanted." Her voice was consoling without being condescending. "I want the same thing."

"And as soon as I find the nice Mormon boy who doesn't freak when he finds out the returned missionary he's out with got her leg blown off by an IED in Afghanistan—and spends less time staring at my prosthetic than he does at the rest of me—as soon as I find that nice Mormon boy? You and I will both get what we want."

This was the first time Connie had voiced these frustrations. Linda's anger immediately gave way to hurt for her daughter.

Angrily wiping tears from her eyes, Connie continued. "As far as how hard the last five years have been for you? I can only make a poor guess. But...you wanna trade your five years for mine?"

Linda's face showed how hard the question hit her.

"Of course you don't," Connie said, softening the blow. "I wouldn't want that either. My point is this: when you look at me, you still see that ninety-pound mess the corpsman wheeled off that C-130 three years ago. These people I work for? When they look at me, they see somebody strapped up, locked and loaded, and ready to go. Time for you to start seeing me the way they do.

"Hopefully, the worst that can happen has happened. But if things—as they say in our business—get ugly, me and 'these people I work for,' and the grace of God, are the only things between you and a body bag."

Silence returned...and camped for a few minutes.

Gently dabbing the tears from her daughter's eyes, Linda finally spoke.

"Strapped up? Locked and loaded?"

Connie patted her mother's hand. "Yeah, sorry about that; it's a Marine thing."

Linda said nothing on the drive back to her house.

When Lonnie started to get out of the car she finally spoke.

"She's fearless. Been like that all her life. Makes me crazy. Then Darcy and Marcus come along...and bring out even more of that in her. Then you come along..."

Lonnie could only nod. *If this is her way of saying "Pigs will fly before I ever consider even thinking about wanting to see you again," it sure is a long, drawn-out, and painful way to do it. Maybe I deserve it.*

"My daughter...what she's become. You and what you are... whatever that is. You both scare me. Consuelo's my daughter. I'm stuck with her, but you—?"

Here comes the kill shot.

Leaning into him, she kissed him on the cheek. "For some illogical reason, part of me wants..." She paused as if saying the words might jinx a possibility. "I don't know. Maybe I'll come to my senses later, but for right now...?"

55

Flying on Marcus's Gulfstream G280 made flying commercial first class seem like riding the city bus.

Stretched out on a stylish couch more comfortable than most beds he had slept on, Lonnie noticed the G280's cabin was as elegantly appointed as a CEO's corner office. Satellite phone and high-speed Internet allowed connection to anyone, almost anywhere on the planet. Push a button on the small control panel molded into the arm of the couch, and cabin lighting dimmed or brightened. Other buttons brought up music, movies, CNN, stock-market quotes—even the flight's progress.

Lonnie tried hard to convince himself he couldn't get used to this. He tried even harder to act surprised when, in conversation with the pilot before takeoff, he learned the G280 was built by IAI— Israel Aerospace Industries—home base for Gulfstream's Aerospace Operations and Israel's fighter-aircraft development center.

On another front, but equally impressive, was the in-depth intelligence report on the man who called himself Kadar. The report came courtesy of Craig Sloat, one of Patino's friends. Sloat was a former Navy SEAL turned ONI "investigator" turned "private security" company CEO. His report included photos, histories, addresses, eating habits, travel schedules, and where Kadar stayed when he traveled.

Recalling his conversation with Patino ten days earlier, Lonnie remembered the edge in her voice and her vague answers regarding Mr. Sloat.

"He'll pick you up when you land in St. Petersburg. Don't worry. You'll know him when you see him."

Nodding, Lonnie had asked her, "How do you know him?"

"Afghanistan."

Old boyfriend? Lonnie wondered, then immediately dismissed the notion. Patino wasn't the mix-business-with-personal-life type.

At six foot five and 240 pounds, there was no way anyone could miss Craig Sloat. He practically blocked out the sun streaming through the windows behind him.

Waiting until he was about two feet from him, Lonnie offered him a handshake. "You must be Sloat."

The former SEAL did a terrible job of hiding the you-gotta-be-kiddin'-me look on his face. Lonnie looked nothing like "the guy you don't want to mess with" description Patino had given him. Nodding as he shook Lonnie's hand, he showed surprise again when the older man's grip was every bit as firm as his own.

"Relax, squid," Lonnie said. "Yeah, I'm old. So get that *Oh, shit* look off your face. Where ya parked?"

Shaking his head, Sloat said, "You read my mind. I'm out this way." He turned and strode off toward the doors.

The small bronze "Gulfside Security Associates" sign at the driveway entrance was the only thing that distinguished Sloat's house from all the other expensive homes on Eden Island. Lonnie paused on the walkway to admire the thirty-five-foot cabin cruiser docked behind the house.

"You know about boats?" Sloat asked.

"Some," Lonnie answered. "Not a lot."

The interior of the house looked more like something out

of NSA or CIA. The furniture and decor made it clear this was a reception area, not a living room.

"This way," Sloat said, nodding toward the back of the house as he headed down the hall. "There's stuff in the galley if you're hungry or thirsty." He pointed to an edgy metal-and-glass kitchen before going upstairs to what Lonnie figured were the bedrooms.

Upstairs, all the doors were closed. A biometric scanner was mounted on the wall beside a door halfway down the hall. Sloat pressed his palm against the scanner, triggering a faint click, and the door opened with a whoosh of air.

The room was a duplicate of the NSA and CIA's T-SAC— Tactical Surveillance and Communications—Center. Running the length of the house, it was equipped with the most sophisticated surveillance technology available. Dozens of TV monitors showed various perspectives of the house from just above street level. Others showed views from space. Some showed graphic readouts Lonnie couldn't begin to decipher, but he'd seen their predecessors years earlier at Langley.

A black guy about Sloat's age but nowhere near his size, wearing trendy glasses and a T-shirt that read *Geekus Mondo Suprimasis*, was sitting at what was obviously the control console. This was his domain. Staying seated, he smiled as he rolled himself over to shake hands with Lonnie.

"Mr. Tate. Doug Jennings." The young guy's good humor was infectious. Lonnie liked him.

"Call me Lonnie."

Rolling back to the control console, Doug spun the empty chair next to him around for Lonnie.

"Lemme show you what we've got, Lonnie." Doug pushed four or five buttons, and the scenes on four or five monitors changed. A larger monitor sequenced through two dozen still photos of a high-end house somewhere on the Gulf.

"Tarpon Springs," Doug announced, "about an hour north of here." He watched Lonnie studying the photos.

Doug clicked to another picture. "Your guys have expensive taste, Lonnie. Here's the floor plan."

"How'd you get this?" Lonnie leaned forward, studying the layout of the house.

"MLS," Doug answered.

Lonnie glanced at Doug, not recognizing the acronym. Doug clarified. "Multiple Listing Service. Real estate. They bought it, or the people they work for bought it about three months ago. Wasn't hard to find the listing...and a bunch of other stuff."

Turning back to the monitor, Lonnie observed, "Looks like two floors."

"That's what we thought at first," Doug countered, "but this shot"—the image changed— "shows it's just a daylight basement, one room, nothing in it but a couple of chairs."

Doug glanced back at Sloat. "Be a great spot for a pool table." Sloat shook his head and almost smiled.

Lonnie leaned back. "The files had a lotta comings and goings—"

Sloat's defenses shot way up. "Yeah?"

"Any chance anyone saw you when you surveilled these guys to get that intel?"

The former SEAL smiled. "Show 'im, Dougie."

56

The screen changed to a black-and-white overhead shot. The angle was wide enough to take in the entire house. People were moving about the house, some sitting. One person was standing in the kitchen, and another was lying down in one of the bedrooms.

Real-time infrared satellite. Lonnie looked up at Sloat.

"I don't guess you'll tell me how you happen to have a dedicated bird watching these people."

Sloat and Doug exchanged smiles.

"Five people, that's all?" Lonnie asked. "No girlfriends, boyfriends, delivery people, cleaning ladies?"

Sloat shook his head. "Cleaning ladies come Monday and Thursday, around ten in the morning, gone by noon. Those five aren't always all in the house, but other than the cleaning ladies, never anyone but them."

"OK." Lonnie studied the big screen. "What's the weather gonna be like tomorrow night?"

Lonnie found Sloat sitting on the stern of the cabin cruiser, nursing a beer in the fading daylight. The ex-SEAL saw Lonnie before he was within thirty feet of the boat. "Join ya?" Lonnie asked. Sloat nodded.

Climbing aboard, Lonnie took a seat in the deck chair across from him. The two men looked at each other for a full minute before Sloat spoke.

"You got a question, ask."

Lonnie took another minute then said, "You owe her."

"That's a statement, not a question, Lonnie."

"It's a fact, Craig," declared Lonnie. "You look at me and this job as a train wreck just waiting to happen. No way a guy like you takes a risk like this just for the paycheck. You owe somebody. It's not Marcus. You have no history with him."

Damned smart old bastard, Sloat thought. *Bad enough I gotta do this, now I gotta explain it?*

Sloat took a deep breath and exhaled slowly.

"You're an asshole, ya know that, Tate?"

Assuming the question was rhetorical, Lonnie didn't answer.

"You're right," Sloat said grudgingly. "I owe her. Twice."

57

THE NEXT NIGHT

Forty minutes after the cabin cruiser cast off from the dock, it tied up next to a 75 Sunreef Power Sportfish catamaran. Two of Sloat's people, Jesse Bernal and Travis Davidson, former SEALS also, were already on board.

A well-muscled six-footer, Bernal looked like the standard-issue ex-SEAL. Travis Davidson, on the other hand, made Craig Sloat look like a normal-sized person. His six-foot-seven, 260-pound frame, combined with his freckles and flaming-red hair, made Davidson look like the love child of Howdy Doody and a female Russian weightlifter.

"Lonnie Tate," Sloat announced to Bernal and Davidson. "Patino says he's a guy we don't want to mess with." Bernal and Davidson chuckled, which was the point.

Lonnie, already in an operational frame of mind, said nothing.

In less than ten minutes they were underway with Davidson at the helm. As they churned out of Tampa Bay, the fog thickened. Once they were in the Gulf, Davidson's eyes scanned the instruments nonstop. Visibility was close to zero, making their boat invisible from shore.

Ninety minutes later, he shut down the twin 1,000-horsepower engines and dropped anchor about two miles offshore.

Sloat, Bernal, and Lonnie had changed into black BDUs and boonie hats, standard issue for SEALs. Sloat and Bernal carried Mini-14s. Lonnie carried his Magnum with the silencer.

Davidson choked back a laugh. "Sure you don't want something bigger, Chief?"

"I'm sure." Lonnie saw Sloat and Bernal rolling their eyes.

Davidson handed each of them an earbud receiver attached to a lip mic with a pigtail cord. "Let's get everybody wired for sound."

As soon as they were hooked up, a sound check was completed. Davidson sat down at a console much like the one at Sloat's headquarters. Flipping it on, he said, "Let's see what's on TV."

The real-time infrared satellite image came up instantly. "Looks like all the boys are home early." The humor was gone from Davidson's tone. "Lemme know when you're feet dry."

The three men looked at Lonnie.

"It's your show, Lonnie. We're workin' for you," said Sloat.

Lonnie nodded. "Let's go."

Davidson lowered the eighteen-foot RIB—rigid-hulled inflatable boat—from the cat's stern. Sloat and Bernal hopped aboard. Lonnie got on more deliberately. Falling in the drink was the last thing he wanted to do.

Bernal took the helm. Sloat offered Lonnie the other seat. Lonnie declined and knelt down by the inflated gunwale, close to the bow. He wanted to see everything, as soon as there was something to see.

In less than two minutes, the house came into view through the fog. Bernal cut the power on the jet-drive engine and the RIB glided to shore. Sloat and Bernal exchanged smiles when they saw Lonnie looking down over the gunwale. They thought he was heaving his guts.

Then their smiles disappeared and their mouths fell open. Lonnie was out of the RIB, grabbing the line, and pulling the RIB onto shore before they had even moved.

"Feet dry," Lonnie whispered into the lip mic.

58

Once at the house, they were relieved to find that the door leading into the daylight basement was a slider. An upscale house like this one would have expensive sliding-glass doors—ones that slid easily and quietly.

Bernal picked the door lock in five seconds. He and Sloat looked at Lonnie, who held up three fingers. Lonnie would count down from three, and they would go. Sloat and Bernal nodded. When Lonnie's hand clenched into a fist, Sloat and Bernal slid the door open and Lonnie vanished.

With Sloat leading the way, he and Bernal silently charged in, wondering where the hell Lonnie had gone. The sound of four rapid metallic spits from the silenced Magnum, punctuated by the sound of bodies falling to the floor, told them.

Hand signaling Bernal to follow him, Sloat moved quickly toward the study. Stepping over a body that lay in the hallway and breathing heavily as they entered the room, Sloat and Bernal were dumbfounded.

To their left, a second man, sitting on the floor leaning against a bookcase—dead, his eyes locked open in a death stare. Blood pooled in his lap from the hole made by the Magnum round that had destroyed his chest.

There was blood spatter a couple of feet in diameter spider-webbing up the bookcase, the result of the head shot that blew out a third man's right eye and ear. Approximately ten feet from that body lay a fourth man, killed in the same way.

Still alive, Kadar was seated in an overstuffed leather chair. The fear in his eyes indicated he knew he was a dead man. Lonnie was positioned in front and about three feet away from him, the Magnum pointed at Kadar's forehead. An iPad streaming porn videos had fallen to the floor.

"What the—" Sloat was working to even his breathing. "You ain't supposed to be able to move that fast, old man."

Not taking his eyes off Kadar, Lonnie said evenly, "Yeah, I know." Then to Kadar, "You put out a hit on me. That was smart. Rumor has it I'm a dangerous man. But the two nimrods you hired were sloppy. Which gives them, you, and your four buddies here"— Lonnie nodded toward the bodies— "the distinction of being the only people I've ever killed for being just plain stupid."

Lonnie fired one round. Kadar's head exploded.

59

ENCINO, CALIFORNIA
ONE WEEK LATER

Back from Florida for a week, packing to go to Australia in a couple of days, Lonnie realized he hadn't called Linda.

Call, say hello, let her know you're back, then tell her you're leaving again. Brilliant. No wonder you've been divorced five times.

Further self-reprimands were interrupted by a voice—the voice of warning. The voice he always listened to when his life was in danger. And completely ignored when it came to women.

Call her. Just to see how she is, it said.

Yeah, why not? he asked himself. *You were thinking about her while you were in Florida, killing people.*

Punching in her number on his cell's keypad, he halfway hoped she had come to her senses and realized that she didn't need him in her life.

She answered on the second note of the *Twilight Zone* ringtone. "This is Linda," she said pleasantly.

The plan was to come back with something witty. But, "Hey, it's, ah, I'm sorry I, ah...it's me," was what came out.

"Ah, well, the voice does sound familiar. I'm assuming we've met?" she returned, unable to stifle a giggle.

Acknowledging the gotcha, he chuckled. "OK, that was good. Very cute."

"'Bout time you called," she scolded.

"Look, I'll, ah, make up for that when...I get back in town. I mean, I'm in town, but I'm, ah...see, I have to leave again, but I didn't want you to think that I—"

"My, my, Mr. Tate," she interjected. "You do have such a way with words."

Lonnie nodded into his cell phone. "Give me a break, will ya? Other than my daughter and your daughter, I'm not used to talking to women who like me, OK?"

"Yes, yes," Linda declared, "once again you find yourself drifting into unchartered territory. Don't worry. You're doing fine thus far."

"You're enjoying my humiliation, aren't you?"

"I'm enjoying talking with a man who can laugh at his humiliation. Not many I've met are secure enough to do that."

Lonnie smiled. "Why are you being so nice to me?"

"Because when you get back from wherever it is you're going, you're going to have to take me to dinner to make up for all of this... whatever it is."

"I can do that."

"Be safe, Lonnie. I mean that." With that, she hung up.

60

Though not as comfortable—make that decadent—as flying on Marcus's private jet, the fifteen-hour Qantas flight from Los Angeles to Sydney in first class wasn't too bad.

A couple of hours into the flight, Lonnie asked the explosives expert the question all Marines ask each other.

"Patino. Why did you join the Corps?"

There was no hesitation in her answer. "My mission. It was the first time I'd been involved in something bigger than myself. I liked it."

She paused, waiting for Lonnie to roll his eyes. He didn't.

"When I got back home, I had no idea what I wanted to do. One day I'm at the mall with some girlfriends I hadn't seen since before my mission. I'm trying hard to convince myself I'm having a good time." Patino shook her head. "But I was bored sick.

"I wanted to cry...or hit somebody." She grinned. "Couple of Marine Corps recruiters—sergeants, a man and a woman—had a recruiting table set up outside the next store we were going to visit. I told the girls I'd catch up.

"While they went off to further immerse themselves in shallow conversation and spending money on a lot of overpriced whatever, I asked the recruiters a few questions, listened to very little of what they said, and"—she smiled triumphantly— "I enlisted."

"No one," Lonnie chided, "joins the Corps on impulse. Certainly no one sober...and with a college degree."

"You're right." She nodded. "Those two recruiters...you could tell they knew they were doing something that mattered."

"Now," Patino declared, "your turn."

"To do what, Jarhead?"

"Why did you get into the Corps?"

"A judge."

Patino ran possible scenarios in her head. Nothing clicked.

"I don't get it. You want to explain?"

"No." He closed his eyes as if he were going to sleep.

"A judge, huh?" She waited until he opened his eyes. "You think I'm gonna let that go?"

He said nothing.

After several seconds, it was obvious she was going to continue staring at him until he gave her something more.

Hoping to end the interrogation, he made a proposition. "Make you a deal. I'll tell you why I got arrested, if you'll tell me about you and Sloat."

As soon as he said it, he felt a tectonic shift in the energy of the conversation.

She looked away, took a deep breath, and exhaled slowly and silently.

61

MARSOC Forward Operating Base Joker
3. 5 miles outside Bagram AFB, Afghanistan
Summer 2011

"**You look like ten** pounds of crap in a five-pound bag," Lance Corporal Connie Patino told Petty Officer Third Class Craig Sloat. "You're hungover. No way you're drivin' my vehicle."

Stumbling toward her side of her MTV, Sloat pushed her aside.

"Just gimme the keys, sweetheart," he belched, "and get yer round little ass in the cab."

She stepped in front of him. "Get over to Hazmat and have them wash out your mouth, Sloat. Your breath's gonna melt the metal plating on the floor of my truck."

This brought laughter from the other Marine MTV drivers, SEALS, and other MARSOC personnel that comprised the convoy detail. One of them, also a SEAL, was a Chief Petty Officer, senior in rank to Sloat.

Sloat tried pushing her aside again.

Grabbing his wrist, Patino pivoted and thrust her hip into the side of his knee, instantly buckling it, which allowed her to leverage him up onto her shoulders. Standing straight up, she pulled his arm down and slammed him to the ground.

Taking a knee on his throat and looking directly at the CPO, "Your man just got tossed by a woman half his size, Chief. You really think he can hold his own, he can ride with you. But not in my truck."

"The Lance Corporal's a little salty, but she's right, Sloat."

The hungover SEAL started to protest, but the chief cut him off.

"You just got your ass kicked by a gir—" He caught himself. "By a Marine." Looking back to Patino, he added, "No gender offense intended, Lance Corporal."

"None taken, Chief," Patino replied, flashing a grin.

"You're sittin' this one out, Sloat," the chief ordered.

Patino climbed into her MTV while the chief went around to the passenger side of the vehicle.

"Mind if I ride shotgun, Lance Corporal?" he asked.

Patino started the truck. "No problem, Chief."

Sloat watched the convoy pull away and then shuffled back to his tent.

Ten miles outside the FOB, the convoy passed a local riding a bicycle.

Immediately, Patino and the chief knew something was wrong. Locals never traveled this road this time of the morning.

Just as she keyed her headset to radio the drivers behind her to slow down and stop, there were two deafening explosions. The MTV jumped up in the air—a chunk of the engine block blew through the firewall and into the cab.

Feeling a burning, wet, tearing pain in her right leg, Patino reached down. She was surprised. Her leg wasn't there anymore.

A small shard of shrapnel blew through the windshield. Feeling it slice through the top of her Kevlar helmet, she thought, *Sloat's a foot taller than me. It would have taken off the top of his head!*

She wouldn't remember vomiting as the MTV slammed back down to the ground, rolled over twice, and came to rest on its roof. But she did remember looking over and discovering that the chief and the passenger side of the cab weren't there anymore.

She wouldn't remember how, through dust and smoke so thick she could hardly breathe or see, she crawled free of the wreckage and began looking for her leg.

She did remember hearing screams from one of the SEALS who had been riding in the back of her MTV.

But she wouldn't remember abandoning the search for her leg when she noticed the SEAL was on fire. She wouldn't remember crawling over to him, pulling him on top of her, and rolling both of them over and over in the dirt to smother the flames, which was why he survived and, three years later, was teaching English and coaching football at a high school in Hanford, California.

Bringing herself back to the present, Patino said in a monotone, "Afghanistan. I kept him off a detail that went south."

Having his own painful memories of ops that went south, Lonnie thought it best to let her non-answer answer be answer enough.

Glancing up, he noticed the flight attendant coming toward them, carrying two trays of food.

He looked over at Patino and smiled. "What say we eat, Jarhead? Then I'll tell you the story about a dumb kid who got arrested for stealing a police car."

62

SYDNEY, AUSTRALIA

It was six-thirty in the morning when they picked up the rental car. Check-in at their hotel wasn't until three o'clock that afternoon, and they were feeling the jet lag.

"So, what are we gonna do for the next seven hours?" Lonnie growled.

"I want to check out my work site," Patino answered.

"You're gonna start putting stuff together now?"

"Oh, no. No way I'm touching explosives after a fifteen-hour flight. But I want to start going over the inventory. Stackhouse always makes sure there's a place I can crash. So you can get some sleep 'til we can check in at the hotel."

The warehouse covered about two-thirds of an acre. Inside, pallets and crates of all sizes took up close to half the space, leaving plenty of room to walk around and between them.

In a corner near the door were a couple of couches and a desk with an office chair. Not waiting for an invitation, Lonnie picked a couch and was dead asleep in less than a minute.

While Lonnie slept, Patino took the encrypted flash drive Stackhouse had given her and plugged it into her laptop. She wanted to do a cursory check of the pieces she would spend the next two weeks assembling and arming. Basic reconning, she called it.

Tomorrow, when she was rested, she'd start getting serious.

Their daily routine was simple: Lonnie would call around lunchtime. They'd meet somewhere, or he'd pick up food and bring it to the warehouse. At the end of the day, Lonnie would come back to the warehouse so they could lock up. Then they would drive back to the car park and walk the few blocks to the hotel.

For dinner, they'd eat at the hotel restaurant or, more often, at one of the dozens of places within walking distance of their hotel.

Lonnie never pressed her on how it was coming. He didn't have to. After the third day, a dozen crates were sealed and marked with big, orange "READY" stickers.

A week of sightseeing and taking pictures had given Lonnie a lot of time to think about the op. The more he thought, the more questions he had.

Who was the real target? Why hadn't Darcy been able to find the SOC's base of operations? What was the plan for handling the SOC?

Most important, if this agency Shapiro was indentured to—this agency with no name—was in fact, the New Millennium version of Dade's Room 319, what was the end game? Why sell a huge amount of dangerous stuff to a bunch of maniacs you were hell-bent on bringing down twenty-five years ago?

Cy Watanabe was right. Something didn't make sense.

63

Thousand Oaks, California

More than forty-five years out of the game and Mary Pentangelo could still spot a tail. Four of them—beige Chevy Impalas—picking her up and handing her off as she drove to the grocery store. Old instincts told her there would be someone inside.

In the produce section of Whole Foods, she sensed him before she saw him. Then she saw him. Close to Marcus's height, this was probably his first field assignment.

Is he kidding? Standing in the produce section and not looking at the produce? Bet he jerks his head away when I make eye contact. She shot him a look. He almost gave himself whiplash turning to look the opposite direction.

Mary's appearance threw him off. The file said she was seventy, but she looked to be in her early fifties. And she was walking straight toward him.

Less than a foot away, she stopped and started sorting through the arugula.

"Everything about you screams 'I work for the government,'" she scolded. She reached past him to get a bag. "What do you want?"

"Give your husband a message," he said, making a weak attempt to mask the intimidation he felt. "We need him and his crew to quit dragging their feet."

"And who would we be?'" she challenged.

"He kno...knows," he stammered.

Tilting her head to the side, she paused to study him.

After a few seconds, she said, "If I were you, I'd find another line of work. Based on what I've observed the last couple of minutes, you're not going to live long. And what makes you think I have anything to do with my husband's work?"

"We know you don't. But your old man likes you doin' your little kids' theater stuff, and you know he'd hate for that to go away."

He leaned toward her. "Wouldn't be good for business," he whispered, "if the mommies and daddies knew their little brats' drama coach was a fugitive suspect in two murders when she was with the Black Panthers." He paused. "Who's to say she got it outta her system?"

Mary smiled and leaned in close to him. "You should keep that in mind," she purred. "I still have the gun. And I still know how to use it."

Taking a step back, she tossed the arugula into her shopping cart and headed for the checkout stand.

At the end of the aisle, she snuck a look back. The color was gone from his face. She stifled a laugh as she went to pay for her groceries.

64

"**Did you see what** he was driving?"

Marcus was angry–angrier than the night he came home from Vietnam. His anger had been so infrequently displayed over the years, seeing it now made her more than a little nervous.

"No," Mary answered. "Why?"

"Because when I find him, I'll kill him."

Getting up from the couch, she crossed to Marcus's recliner, sat in his lap, and leaned her head against his neck.

"They'll just send someone else, babe. Or send something to the media."

She felt him sag, emotionally and physically.

Sitting up, Mary took her husband's face in her hands. "Marcus, you are far too decent of a man to let anyone get to you so badly you'd go back to being what you used to be."

"And you," he said indignantly, "damn sure don't deserve to be held hostage the rest of your life for things that happened when you were serving your country." He straightened up and looked into her eyes.

"Howard Dade used you...he used me."

"No, babe," she countered. "We can't play the victim card."

"What we did back then had nothing to do with us as people, Mary."

"Oh, sweetheart, what we did back then had everything to do with us as people. I was a girl from Middle-of-Nowhere, Montana, working directly for the director of the CIA. Up until Chicago, that was very much who I was, and I loved it."

She laid her head against his shoulder.

"You were the son of an esteemed Ivy League professor so far left that he had the right-hand turn signals removed from the family car. And his only son joined the *Marine Corps*?" Mary laughed. "You've never told me why on Earth you *did* that, Marcus."

Marcus got a far-off look in his eyes.

"I'm a freshman at Harvard. One day, I'm reading an article in the *Globe* about troop buildups escalating past 200,000.

"I started thinking about all the black kids in Roxbury and all the white guys in Southie who were getting drafted." Marcus shook his head and looked at Mary. "They damn sure weren't drafting any of us privileged punks_in Cambridge." He paused. "It just didn't seem right. Hell, it *wasn't* right. So I enlisted." He closed his eyes for a few seconds. "The ol' man wouldn't speak to me for a week."

Tracing the tip of her index finger across his chin, she said, "And yet he cried like a baby when you came home from Vietnam.

"And you loved being there, Marcus. By your own admission, you loved the adrenaline rush, the camaraderie you had when you were in country. You needed *something* to replace it after you came back. And Howard Dade provided it.

"We were young and more than willing. We hoped it wouldn't come back to bite us, but now it has."

His arms around her, he asked, "So... what do we do?"

"We get out," she whispered, without looking up.

Marcus didn't respond right away. His strategy wheels were turning.

65

ANOTHER PART OF L.A.

Without breaking stride, an irate Brian Shapiro walked past her desk on his way to the Coordinator's office.

The administrative aide was on her feet. "You can't go in there, Mr. Shapiro."

"I'm sorry, sir," she said as she followed Shapiro through the doorway. "I told him he—"

"It's all right, Maureen," said the Coordinator as he came around the desk. Taking her by the elbow, he guided her to the door. "I've been expecting Mr. Shapiro. I'm sure I told you."

They both knew he hadn't told her any such thing.

Pacing back and forth, Shapiro began talking before the Coordinator was back behind his desk. "I just had a call from Marcus Pentangelo. He tells me one of your Hitler Youth hassled his wife while she was grocery shopping."

The Coordinator sat down, giving Shapiro a bemused smile.

"Do not screw with these people," Shapiro warned. "You won't like where it leads."

Making no attempt to be anything but the arrogant ass he was, the Coordinator asked, "Why? Is his thug friend Tate going to come in here and choke me?"

Shapiro rubbed his forehead, then spoke slowly, as if talking to someone who couldn't understand him.

"First rule in sales, keep talking after the prospect decides to buy, and you'll kill the sale. Pentangelo is in. If we execute the plan that's been developed, and if elements of this unit who have, at best, negligible field experience can resist the urge to slap their fingerprints all over the operation before their participation is called for"—he paused, hoping the Coordinator's air of superiority would fade a little— "there is a good chance this will work."

"I'm not sure the Pentangelo Group"—the Coordinator sarcastically emphasized the name— "is proceeding with all the urgency it could. What's the problem with applying some pressure to get them up to peak efficiency?"

He leaned forward and jabbed a finger at Shapiro. "Your old Vietnam buddy needs to quit calling and crying to you because somebody picked on his wife."

Shapiro closed his eyes and shook his head.

"He didn't call to cry. He was calling to warn," Shapiro growled. "I've invested three years and substantial resources in this operation, and so far, everything that needs to happen is tracking according to plan. What does not need to happen is someone with no clue about how this is going to unfold, thinking they can make it go faster."

The Coordinator glared at Shapiro.

"Brian," he said, in his best condescending voice, "I'm afraid you're so caught up in this operation on a personal level, you're blind to the opportunity we have here."

"So enlighten me."

"What obviously hasn't occurred to you," the Coordinator continued, "is the natural progression of Pentangelo's resources becoming our resources.

"We've compromised him. Now, we poke him. See how he and his people react. I'll concede that he's had some degree of success staying under everyone's radar. Not a bad achievement, but beyond that...."

Shapiro was incredulous. "Some degree of success? For more than forty years, the Pentangelo Group has grown to become the largest independent arms supplier—to a major U.S. ally. The first ten of those years, they operated within a shuttle flight of the seat of the United States government. You didn't know that until I told you three months ago. Hell, the rest of the feds and all the international intelligence services still haven't figured it out."

Shapiro was shouting. "Then Marcus decides to relocate, and to where? The Caymans? The Middle East? Hell, you thought he might be in Cuba. I start snooping around, and what do I find? He's set up shop in the parking lot of a hamburger joint in the San Fernando Valley. And that's where he's been for the last thirty years."

The Coordinator eyed Shapiro coldly.

"You forget yourself, Brian," he hissed.

Shapiro smiled.

"You mean I forget my place, don't you? You like it better when I'm not being the pushy Jew you think I am?"

"Well, Brian. Since you're playing smartest guy in the room...tell me, how many people are in your old Marine buddy's organization?"

"I don't know," Shapiro replied. "And neither do you."

"Not yet." The Coordinator smiled with a self-satisfied glow. "But we're getting close."

"Do tell," Shapiro said, thinking to call the Coordinator's bluff.

"Given what he's provided to Israel, and the scope of what he's gathering and preparing to supply this bunch of bandits, we're sure he has at least a hundred full-time operatives, and probably twice that many. Or did you think those car club has-beens did everything?"

Shapiro didn't answer. *He isn't bluffing*, he thought, *he's just full of shit.*

"Oh my God." The Coordinator started to laugh. "You did. Oh, Brian."

Just keep letting him underestimate you, Brian, Shapiro told himself. *Eating his crap now will pay off later.*

"For the record," Shapiro stated, "no, I don't think the six employees we know about are Pentangelo's whole team. He's gotta have more, and, hey, you could be right."

A triumphant smile spread across the Coordinator's face.

"Well, it's refreshing to hear you say that, Brian."

"But I know this." Shapiro dropped the conciliatory tone. "Intelligence directors a lot savvier than you trusted Marcus Pentangelo to run operations when he was in his twenties. Staying off everybody's radar for over forty years? Probably a good indication he's even smarter now."

The Coordinator's smile disappeared.

"The Pentangelos," Shapiro hissed, "have enough money to live very well, for the rest of their lives."

"Not if I freeze their bank accounts, credit cards, and lines of credit," the Coordinator disputed.

After all this time standing, Shapiro sat down in a chair across the desk facing the Coordinator. Leaning forward and grinning, he picked up a pen and a folder from the Coordinator's desk.

"Let me save you some time." He scribbled the name of Marcus's bank and several account numbers on the folder and tossed it back on the desk.

"Citizens Business Bank on Ventura Boulevard in Encino," Shapiro said with an exaggerated air of triumph. "Have your financial weasels tie up the six thousand each of them has in checking. And the twenty thousand and change they each have in savings. That'll show 'em."

The Coordinator inhaled slowly to make sure he was in control before saying anything.

"You left out your friend's business account," he said with a smug smile.

Shapiro grinned. "It's offshore."

"Wonderful. We'll get the IRS to work on this right away."

Shapiro chuckled; "The IRS already knows Marcus doesn't launder or hide anything that's taxable here in the States. The Pentangelo Group is incorporated in the Caymans."

His tone became matter-of-fact. "You don't know Marcus Pentangelo like I do. Keep trying to intimidate him. He...his business...the six or two hundred people that work for him? They will disappear and live very nice lives."

A minute passed before the Coordinator spoke.

"Then, Brian, you'll make sure that doesn't happen, won't you. Because we both know that your family's fortune"—he arched his eyebrows— "is not offshore, nor is your family's reputation."

Shapiro closed his eyes and leaned his head against the back of the chair. "I've been hearing that same damned threat for forty-six years." Opening his eyes, he glared at the Coordinator. "You're just the latest in a long line of officious pricks that have made it."

Shapiro flashed the Coordinator a look of contempt, which was suddenly replaced by a feeling that a weight had been removed from his shoulders.

"Go ahead. Expose my dead grandfather. Destroy the foundation and ruin my brother's life, and his kids' lives. Once you do that, I can walk away. Because I won't have anything to lose."

The Coordinator turned to the computer screens behind his desk.

"Get the hell out of my office."

66

SYDNEY, AUSTRALIA

More than three hundred crates were tagged and ready to be shipped. Stackhouse would have six container trucks at the warehouse tomorrow morning for pick-up.

Over the past two weeks, the three-minute walk from the car park back to the hotel had been a pleasant ritual to wind up the day. Tonight, they had gorged themselves at Patino's favorite Italian restaurant, a trendy little place in Leichhardt. So they needed a lot more exertion. Instead of turning right at William Street and heading back to the Boulevard, they turned left, toward Hyde Park.

The extended walk along the south and west sides of the park helped relieve Lonnie of the feeling that he was walking around with a bowling ball in his stomach. They were past St. James Station, across from Hyde Park Barracks, when he felt the twitch in his back.

Keeping an even tone in his voice, he said, "I don't want to sound like an alarmist, but I think…" He paused, hearing three sets of footsteps, some twenty yards behind them.

"You think what?" Patino asked.

"Three idiots coming up behind us, in the trees between the fountain and the sidewalk."

"Oi bet she ain't wearin' nothin' under them white daks," a loud voice announced.

"Crap," Patino scolded herself, "shoulda worn jeans."

Instinctively, Lonnie and Patino moved to position themselves back-to-back.

"Hey, luv," said one of the idiots. "Why don'tcha send Granddad home, and let's go rage! It's Friday night, yeah?"

They looked to be in their early twenties. Idiot A, the loud one, and Idiot B strolled up to within a couple feet of Patino. Both were about five feet eleven and thin. Stepping around his two idiot friends, Idiot C positioned himself directly in front of Lonnie. He was six-feet-three, probably 220.

Big, but soft, Lonnie thought. *Probably been intimidating smaller guys with his size since he was twelve.*

Sliding his hands in his pockets, "We're all going to be a lot happier if you leave us alone, big guy," Lonnie warned.

"'Ow the 'ell do you know what'll make me 'appy, you old turd?" he snarled.

"You're right," Lonnie replied as he extracted his key ring from his left pocket. "I don't."

Instantly, the air smelled and tasted like pepper.

Idiot C's eyes burned and teared up to the point he couldn't see. The skin on his face burned. His nose was running so badly that he was spewing and choking on his own mucus. His hands clawed at his face, which only made his skin and eyes burn worse.

Taking a short, quick step forward, Lonnie landed a haymaker to Idiot C's left jaw, sending him to the ground, out cold.

Idiot B just stood there wide-eyed and disoriented.

Idiot A, the loud one, was flat on his back, his sternum fractured as a result of Patino taking a quick step forward, high-kicking, and driving her titanium prosthetic leg into his chest.

Idiot B had seen enough. He started to run. Four steps into his escape, Patino had him by the back of his leather jacket, yanking him to the ground.

Bracing her left knee across his chest, she pinned his hands above his head.

"Where's your mo-bile?" she barked.

His mouth moved, but nothing came out.

"I said, where...is...your...mo-bile?"

"It's-it's-it's in moi p-p-p-pocket."

"Get it," she ordered, rising to her feet.

Rolling onto his side, he started to get up.

"I didn't say 'get up.'"

He held his hands up in front of him. "It's in m-m-m-m-moi back pocket."

Narrowing her eyes so she wouldn't laugh, she asked, "Then what's that in your hand?"

He was so rattled he didn't realize he was holding it.

Attempting to imitate Lonnie's soothing tone of voice, she said, "Call triple-zero." It sounded like a bad feminine imitation of Clint Eastwood.

Lonnie rolled his eyes. "You're a regular Rich Little, aren't ya, Jarhead?"

"Who's Rich Little?"

She turned her attention back to Idiot B. "Tell 'em one of your mates has been pepper-sprayed; probably has a broken jaw and a concussion. The other has a fractured sternum, and they need ambos right now—got it?"

The punk nodded.

"Call, you twit!"

It took him four tries to punch the 0 key three times in a row. "Oi-oi-oi-oi n-n-n-need a-a-a-ambos."

Snapping her fingers in his face to get him focused, Patino mouthed, "Ster-num."

"Moi mate's got a sternum!" he shouted.

She rolled her eyes. "Fractured sternum," she stage-whispered.

"It's fractured. God! Oi dunno. They's 'urt, dammit! Jes' layin' on the footpath…where?" He paused, looked around. "Uh, at…uh…"

She grabbed his wrist and pulled the phone close to her mouth.

"College Street and Prince Albert," she said, affecting an Aussie lilt. "East side by Hyde Park. Two males, early twenties. Male number one: approximately one-point-eight meters tall, seventy-two to seventy-four kilos, probable fractured sternum and possible internal injuries. Male number two: about one-point-nine meters, one hundred kilos. Eyes and mouth irritated by pepper spray, probable concussion, probable fractured jaw." She paused while the emergency dispatcher asked her something.

"Because." She dropped the Aussie lilt and replaced it with no-BS American English. "The smaller one tried to rape me. My granddad"—she winked at Lonnie— "pepper-sprayed and punched the big one out. Get ambos here quick."

She let go of the punk's wrist and glared at him. "You stay right here, and you tell the ambos everything they ask. Got it?" He nodded.

Standing up, she looked at Lonnie. "Can we go now?"

"I'm just waitin' on you, Jarhead."

Ambulance siren blaring in the distance and getting closer, Patino took the lead. She and Lonnie needed to be gone when the paramedics arrived. Keeping a pace that was neither hurried nor relaxed, she knew not to take a direct route back to the hotel. Each time they came to a corner, she turned.

While waiting for the light to change so they could cross busy William Street, Lonnie grinned and asked, "Pucker factor?"

Patino shrugged. "'Bout two point oh."

"Charlie that," Lonnie replied.

67

THE WAREHOUSE
7:00 A.M. THE NEXT MORNING

Six semis hauling shipping containers were idling in the parking lot when Lonnie and Patino drove in. A seventh was hooked up to a flatbed trailer carrying loading gear. A medium-tall man Lonnie guessed to be in his mid-forties was leaning against the building, next to one of the roll-up doors. He smiled and waved.

"Morning, Con," he called out as he walked toward the car. He and Patino shared a brief hug. She took his arm and led him to Lonnie, who was getting out of the car.

"Mike, this is—"

"The legendary Lonnie Tate," Mike cut in. He stuck out his hand and winked as they shook hands. "Stack told me all about you, mate. It's an honor."

Mike was six feet one and weighed maybe two hundred pounds. Lonnie was sure the strength in his handshake came from hard work, not lifting weights in a gym. Lonnie liked him immediately.

"This is a first, Lonnie," Mike said, putting his arm around Patino's shoulders as they walked to the warehouse. "Usually, Con's waiting for us. D'jou keep her up late?"

"No, I'm still getting over all the Italian food she stuffed into me last night."

"Little Sicily?" Mike asked, looking at Patino. She grinned and nodded.

Mike glanced back at Lonnie. "You're lucky you can move at all, mate."

With Patino noting the information on the outside of every pallet and crate of explosives on her laptop, Mike's crew had all six trucks loaded in less than two hours.

68

PENTANGELO GROUP OFFICES
FRIDAY AFTERNOON

It was a standing invitation: if Marcus's office door was open, no need to knock before entering.

Doyle Stackhouse leaned against the frame in the open doorway and knocked anyway, as he always did.

"Got a minute?"

Marcus looked up from the papers spread out on his desk and smiled. In spite of the open-door invitation, he had come to appreciate the logistics man's gracious manners.

"Tell me something good, Doyle."

"Trucks are loaded and headed to the shipyard." He shook his head and smiled. "I wondered if she could get everything ready in two weeks. "I should know by now. The difficult Patino does immediately. The impossible takes her just a skosh longer."

Marcus pursed his lips, fighting a grin.

"What?" Stackhouse said.

"I'm betting she picked that up from you, Doyle."

Stackhouse looked down. He knew how well he did his job, for which Marcus compensated him handsomely. But it was nice to hear the compliment.

"I expect to hear from her a little after ten tonight," Stackhouse explained, "after the loads are squared away."

"What's the time difference?"

"Eighteen hours. It's Saturday morning there now and—"

"They get back here when?" Marcus interrupted.

"Sunday evening. And there's only one flight out each day from Eden—or some little airport near there. I think it's the same with the flight back to L.A. Connie handles that, so I'm not completely sure about the times."

Marcus knew better. The logistics expert was always completely sure about "the times," but he made a point of not sounding like a know-it-all.

"What's next?" Marcus asked.

"You tell me." Stackhouse smiled. "Our...uh...customers tell you when they want this stuff, and where?"

Marcus shook his head. "Not a word, and I hope I don't hear from them until Cy and Lonnie have the weapons ready to ship out...or are at least getting close." Marcus looked troubled, and it wasn't about the weapons.

"Never seen Russell so focused," said the logistics expert. "He's putting in twenty-hour days. Can't say he's happy about it, but he's damn sure engaged. I don't know what you told him, but he's working like a man possessed."

"Have you talked with him?" Marcus wondered.

"I bring him lunch or dinner every other day." Stackhouse shook his head sadly. "And listen to him vent."

"About me, right?"

"Not really. Well, not that much about you," he chuckled, then sadness crept into his tone. "Not that he'd ever admit it, but this whole thing scares him—been that way since before Lonnie got the list."

Marcus stood and walked over to the window. Stackhouse could sense how much it had pained his boss to have pushed the computer genius so hard.

"He'll be OK, Marcus. Shoot, this whole thing's gonna be OK."

Marcus flashed Stackhouse an appreciative smile. "How about you, Doyle? I can't imagine how complicated this thing is on your end."

"Well, it's certainly different." He had never had to make sense of a supply-chain process with so many moving parts. "I'm gonna be making it up as we go, pretty much."

"Using one of those supply-chain software outfits you usually work with?" Marcus asked as he sat back down.

"Not this time."

"Can't they handle it?"

"I'm sure they could; it's just…." Marcus felt the chill of Stackhouse's unfinished sentence.

"Just what, Doyle?"

"On the off chance this thing goes sideways, and I'm sure it won't"—he smiled without conviction— "I'd rather it didn't come back on any of 'em. Know what I mean?"

69

EQUIPMENT DEPLOYMENT FACILITY
EDEN, AUSTRALIA

As Patino pulled up to the security checkpoint, a guard stepped out of the guard shack, clipboard in hand.

"Good t' see you again, miss! It's been a while."

"Too long." Her smile made his day.

Taking a step back from her car, he waved her through.

In the last two weeks, but especially today, Lonnie had developed a new appreciation and respect for Doyle Stackhouse. Logistics was an exact science of procuring, warehousing and staging people and equipment and all the necessary support elements; then moving and tracking those elements from one location to another within a very specific time frame.

It was one thing to do it with racing cars. It was quite another to do it with the freight Stackhouse had been moving for the past thirty-plus years.

As if knowing what Lonnie was thinking, Patino said, "Marcus says Doyle is the Einstein and da Vinci of logistics."

Even more mind-boggling was how Stackhouse had put together such a highly efficient and trustworthy network of port-security officials, transportation personnel, and dock workers to make it work.

Some folks must be getting paid a lot of money to take that kind of risk, Lonnie said to himself.

Mike and his crew had the containers off the trucks and staged in the cargo storage area in less than forty-five minutes. Half an hour later, Mike gave Connie a hug, shook Lonnie's hand, and wished them well.

As the big Qantas 747 went wheels up from runway 3 Alpha at Melbourne Airport the next day, Lonnie glanced out the window and promised himself he'd be coming back to Australia someday. Maybe Linda would want to come with him.

Yes, he missed her. They'd be back in L.A. Sunday night, and he'd call Monday—no—Tuesday, after the jet lag wore off.

He did call her on Tuesday, but it was to apologize for delaying their next get-together for another week. His daughter had called.

70

Dad, let me spoil you for a weekend" He could feel the excitement in her voice through the phone. "The firm has condos in Sedona that the partners can use, and I reserved one for us."

"It's August, kid," he protested, "and you live three blocks from the sun."

"In point of fact," she said in her high-powered attorney voice, "I live at least ten blocks from the sun." Hearing him laugh, she knew she had him. "Sedona is over

four-thousand feet elevation, so it's only going to be in the eighties. And"—she paused for effect— "I guess word hasn't gotten to Southern California yet, but we have air-conditioning here."

"OK, OK," Lonnie chuckled. "We celebrating something?"

"Actually," she said, sounding more serious than she intended, "I just wanted to show you how much I appreciate you taking care of that email stuff."

"You hear any more about it?"

"Nope." He could hear the relief in her voice.

"OK." Lonnie tried to sound reluctant, but no way was he going to pass up spending the weekend with her. "So, what are we gonna do in Seh-doh-na?" He drew out the middle syllable sarcastically.

"Oh, Dad! It's gorgeous," Donna said excitedly. "The colors are just spectacular, and there's all kinds of great hiking trails, and—"

Lonnie cut her off. "Donna…?"

"Yeah, I know." She dropped into her Lonnie Tate imitation.

"'Donna, I did all the hiking I'm ever gonna do in the Marines.' So, Dad…how about taking a Jeep tour out to the red-rock country—"

"Sweetheart," he interrupted her again, "I did all the Jeeping I'm ever going to—"

"You're a vacation planner's worst nightmare, you know that? How about a helicopter tour? And don't tell me you did all the helicoptering—"

"They're called choppers, sweetheart. And I'll never turn down a ride in a chopper. See if you can make it a Huey."

"Really?" Donna said, with enthusiasm. "What's a Huey? Never mind, the helicopter—excuse me—the, ah, chopper people will know what a Huey is, right?"

The carousel started moving, and the revolving red light signaled that baggage from Lonnie's flight was coming out. The flight to Sky Harbor Airport in Phoenix had been less than half full, so Lonnie knew he wouldn't have to wait long. His red-and-black canvas bag showed up just as his phone rang. He grinned. It was Donna.

"Hey Kiddo," he said, walking to the quieter side of the carousel.

"Sorry, I'm running late. I should get to you about the time your bag shows up."

"It's here, hon…I'm just waiting for it to make the turn on the carousel."

"Oh, shoot. I'm just pulling into the garage. Do you mind waiting by baggage claim? I'll be there in five minutes—seven tops."

"How 'bout you tell me which level you're on. I'll come to you." Lonnie picked up his bag. "Save you a couple bucks on parking."

"Um…OK. I stopped by the office to pick up my membership card for the place we're staying. I forgot the damned thing when I left last night. I'm sorry, Dad."

"No worries. I'm enjoying the air-conditioning I didn't know you guys have in this skillet you call a city."

Looking for signage, she piloted her Lexus toward a parking place close to the elevators.

"I'm on level four. Take the elevators at the east end of the building, away from where you came down the escalator."

"Yep, I see 'em." Lonnie headed that way. "I'll see you in a couple of minutes."

Finding a men's room along the way, Lonnie hustled in and went to the pull-down diaper-changing table mounted on the wall near the sinks. He hoisted and unzipped his bag, clearing away the layers of clothes covering his Magnum, cylinder, and silencer. After inserting the cylinder, he screwed the silencer onto the barrel. He started to slide the .357 into its holster at the back of his waistband, but the little voice inside him said, *Leave it in the bag and leave the bag open.*

Donna grabbed her weekend bag off the passenger's seat and got out of the car to stow it in the trunk. Shutting the trunk lid, she gasped. Standing there smiling was a woman—the woman from the hotel room.

Taller than Donna remembered, she wore a sleeveless dress. Her heavily muscled arms glistened in the heat.

"What you did to my company's email made some people really angry," she said casually as she came around the car.

Grabbing Donna by the arm, she spun her around and yanked her in close. Keeping a tight, painful grip on her arm with her left hand, the woman took Donna's chin in her right hand and jerked her head back.

With Donna's neck pinned against the woman's shoulder, she whispered, "That got me in a lot of trouble, bitch."

71

The elevator doors opened. Donna and the woman looked up. The woman's right hand went to Donna's throat and squeezed.

The squat-framed man stepping out of the elevator, wearing a green Hawaiian shirt, khaki slacks, and a beige Panama hat, looked about as intimidating as a door greeter at Walmart. The woman almost laughed.

Carefully approaching them, Lonnie stopped about ten feet away. "Well, look who's here. The Phantom of the Law School. You can let go of my daughter now."

"I'm not going to do that," she replied, "but you can put your bag down."

"Not on your life," Lonnie countered.

"Come on, now. This is the wrong time for Daddy to try and play hero. Put the bag down—now. Or I'll crush your little girl's throat."

Lonnie leaned over and set the bag down on the pavement. When he straightened up, the Magnum was in his hand and pointed at the woman's head.

Keeping her eyes on Lonnie and squeezing his daughter's throat tighter, she hissed, "Daddy's dumber than he looks, honey."

Donna looked at her father, her eyes wide with fear.

"I'm sorry, sweetheart," Lonnie said sadly.

The Magnum made a spitting sound. The woman's hands flailed away from Donna's neck and arm. Something warm, thick, and wet oozed down Donna's neck.

As the body hit the pavement, Donna looked at her father. He felt sick to his stomach. She ran to him and buried her head against his shoulder.

Looking down at the body, he put his free arm around his daughter's waist and held her close.

"God, I never wanted you to…" He couldn't finish the sentence. Donna didn't care. He didn't need to apologize. The only thing Donna Tate cared about was that her dad was alive.

The security video wasn't any help. Airport police detectives couldn't enhance it enough to read the license plate of the car from any angle as it drove out of the parking structure.

It was as if the perp knew there were security cameras. He never looked up, so they couldn't see his face. Didn't matter. As far as they could tell, his general description fit a thousand men who passed through Sky Harbor International Airport that day: medium height, stocky build, wearing a green Hawaiian shirt, khaki slacks, and a beige Panama hat.

As for the victim: no ID. The M.E. logged in the remains as Jane Doe #19.

72

A WEEK LATER

Grocery shopping was the last thing Lonnie wanted to do. But after spending two days sleeping off jet lag, and his trip to Arizona, grocery shopping had evolved from the thinking about it stage to the urgent necessity stage.

The store opened at 5:00 a.m.; Lonnie pulled into the parking lot at 5:05. Half an hour later, he was pushing a full grocery cart back to his car.

The sun was just starting to rise, leaving most of the parking lot still in shadows. Lonnie heard the unmistakable rumble of a large-displacement American car engine before he saw the car.

It was a Dodge Viper, competition yellow, with a V10 engine that put out 640 horsepower. The low-profile, wide-stance supercar was rolling down the lane nearest the store as if it were on the prowl, looking for any car that dare try to share the lane.

Lonnie felt the twitch in the small of his back. *Nobody who drives a car like that goes grocery shopping—not before six o'clock on a Monday morning.*

The twitch turned to throbbing as he watched the Viper turn into the lane at the far end of the lot. Right where he had parked his Bimmer.

Retrieving the Magnum from under his shirttail in the small of his back, Lonnie rested the handgun on top of the shopping cart and continued walking toward his car.

As the Viper pulled in one space over from his BMW, Lonnie stopped, took aim at the driver's-side door, and clicked off the safety.

The door opened. Lonnie took a breath, exhaled, and took up the slack on the trigger.

With arms out to his sides, the palms of his hands up and open, Brian Shapiro stepped out of the car.

"You gonna let me live?" he asked. Then he smiled. "Or are ya gonna tag me and get yourself a new ride?"

From the sculpted racing-style seats to the dashboard instrument panel, the Viper was all business. As was its driver, Brian Shapiro.

"The woman at the airport in Phoenix."

Lonnie remained silent.

"As soon as Beck found out what happened," Shapiro resumed, "he was in my office begging me to get word to you that he had nothing to do with her. He even had the airport security video of you tagging her."

Lonnie gave Shapiro a hard look.

"How'd he know about it so quick? Where did he get the video?"

"Lonnie…are you kidding? It's black, black ops. Everything is monitored."

Lonnie accepted the obvious logic.

"This wasn't the first time she'd caused us problems," Shapiro continued, "By the way…I don't know what you had Branco do," Lonnie didn't ask how Shapiro knew Branco was involved. "but it sure played havoc with our email. The bosses blamed Beck. He dumped it all on her. He brought her in, and all the heavyweights—the IT chief, even the Coordinator—ripped her a new one."

Lonnie made no attempt to hide his skepticism. "If she was that much of a problem, why the hell didn't you guys—?"

"You got to her before we could," Shapiro cut in. "Not that it's worth anything, but thank you."

Closing his eyes; Lonnie shook his head, "My daughter, Shap… she saw…what I do."

"I know." Shapiro's voice broke. "I am so sorry, Lonnie."

Lonnie was taken aback at the sadness and regret he felt coming from his old comrade-in-arms. It was as if Shapiro was holding himself solely responsible for what had happened.

"The game sucks, Lonnie."

"Yeah," Lonnie agreed, "Always did, Shap."

"On my grandfather's soul, Lonnie, I did everything I could to keep this away from her."

Lonnie wasn't so sure. "This from the guy who died forty-six years ago…but isn't dead anymore."

Shapiro just looked at him.

"Forty-six years, Brian! All our time in 'Nam…and after. And you didn't think you could trust us?"

Shapiro felt his voice catch. "I stayed quiet because any contact with either one of you…they would have done to you what they did to me."

Lonnie shifted his gaze away from Shapiro. "So you were protecting us."

"Yes, I was trying to protect you." His chin started to quiver. "And I am so goddamn sorry I did such a piss-poor job."

Neither man spoke for the better part of five minutes.

Lonnie looked at his old friend. For the first time since their reunion, he realized that Brian Shapiro did, in fact, die forty-six years earlier. God just hadn't shown him the mercy of taking him.

"Thanks for finding me, Brian—I mean that." Shapiro's head jerked up in surprise. Lonnie reached out his hand. "Thanks for talking to me this morning. It means the world."

"You're welcome, Lonnie," Shapiro said as they shook. "I'm trying to make this right."

"Well… there is one thing that could take care of that. In fact…I'd owe you."

"Name it."

Feigning sincerity, Lonnie paused and looked at Shapiro; then his face broke into a wide smile. "Whatever you have to do…get those two mouth-breathers posing as managers outta my building so the property-management company will bring in people who really know how to run an apartment complex, would ya?"

Shapiro threw back his head and laughed. "Done. I'll call 'em right now."

Enjoying the sound of Brian Shapiro's unrestrained laughter—a sound he hadn't heard since Vietnam—Lonnie climbed out of the Viper feeling more resolve than he had in years.

73

Branco pulled into the grocery-store parking lot just as Lonnie was pulling out. Lonnie nodded and gave a two-finger salute as they passed, but Branco didn't see him.

Typical engineer, Lonnie thought, *focused only on what's in front of him.*

Back home, he had just finished putting away the last of the groceries when the voice in his head said, *Check on Branco.* Lonnie grabbed his keys and left.

Stopping for the light at Coldwater Canyon and Ventura Boulevard, Lonnie spotted Branco's Buick heading south. Traffic was heavy enough, even at that early hour, that it took more than a minute for the sensor to give him a green light. By then he'd lost sight of Branco's car. But he wasn't worried.

Closing the distance quickly, Lonnie saw the Buick rounding into the curve. Thirty seconds later he watched Branco turn into what had to be his driveway.

As Lonnie pulled in, he couldn't help but notice the tricked-out Camaro parked next to Branco's car. The twitch in his lower back came on with a rush. If Branco had any friends, it was a safe bet none of them drove a Camaro. Snugging the BMW up close behind the Buick, Lonnie made a phone call before getting out and going around to the back of the house.

He heard the arguing even before he opened the back door. Something about computer codes, and it was getting intense.

The guy arguing with Branco was a little over six feet tall. Lonnie nicknamed him "Camaro Guy."

Camaro Guy was tan, fit, and looked to be in his thirties. He wore a sport jacket and was not the least bit concerned when Lonnie walked in.

He should have been, because Lonnie took three steps and drove his fist into Camaro Guy's solar plexus. As Camaro Guy doubled over in pain, Lonnie grabbed the sport jacket's lapels and jerked them down off Camaro Guy's shoulders, immobilizing his arms.

Shoving him to the floor, Lonnie leaned down and got in his face. "Don't try to talk. Just nod if you can hear me." Camaro Guy nodded as a stunned Branco looked on.

"Couple a things," Lonnie said as he took a knee on Camaro Guy's head and neck. "You're with the guys that are leaning on Pentangelo, right?"

Camaro Guy responded with a loud, painful grunt.

"I'll take that as a yes" Lonnie commiserated. "And in case you're wondering, you should know that I got no problem hitting you again. Capiche?"

Camaro Guy grunted.

"Okay, now, second"—Lonnie nodded toward Branco— "Branco and I aren't friends. He doesn't like me. I'm OK with that, because Russ doesn't like anybody—especially you. Right, Russ?"

"Damn straight," Branco barked.

"But it's my job to look out for him. Now, Russ really hates what you clowns have him working on. He knows he's gotta do it, and he will, but he just really hates it, understand?"

Camaro Guy grunted a little quieter.

"So in the spirit of you not getting hit again, understand that leaning on him isn't gonna make him do it any faster. It's just gonna piss him off even more." Lonnie glanced over at Branco. "Right, Russ?"

"Damn right!" Branco barked.

Lonnie continued. "Then two bad things happen. One: you have to deal with me. And two: Russ is gonna start screwing with your computers.

How does he know I'd do that? Branco wondered.

"See, ol' Russ here is like a cyber savant. He starts digging into your computer systems, he can screw things up so bad that when you open a program, all your toilets will back up." Lonnie looked up at Branco.

"Right, Russ?"

Branco just nodded. He was afraid to tell Lonnie that what he had just threatened was impossible.

Helping Camaro Guy to his feet, Lonnie said, "You have to go now." Addressing Branco but keeping his eyes on Camaro Guy, he added, "Ya want to get the door, Russ, please?"

"What the hell's a tow truck doin' here?" Branco yelled as he opened the door. A wrecker was lifting the back of the Camaro.

Straightening Camaro Guy's jacket back over his shoulders, Lonnie walked him to Branco's front door. "You'll have to pay 'em for coming out. If…you can convince 'em not to tow you."

They watched as Camaro Guy argued and pleaded with the tow-truck driver, who eventually gave in—but doubled the cost for coming out.

"Thanks, Tate," was all Branco managed to say. But he said it with a sincerity that was rare for him.

Lonnie smiled. "You're welcome, Russ. Like I said, it's my job."

Branco was grateful for Tate getting rid of the guy. He was just as grateful to see Lonnie get in his car and leave.

It wouldn't occur to him until later in the day to wonder how Lonnie knew where he lived and how he just happened to show up when he did.

74

TWO NIGHTS LATER

The evening weather was perfect. Lonnie and Linda shared easy conversation on the fifteen-minute walk from the Lebanese restaurant back to his apartment.

"Great dinner." Linda said. "And what a place."

Lonnie handed her the boxes of leftovers so he could unlock his front door. "Yeah, the place is a zoo because the food is so great. I always go home with enough to feed me 'til I go in again." He motioned for her to go inside.

"And how often is that?" she asked, waiting for a punchline.

"Couple a weeks," Lonnie deadpanned.

Since his last divorce, Linda was the only woman other than his daughter that Lonnie had invited to his place.

As she stepped inside, music from smooth-jazz pianist David Benoit started playing on the motion-activated Bose Surround System.

Smooth jazz and Lonnie? Yes, she could put the two together. Expecting the no-frills, just-the-essentials decor she envisioned a man like Lonnie would call home, she was visibly surprised. The living room was bright, open, and inviting. The Copenhagen sectional couch, coffee table, and end tables sat low to the floor—their design clean and sleek. Modern but not sterile, expensive without pretension. Large live-action photographs decorated the walls: Andre Agassi delivering a vicious backhand at Wimbledon, Jazz artist George Benson at the Universal Amphitheatre. Country-music artists Brooks and Dunn, and Kenny Chesney.

Jazz and country? Linda asked herself. *Never saw that coming.*

The photo that stood out the most was that of a book cover: Jimmy Buffett's *A Pirate Looks at 40.* In the bottom right-hand corner Buffett had written, "Damn good thing we didn't grow up together. We'd both be pirates! Jimmy."

Throwing his keys on the coffee table, Lonnie said, "The head is…" He caught himself. "Excuse me, the, ah…"

Turning her head away from the book-cover photo, Linda grinned. "I know what the head is, Lonnie. First time you hear your returned missionary daughter turned Marine call a bathroom the head, you don't forget it."

"I bet." He laughed. "Well, whatever you want to call it, if you need to freshen up, it's down the hall." He pointed over his shoulder. "First door on the right." Motion-sensor lighting lit the hall as she made her way to the bathroom.

Returning a few minutes later, she gave him a curious smile.

"I don't want you to think I was snooping," she began as she sat down on the couch next to him. "OK, I was."

Lonnie's face smiled, but not his eyes.

"In the hallway you have some pictures on the wall. One is of the Eagles, has to be from the seventies, and there's a guy—obviously not a musician. He looks like you might have looked back then? Maybe?"

"Yeah," he grinned. "That's me."

"What did you do?"

"Rock-concert security. I was their tour security supervisor. I had to be with them when they'd go to the venues to do sound checks. During the concert, another guy and I rotated running backstage security and the guys we had working out front."

"How was it?" she asked.

"The tour was great. One of the best I ever did." He shrugged. "The job itself...did it for four years. But after six months, being a high-paid babysitter starts to wear on you. I stayed for the money."

"Then you quit?" she asked in her mom tone.

"Yeah," he answered, remembering the incident that had made the great money not worth doing the job anymore.

"From bodyguard to advertising. Just like that?" She knew he was leaving something out of the story.

He wasn't about to tell her about the broadcasting-school crash course that led to a DJ job in Rigby, Idaho. That was the first and—he swore a blood oath to himself—last time he'd live anyplace where the temperature fell below fifty.

She nodded and gave him a pursed-lip smile that said, *Let's see if I can ask something you will answer.*

Getting up from the couch, she took him by the hand and led him to the hallway.

"Tell me about these other pictures." She gestured to a series of framed photos, some yellowed with age.

Lonnie had shot most of them. One, taken from a chopper—a beautiful panoramic shot of smoothly-terraced rice paddies in Vietnam. A peasant woman walking a narrow rice paddy dike, balancing a large basket on her head was the subject of another. A third, a little Vietnamese boy who couldn't have been more than four or five years old, sitting atop a water buffalo.

Her attention was suddenly drawn to another photograph.

"Wait. Oh my gosh, Lonnie. Is that—"

It was the picture of Lonnie, Marcus, and Shapiro in Vietnam, where he was flipping off the camera—the same picture he had told himself to take down before he brought her here.

"Yeah," Lonnie said, trying to cover his embarrassment. "That's me, Marcus, and our other team member, a guy named Brian Shapiro." He paused. "I was having a bad day."

She laughed. "Yes, from the looks of things, I guess you were."

"You said you were a team?"

"I-T-T, Interrogator, Translators," he replied offhandedly.

"Now, I'm even more impressed."

"Yeah, well"—he shook his head—"fancy title that translated—pun intended—to being a grunt that could speak Vietnamese."

"You and my daughter," she scolded. "The bigger the accomplishment, the less you talk about it. I thought Marines were more arrogant than that."

"Oh, we are." Lonnie laughed. "Some of us just hide it better than others."

She gestured to Shapiro. "This other Marine, Shapiro, right?"

"Yes."

"Have you and Marcus had a chance to get back together with him since the war?"

Lonnie showed a slight grin. "Interesting that you asked. The three of us caught up just a few weeks ago."

"That's wonderful, Lonnie. How was it?"

After taking a few seconds to come up with the right words, he answered, "The guy's had a hard life."

"I'm sorry to hear that, Lonnie. The three of you were quite close?"

Looking at the picture, he played back their meeting in his mind. "In some ways…triplet sons of different mothers," he said answered; "In other ways…as different as a Nash Rambler and a Rolls-Royce."

Linda sensed she needed to take the conversation elsewhere. "Tell me about this picture. The three men standing with you in… where is that, a consulate or something?"

"Vietnam, 1995," he replied. "The Ministry of Finance in Saigon: a.k.a. Ho Chi Minh City. I was translating for an American company. It was the start-up phase of their doing business with the Vietnamese government."

"The guy standing on my right," Lonnie continued, "was my counterpart for the Vietnamese government—heck of guy—former NVA—North Vietnamese Army. The guy on the left was the president and CEO of the company setting up shop there. The guy standing next to him is an old friend of Marcus's and mine, Cy Watanabe. He was doing something with the State Department."

Internally, Lonnie grinned. To this day he still wasn't sure what Watanabe was really doing while they were there. Cy never volunteered an explanation.

Taking her by the hand, Lonnie walked her back into the living room.

"It's late, and I should get you home. Don't get me wrong; I enjoyed the evening and enjoyed showing you my place. Surprised you, didn't it?"

She blushed and smiled. "Have to admit, it's a far cry from the sandbags and concertina wire I thought I'd see."

Gently pulling her closer, "Now what's a nice lady like you know about sandbags and concertina wire?" he asked.

She laughed. "You forget"—they kissed— "you're not the only Marine in my life."

Gently pulling back from him, she felt safe. Lonnie felt the same way. The unspoken mutual awareness was electric—and nurturing.

75

Taking her keys, Lonnie unlocked and opened Linda's front door. She leaned into him as she took them back. He put his arm around her shoulders.

"So what do ya think? Make up for after I came back from Florida?" he asked.

Gently placing his arms around her waist, she teased, "When you'd been back close to a week? Then finally called to let me know you were back? Then told me you had to go out of town again? To be honest, I'd completely forgotten about it."

Lonnie laughed and shook his head. "I swear you missed your calling. You should have gone into stand-up, ya know?"

Heaving an exaggerated sigh, Linda countered, "So many talents. What's a girl to do?"

"Plan on another make-up dinner, because I have to go out of town again. I can send you a list of restaurants."

"Won't be necessary," she quipped "I have a list of my own. I'll surprise you when you get back. Unless," she warned playfully as she opened the front door, "you're leaving to see another woman. Then you're on your own."

Lonnie replied, "To be honest, Linda, I am. Been seeing her for quite some time," he stated as if it was common knowledge to the whole world. "I told you about her."

Her shoulders tightened. She took a step back. "No, I would have remembered if you did, Lonnie."

She was surprised and disappointed—mostly at herself. Granted, she hadn't done much dating, especially since she'd become adept at discerning when a man was a player. She had no doubt that at one time in his life, Lonnie had been a player. But not now, unless—

"You sure I didn't mention my daughter, Donna? I could have sworn…"

Her shoulders relaxed. A look of obvious relief, and embarrassment at showing it, swept across her face.

"…I told you about her," he continued as he stepped out onto the stoop.

Pursing her lips and crossing her arms in front of her, she said, "You think you're cute, don't you?"

"Gotcha," he returned, with a Cheshire-cat grin.

"Well…you are," she said begrudgingly, "in an obnoxious sort of way."

He let the moment hang in the air. Which gave her time to replace the feeling of wanting to kill him with a feeling—a stirring that she hadn't felt in a very long time.

He felt the same thing. She knew it. It made the moment more intense, and at the same time, more pleasant and comfortable.

"I need to see her, Linda—to check on her, I guess. I've never done that. She has always been the one to—"

Lightly touching an index finger to his lips, she said, "No explanation necessary. It's called taking care of your daughter. That's what good dads do." She moved into him, placed his arms around her waist again, and looked into his eyes. "I think that's what Lonnie Tate does with the very small circle of people in his life that he loves. He takes care of them."

Putting her hand over his heart, she continued. "I see, and I like the man who's in there, Lonnie. You need to do the same."

Reaching up, her hand on the back of his neck, she kissed him. Then she stepped inside and closed the door.

76

Palm trees two stories tall flanked the glass-and-steel high-rise in the heart of Biltmore Center, Phoenix's version of Beverly Hills.

Riding up in the elevator, Lonnie rehearsed how he was going to tell his daughter what she deserved to know.

The elevator doors opened on the tenth floor, where a fifty-something receptionist eyed Lonnie suspiciously. He could tell it was dislike at first glance.

"Can I help you?"

"Yeah," he said, "tell Ms. Tate her father is here."

Glaring at him, the receptionist keyed Donna's extension.

"Thank you," Lonnie said, smiling just to annoy her.

"Ms. Tate. Your…father…is here. Hello? Donna?"

Lonnie's smile grew bigger as he heard the double-time click of high heels approaching. Knocking him back a step as she threw her arms around his neck, Donna hugged him for a full minute before she leaned back.

"Wha…I didn't…" was all that came out as she shook her head and smiled.

"Can I buy you lunch?" Lonnie asked. Donna took his arm and led him back to her office.

"By the way, where'd you find Mary Poppins?"

"Who?" Donna replied.

"Your receptionist."

Casting a quick glance back, Donna whispered, "You mean

Helen—the Dragon Lady? Don't mind her; she doesn't like anybody unless they're a client, or they look like a potential client."

"How does she know I'm not?"

Donna smiled. "Dad, you know I love you. But even in your grown-up clothes"—she played with his tie— "which look great on you, by the way—you still look more like a well-dressed bouncer than you do a potential client. Now as far as lunch, let's order out and take it to my place."

Twenty minutes later, she proudly opened the door to her condo.

"Come on in. Let me give you the fifty-cent tour, then we'll eat."

Walking him down a short hallway to a nicely-furnished guest room, she had him toss his bags on the bed. She could see he was pleased that she had framed and hung some of the photos he had shot on their chopper ride over the red-rock country around Sedona. Another five minutes of walking him through the place and they were back in the front room.

"Well? What do you think? Nice digs, huh?"

Lonnie nodded and smiled. "Compared to that, uh, other… uh…"

"Place?"

"That isn't the word I was going to use, but, ah…" He shrugged. "This place has class."

She laughed as she stepped into the kitchen. "You hated my old place," she said, lifting her salad and Lonnie's burger out of the takeout bag. "Let's eat."

77

Donna waited until they were finished eating to ask her question.

"OK, Dad. Why are you here? I love that you're here." She paused. "But you hate the desert. You hate lawyers, except for me. And you never come and see me. I come and see you."

"I wanted to meet the Dragon Lady." Lonnie enjoyed her directness. "Heard a lot about her," he said, "and since you two work for the same—"

She leaned forward and kissed him on the cheek to cut him off. "Dad?"

He took a deep breath and exhaled. "I came here because you need and deserve to know more about me than you do, hon."

She took his hands in hers. "Are you sure you want to do this?"

Seeing his look, she pulled her cell phone from her purse and speed-dialed her office. "Helen? This is Donna Tate. Let my assistant know I'll be back late this afternoon, please. Thank you."

Tossing the cell back in her purse, she looked at her father. "I've been waiting for this conversation for a long time."

For the next three hours, she sat fascinated, intrigued, yet hardly surprised. Everything about her father started to make sense. His attitude toward people and life. Why he and her mother couldn't make their marriage work, although as point of fact, she found it odd that they had gotten together in the first place.

When Lonnie finished, she sat quietly.

Donna's silence was killing him. If she was going to tell him she needed time to decide if she still wanted him in her life, he could live with that. If she decided she wanted nothing to do with him, as painful as it would be to hear, he would live with that also.

Finally, she spoke. "Mom and I were at odds with each other one time. We were at odds with each other a lot of times, actually. I don't remember what this one was about. But I do remember that that was the first and only time I ever heard her say, 'You're just like your father.'"

She stopped. A look of surprise came across her face as she realized she was about to voice something she had been thinking ever since that day at Sky Harbor Airport.

"I wish you hadn't killed that woman, Dad."

His heart sank.

"I wish *I* could have killed her." A wry smile crossed her face. "I guess Mom was right, huh?"

Giving him another kiss on the cheek, she said, "I'm going to go back to the office and finish up some things. You know where the guest room is. I'll fix us some dinner when I get back. Then you're going to tell me about what's new in your life. I love you."

Lonnie watched her grab her briefcase and head out the front door.

78

THE CHURCH BUILDING
NEWPORT BEACH
THAT EVENING

After dropping off some paperwork for her bishop, Linda Patino
was on her way to her car when she heard a man's voice coming
from behind her.

"Excuse me."

She turned to see a man in his early forties, maybe older—
maybe younger. He wasn't tall, but he wasn't short. He wasn't heavy,
nor was he thin, except for his hair.

"I'm, uh, new in the area," he said in a voice neither loud nor
soft, neither cordial nor dismissive. "I was wondering; what time
are services?"

Despite his nonthreatening appearance, her internal caution
meter jumped.

"Well, we have two wards that meet in this building," she
answered in a tone more civil than friendly. "Where do you live?"

He paused before answering. "A few blocks down...and over
toward the freeway."

Knowing the area well, Linda tried to visualize the streets. But
his vague answer made it impossible for her to do anything but guess.

"Sounds like you might be in the Newport Beach First Ward.

They meet at nine. But you could be in the Second Ward. They meet at one. The boundaries are kind of funny." She smiled. "The best thing? Go on the church website. Click the 'Worship with us' tab and type in your address." She saw confusion in his eyes. "You are LDS, right?" she asked.

"Uh, ah, yes…of course. Thank you, I'll do that. Ah, I'm sorry, what ward did you say you were in?"

Her caution meter spiked again. She had never mentioned her ward.

Moving more quickly toward her car, she said, "You know, I hate to dash off, but I'm running late and—"

"Oh, no problem." He was following her. "You've been lots of help—"

"Just check the website." She forced a smile as she unlocked her car door. "It'll help a lot more than I did."

"You're very kind. Are you the pastor?" he asked as Linda got in the car.

Her caution meter pegged all the way into the red; Mormons don't have pastors.

Feeling like her insides were going to fall out, she nervously twisted the key and drove away without putting on her seatbelt.

"Darcy…it's Linda Patino." She was calling from her car, which she never did. She didn't even like answering calls when she was driving. "Do you have time to get together and talk?"

Forty-five minutes later, Darcy pulled into the parking lot of a Starbucks near Disneyland. *I wonder if she's still mad at me?*

Linda's smile and warm hug answered that question. But Darcy felt her trembling.

"Linda, what's wrong?"

Linda thought telling Darcy about meeting the man she called

"Mr. Average" would help her calm down. It didn't. In fact, Darcy's unconscious attitude shift from concerned to fact-finding served to turn up the heat under Linda's discomfort.

"What did this guy look like?" Darcy asked.

Linda thought for a moment. "Well…he looked like the president in *Dr. Strangelove.*"

Seeing Darcy's expression gave her goosebumps.

"What? C'mon, Darcy," Linda said. "It was just a dumb joke, but—"

"No, it isn't that, Linda," Darcy interrupted. "Your description of Mr. Average? That's how Marcus described one of the government flunkies who got us into this."

79

PHOENIX

Looking up from her food prep, Donna shot her dad a big smile as he shuffled into the kitchen.

"Hey."

"Guess I fell asleep for a while. Work didn't take as long as you thought it would?" Her smile widened.

"Actually…it took longer than I thought it would."

Lonnie sat down on one of the barstools by the counter. "How much longer?" he asked, realizing his sense of time was shot.

"Two hours after most everyone went home. It's eight o'clock, Dad."

Lonnie looked at his watch.

Seeing her always-in-control father feeling disoriented touched a tender place in Donna's heart.

"We're having Asian," she said as she rinsed her hands in the sink. "I got a really good recipe for hot-and-sour soup. That's still your favorite, right?"

They ate in companionable silence, enjoying the closeness and the good food. When they finished, Lonnie cleared the table and started rinsing off the dishes.

"So…what's new in your life?" Donna asked.

"Since we last talked a couple of hours ago? I took a nap."

"That's not what I meant."

"What did you mean?"

"Dad?"

 He didn't answer.

"I knew it!" she shouted, clapping her hands together. "Who is she?"

"What makes you think I—"

"Where'd you meet her?"

Lonnie sighed. "We've been seeing each other for a couple months. I work with her daughter."

"Her daughter works for your gun-runner buddy?"

"He's an arms dealer. There's a difference," Lonnie corrected. "Her daughter is our explosives expert."

"OK, then…well, what does your explosives expert think about—"

"She set us up."

"What does your explosives expert's mother do?"

"Her name is Linda," Lonnie began. "She's a life and business coach." He spent several minutes detailing what he knew of Linda's life. Donna's smile grew softer the more he talked.

"She sounds impressive, Dad. Does she have a last name?"

"Patino." He paused. "P-A-T-I-N-O. Because I know you're gonna Google her before you go to bed."

"Not necessarily," she protested.

Lonnie pulled his glasses down his nose and looked at her over the top of the frames.

"Oh, all right," she admitted. "Yeah, I'm gonna check her out."

He shot her a self-satisfied smile.

Pretending to scold, she said, "You never talk about the women in your life."

"Not with you. You're my daughter."

She took his hand in both of hers. "She must be some lady."

A wistful smile crossed his face. "Never met anyone like her."

"And…?" Donna invited.

"And"—he sat back— "that's why I don't belong in her life."

She looked at him skeptically.

"C'mon, sweetheart, we're talking about someone who…builds people up. I'm about as far from that as it gets." He paused. "I'm a complication. She doesn't need that."

"Has she told you that?"

He shook his head.

She arched her eyebrows. "But you've decided to make up her mind for her."

"OK." He sounded resigned. "No, I don't think she thinks I'm a complication…although I'm damned if I know why."

Sliding her chair closer, she said, "She knows your secret, Dad." Donna put her hand on her father's chest. "She knows what's really in there. Wouldn't hurt for you to start doing the same thing."

80

ONE WEEK LATER

Lonnie knew he hadn't been tailed, but that didn't mean the no-name agency—or somebody else—didn't have someone sitting on Linda's house. He did a quick look up and down the street just in case.

Just as he he went to ring the doorbell, she opened the door. Smiling, she stepped out, wrapped her arms around his waist, and laid her head against his chest. Her very public welcome was a pleasant embarrassment.

"So I guess this means you missed me," he said, putting an arm around her shoulders.

"I'm so glad you're back." She blushed. "C'mon in. Lunch is ready. I hope you like Mexican."

Whatever was going on, he didn't want to press her on it. It was nice to see her again—and the smells coming from the dining room reminded him of how hungry he was.

The table was filled with more Mexican food than he'd seen since his last trip to Mexico twenty years ago.

"Who else is coming?" he asked.

"Uh, just us." Linda blushed again. "I get kind of compulsive when I'm upset. This time I happened to be in the kitchen." She looked over the spread. "Be sure to try the tamales." Pulling out a chair for Lonnie, she said, "We better eat before it gets cold."

Linda might have hoped all the food would distract Lonnie from her comment about being upset. He let her think that through the first few courses.

"What's bothering you?" he finally asked, not sure he wanted to hear the answer.

Setting her fork down, Linda looked over the table before turning to answer his question. Tears in her eyes, she told him about Mr. Average and the conversation with Darcy.

Lonnie waited half a minute before responding, partly to think, but mostly to dial back his anger at himself for getting her into this.

"Do you think he'll come back?" she asked.

"No," Lonnie said calmly. *Neither will anyone else*, he said to himself.

"I thought these people"—Linda's voice grew louder— "are supposed to be smart. What do...whoever these people are...want with me?"

"Truth of the matter? In intelligence, with few exceptions, the smart and cunning people work in the field. The ones who will get you killed work at a desk, pushing paper and issuing orders. This guy—Mr. Average?" Lonnie continued. "He was leaning on us by scaring you."

"They think scaring and harassing...civilians...like me is going to make you and Consuelo do what they want faster?"

"He was posturing," Lonnie stated flatly. "If he wanted us to take him seriously, he would have killed you."

His matter-of-fact tone sobered her.

"Lonnie...keep these people away from me," she said, shaking with fear and anger.

"They won't be back."

81

He was unlocking his car when he felt the twitch. Doing a subtle visual recon up and down both sides of the street, Lonnie sang to himself, *Come out, come out, wherever you are.*

Mr. Average was parked half a block down from the street where Linda lived. That way, he would see Lonnie's car as it went by, but Lonnie wouldn't see him.

Backing up into Linda's driveway, Lonnie pulled out and headed the opposite direction from his usual route back to the freeway. At the end of her block he turned left, then left again on the street one over from Linda's. At the end of the block, he noticed the white late-model Impala parked halfway up toward Linda's street. The twitch in his back spiked.

Mr. Average wasn't checking his rearview mirror, so he didn't see the BMW pull to the curb some ten car lengths behind him. Nor did he see the stocky-built man climb out.

A few seconds later, Mr. Average jumped when something rapped on his window. A stocky-built man stood there, opening and closing a butterfly knife. Mr. Average rolled down the window.

"You're closing down any and all further surveillance on Linda Patino. You understand?"

The lethal edge in the stocky-built man's voice made it clear that there was no room for debate.

"Do you understand?" The stocky-built man repeated.

Mr. Average couldn't take his eyes off the knife. He swallowed hard.

"I'll take that as a yes," said the stocky-built man as he turned.

"One more thing," the stocky-built man called over his shoulder as he bent down and drove the knife into the left rear tire.

"This tire's a little low."

82

THE NEXT MORNING

The Gulfstream G-280 went wheels-up from Van Nuys Airport just as the sun appeared over the horizon. The flight crew wanted to get away before the private charters hauling Hollywood types, politicians, and captains of industry started jamming things up.

"What are they buying?" Lonnie asked.

"Crude stuff," Cy replied, "a lot of crude stuff."

"How crude and how much?"

"Ninety-five hundred AK-47s—five hundred RPGs—and ammo."

Lonnie raised his eyebrows. "You making any modifications?"

Cy shook his head, "Nope."

"Why Vietnam?" Lonnie asked. "We're flying damn near eight-thousand miles just so you can look inside a few hundred crates of weapons?"

The old Marine held off answering the question. It wasn't that he didn't trust Lonnie. Watanabe was old-school. Controlling information was in his DNA.

"We're installing tracking devices in the crates."

Lonnie suspected that was only partly true. "Define installing tracking devices in the crates."

"Open the crate, screw the thing into place. Close the crate, move on to the next one." Cy gave Lonnie a challenging glance. "Too complicated for ya?"

"That's a lotta crates for just two people to open and close."

Cy smiled.

"That's why I contracted your old buddy, Vuong Nguyen. He's got some guys that will handle the opening and closing."

The mention of Vuong Nguyen brought a smile to Lonnie's face. He and the former NVA officer first worked together in 1995, when Vuong was top man in the Vietnamese Ministry of Finance.

Over the past twenty years, Vuong had helped Watanabe cut through miles of red tape on a few "special priority" projects.

They would be on the ground at Kona International Airport at Keahole, Hawaii, maybe two hours—just long enough to fuel up, stretch their legs, and give the crew a little bit of downtime.

Sitting in the lounge, Lonnie nodded at two Sikhs walking past him, animatedly speaking Punjabi. The turbaned men nodded back. They didn't hear the man sitting across the lounge call out, "Hey, towel head! How'd you two get outta Gitmo?"

"Damn, Z. Chill." exclaimed the man sitting next to him.

Z smiled back at his buddy, obviously pleased with himself.

Watanabe wrinkled his nose and sniffed loudly.

"You smell that, Lonnie?"

"Smell what?"

The old Marine exaggerated sniffing the air again.

"Smells like…stupid." His voice was loud enough for the man named Z and his friend to hear. "Yeah, and it's comin' from"—Cy pointed to Z— "the guy in the purple shirt."

Z's mouth gaped open.

"You talkin' to me, Chink?"

Watanabe smiled back.

"I'm talking about you."

Z stood up and walked over to Cy and Lonnie.

Still smiling, Watanabe calmly stood up. Lonnie stayed seated, his attention on Z's buddy, who was about to join them.

"You got a mouth on you, old man," the six-foot-two, 220-pound-plus Z snarled.

"Yeah, I do," the old Marine replied. "And I'm half your size and twice your age. That should make you wonder what I know that you don't." Cy's smile widened in a way that wasn't at all friendly. "Care to find out…Z?"

Lonnie noticed uncertainty beginning to show in Z's eyes. His buddy had the same look. The smarter of the two, the buddy put a cautioning hand on Z's shoulder.

"Come on, Z, let's get outta here. The old man's crazy."

The man called Z paused a couple of beats, slapped his buddy's hand away, and the two of them stalked out of the lounge.

As Watanabe sat back down, Lonnie queried, "I assume that you had a plan if that guy came at you?"

Watanabe laughed. "Yeah, I planned to stand aside and let you kick his ass."

The flight from Kona to the Marshall Islands was about the same distance and duration as the Van-Nuys-to-Kona leg. Cy was asleep soon after takeoff and didn't wake up until they were less than an hour from landing.

Confident he wasn't going to get much of an answer, Lonnie decided to ask the question anyway.

"What was that about, with the asshole back at Kona?"

The old Marine looked at Lonnie for several seconds.

"Honoring a promise I made to myself in boot camp," he replied.

"And that was…?"

"Never tolerating anybody's crap."

Thinking about it, Lonnie realized that as tough as Marine

Corps boot camp had been for his generation of recruits, in Cy's day it had to have been much worse—especially for a Japanese-American.

"You joined in '50, right?" Lonnie asked.

Cy smiled.

"Four July 1950. The first day of sixteen luxurious, fun-filled weeks at MCRD, San Diego."

Five years after the end of World War II, the majority of Marine Corps drill instructors at San Diego and Parris Island were veterans of the Pacific. Then-Private Watanabe looked like the guys they had fought as they slogged from one island hellhole to the next.

"Post-World War II Japanese-American kid? MCRD, San Diego?" Lonnie mused.

"Ain't no Japanese or hyphen in front of the word American, Slick," Watanabe scolded. Never has been—never will be."

"Yes, sir." Lonnie saluted.

Cy smiled. "Don't call me sir. I work for a living."

Both men laughed.

"Ya know, Cy. I've never asked you. Why did you join the Corps?"

"North Korea invaded the South right after I finished at Boise JC. I didn't want to get drafted."

That answer didn't make sense to Lonnie.

"They were sending everyone to Korea. Why'd you think enlisting was better?"

Watanabe's eyes narrowed. "I wanted some say, however small, in what I was going to be doing for the United States government." He looked out the window. "They put my family...in Tule Lake. They sent my uncle, my dad's brother, his wife and kids, to Manzanar. After that, I'd had a bellyful of the government making all the decisions about my life."

It took Lonnie a moment. *Tule Lake? Manzanar?* Then it hit him—*the internment camps.*

83

WAREHOUSE
TIEN SA PORT, REPUBLIC OF VIETNAM
0500 HOURS

Two guys—five hundred crates—damn! Lonnie said to himself. Then he remembered: *Vuong Nguyen's guys are coming to help. Better be a lotta guys.*

"You talked to Vuong, right?" he asked.

Cy shook his head. "I think Stackhouse got in touch with him." Cy could guess what was going through Lonnie's mind.

Stackhouse doesn't speak Vietnamese. Vuong speaks English—but only after he's worked with you face-to-face. So who did Stackhouse talk to, and what did he tell 'em?

A doorbell that sounded like a fire alarm went off. Cy arched his eyebrows and smiled at Lonnie.

"That'll be our guys."

"*Anh trai tôi, Anh trai tôi!*" Vuong Nguyen shouted before he and Lonnie were close enough to share a heartfelt hug.

"*Anh trai tôi*" was Vietnamese for "brother"—an appellation not easily bestowed on a man outside the actual family, especially an American.

Vuong's loud, uninhibited greeting told the cluster of more than fifty men standing a few feet behind him that the short, stocky man with bushy gray hair was a man of "*kính trọng*"—respect—and just not because he was older.

"It's good to see you," the one-time NVA colonel said.

"You also, *anh trai tôi*," Lonnie replied with mutual respect and affection.

Almost twenty years earlier, the two men first met on the tarmac at Da Nang International. Vuong Nguyen was Vietnam's minister of finance. Lonnie headed a team of interpreter-translators for a large American conglomerate about to open offices in Ho Chi Minh City, formerly Saigon.

Impressed with Lonnie's grasp of Vietnamese, Vuong had commented that Lonnie had probably learned the language in the military. Lonnie confirmed the observation. Vuong further observed that, based on Lonnie's general presence and demeanor, he had most likely been a Marine.

Impressed with the minister's intuition, or lucky guess, Lonnie confirmed that observation also.

Further discussion revealed that Vuong and Lonnie had fought in Quang Tri Province during the same time period. The former NVA colonel laughed. "Perhaps we took shots at each other from time to time," he offered.

Returning the minister's smile, Lonnie said he didn't think so.

When Vuong asked why that wasn't a possibility, Lonnie responded in Vietnamese, "*Bởi vì bạn vẫn đang ở đây.*" Translation: "Because you're still here."

Vuong doubled over in laughter. Straightening up, he put his arm around Lonnie and insisted that while in Vietnam, Lonnie should make the minister's home, his home.

That experience and others they shared during the five months Lonnie was in country were now distilled to profound respect and admiration.

"Please"—Lonnie stood aside— "come in."

Taking a place beside Lonnie, Vuong nodded for his men to enter.

Voung's men were divided up into teams of twos. One team opened the crates. Cy and Vuong affixed small plastic tracking devices to the underside of each lid. The other team resealed the crates. Once that was done, Vuong selected eight men, including himself, to inspect each closed crate to make sure there was no visible sign that the crate had been opened. The process took four days.

Over that time, Lonnie experienced intermittent flashes of concern. Something regarding the op. Something that wouldn't go away.

84

Lonnie had just come back from the head when he noticed Cy studying him.

"What?"

"You've been chewing on something since we started working in Da Nang," Cy said.

Looking out the window, Lonnie nodded. "Watching those guys in the warehouse?" He turned back toward Cy. "They have something to do with this op."

Cy just listened.

"Don't ask me what it is," Lonnie added, "but they do."

The old Marine pursed his lips. "You keep chewin' on it, you're gonna drive yourself—and me—up the wall. Relax. It'll eventually come to you. In the meantime, if I were you, I'd take a break and think about letting Corporal Patino's mother make an honest man outta you."

"That," Lonnie looked out the window, "is the last thing I need to do."

"Why?" Cy asked, with some force.

"You haven't met her."

"So?"

"So"—Lonnie leaned into the argument— "she's about as far from what we do as it gets. And further from me than anyone I've ever met."

After a few seconds' pause, Cy said, "Ya know… you've always had this gift for seeing right into the essence of a situation—"

"Then you know what I'm talkin' about," Lonnie interrupted with sad satisfaction.

"Except for this situation."

"What?"

"Did it ever occur to you that this time you might be wrong?" Cy challenged.

"Not when there's five ex-Mrs. Tates who can prove otherwise."

"Yeah." Watanabe chuckled. "Five women who were much bigger train wrecks than you were.

"Allow me," Watanabe went on, with an exaggerated air of superiority, "to update you on your former partners in wedded bliss.

"Ex-wife/train wreck number one: The one who threw heavy pointed objects at you? She's doing twenty-five to life at the California Institute for Women, something having to do with killing one of her other exes.

"Ex number two, your daughter's sainted mommy. She hasn't been seen or heard from since she drank away the last child-support check you sent, which arrived the day after Donna left for Berkeley— what—twenty years ago?

"Moving on…ex-Mrs. Tate number three; the one that met an untimely end when her boyfriend, who was also her boss, found out she'd been skimming money from his auto-repossession business.

"Number four OD'd on a hit of the heroin she'd started selling a few months before your eight-month union ended.

"Last, and my personal favorite…ex number five: Rumor has it the FBI is curious about why she went to Syria."

Lonnie looked at Cy with the same mix of emotions he had the first time they met. And like that first time, Lonnie wanted to shoot him.

"You screwed up, Slick," Cy said. "You went out and got yourself involved with a woman who isn't an axe murderer, and you don't know how to handle it."

Lonnie glared at Cy, saying nothing.

"You got a choice, Slick." Cy continued. "You can go back to holing up in your apartment by yourself. Going out to dinner—by yourself. Driving up and down the coast—by yourself. Shooting pictures—by yourself. And growing old—by yourself. Or…you can have a happy life."

Lonnie's countenance was dark. "Please…feel free to start minding your own business."

Cy smiled. "You are my business, Slick."

"Then Marcus needs to give you more to do."

"You've been my business," Cy went on, as though Lonnie hadn't said anything, "since DCI Dade called and told me about this kid—a real talent—going through a rough patch." He paused and smirked. "That's up to, what, forty-six years…and counting?"

"Dade's dead," Lonnie said sullenly.

"You're close," Cy shot back. "But I'd like to think that sometime before you actually stop breathing—you'll use your gift and take an honest look at yourself."

"I have," Lonnie said, feeling very tired, "and it's a pretty crappy picture."

"I said honest," Cy corrected. "Not the skewed mirror you're always holding up."

Lonnie turned and looked out the window, but Cy knew he was listening.

"Quit comparing yourself to people who don't bring half what you do to the table."

"That would be people who don't know how to kill someone without even thinking about it," Lonnie replied.

"That would be"—Cy's tone softened— "people who didn't eat a mountain of crap to find high-five-figure ad-agency jobs for more than a dozen people when your own job was going away."

Lonnie said nothing.

"That would be people who have no idea what it is to be loyal to the people you care about, even people you barely know…even when there's nothing in it for you. Which includes Shapiro. And, Lonnie…it includes Marcus."

Lonnie slowly turned his head, giving Watanabe a hard look.

"Yeah, I know he's a brother-in-arms, and you love him. And he's almost the best person I've ever met. But Marcus uses people, Lonnie. Not because he doesn't care, because he does. But he's a master strategist, and he makes the most of resources…including people.

"Lonnie Tate would never do that." Cy leaned back. "I'll tell you something else, and pay attention because this is important. You listening?"

Lonnie nodded.

"Lonnie Tate is the only person I've ever met…the only person… that I trust without reservation."

85

PENTANGELO GROUP OFFICES
TWO DAYS LATER

Everything was ready. The tension was thick, but the funereal mood that had saturated the last meeting was absent.

Referring to Lonnie, Marcus said, "The new guy has found the missing piece of the puzzle." All heads snapped toward the end of the conference table where Lonnie was sitting.

"Darcy?" Lonnie leaned back in the chair. "I figured out why you couldn't find all the Caliphate guys."

She gave him a curious stare. "Do tell."

Grinning, Lonnie proclaimed, "You were right."

"Right about what, Tate?" Branco demanded.

"About assembling their troops," Lonnie replied. "It's the just-in-time inventory concept applied to building an army."

"What's just-in-time inventory?" Patino asked.

"Manufacturers have been doing it for years," Lonnie explained. "They have materials delivered just before they turn them into product. They don't build things until they're ordered. Eliminates having inventory sitting on the shelf, tying up money."

Stackhouse closed his eyes and smiled.

Lonnie continued, "The Japanese came up with it back in the sixties. Everyone does it now.

"These Caliphate guys…are waiting until the weapons, explosives, and computers are on the way before they start calling up troops."

"How do you know this, Tate?" Branco asked, in a voice only half as grouchy as usual.

"When Cy and I were in Da Nang, our contact told me how happy he was when he found out we were coming. That was a couple of days before we got there. I've known this guy for close to twenty years. He's a one-man shop. Yet, with just two days' notice, he had near a platoon of guys to help us out."

Lonnie looked at the faces around the table. They were beginning to connect the dots.

"Over the four days we were in there, the more I watched Vuong's guys working, the more I knew there was some connection with what we didn't know about the Soldiers of the Whatever—I just couldn't put it together.

"Yesterday, it hit me. If Vuong could assemble a platoon-sized group of laborers just in time to do a job, why couldn't you put together an army of terrorists the same way? It's the only thing that makes any sense."

Patino nodded. Stackhouse was beaming. Branco leaned back in his chair and gave Lonnie a quick thumbs-up.

Lonnie glanced at Darcy. "You were right, Darce." He shifted his focus to Cy. "You were both right. We were paying so much attention to what we thought wasn't there, we couldn't see what was missing."

86

Encino Park
That afternoon

The text message was cryptic.

Encino Park: Near northeast corner—3 pm—Discuss final arrangements.

In their CIA days, Shapiro's incessant reviewing and re-reviewing the planning for an op drove Lonnie and Marcus crazy. But it always revealed one or two minor, yet very crucial adjustments that needed to be made.

Marcus parked his Lexus in the shade of the big trees that lined the east side of the park, then got out and scanned the benches and picnic tables, looking for Brian.

At his three o'clock, in a shaded area, sat an old man at a picnic table, weakly waving to him. He was wearing what Marcus always thought of as the uniform of old men in parks everywhere in Greater L.A.: muted plaid long-sleeved shirt buttoned at the neck, faded sweater vest, buttons not quite synched with the buttonholes, and an old Dodgers cap.

The old man waved again, nodding his head and beckoning.

A second look revealed that the old man at the picnic table was Shapiro. He had aged even more since Marcus and Lonnie had met with him a few weeks ago.

"I never would have recognized you, Brian," Marcus admitted as he came over and sat down. "What would you have done if I'd gotten back in the car?"

"Sent you a text. Already had it ready, see?" Shapiro showed Marcus his phone screen: "Old man at picnic table—me."

"This is awfully public," said Marcus. "Can't people pick up whatever we're going to talk about?"

Brian shook his head slightly. "You watched *The Conversation* too many times, Marcus."

He lifted the bottom of his sweater to reveal what looked like a plastic cell-phone holster on his belt. "This emits a tone that interferes with electronics anywhere within a hundred meters. No one's gonna hear us."

"And the trees block anyone across the street from reading our lips?" Marcus offered.

"Very good, Marcus. You sure you're not interested in a career in the clandestine services?" Shapiro teased.

It was hard for Marcus. The voice of his old friend sounded the same as when they were in Vietnam: quiet but strong, powerfully self-assured. A young man's voice that had no business coming out of the sickly old man sitting next to him.

After looking at Marcus for what seemed like a long time, Shapiro smiled. "Everything you and your team have done is brilliant, Marcus. And from what I understand, thanks to Lonnie, the Soldiers of the Caliphate are down a few troops."

Marcus chuckled. "Yes, they are. But why the attempt on his life?"

Shapiro smiled. "They're afraid of him. And…" He let it hang in the air.

"And what?" Marcus asked.

"Come on, Marcus. We're talking about Lonnie Tate."

"The man does have a talent for pissing people off," Marcus conceded.

"Doesn't even have to say anything."

Marcus nodded agreement. "He just has to be in the room."

Both men laughed, Shapiro even more than Marcus. This caused Shapiro to start coughing so hard that it scared Marcus.

"Are you OK?" Marcus reached into his jacket pocket for his phone. "I'm calling 911."

Shapiro put a firm hand on Marcus's forearm.

"Of course I'm not OK," he wheezed. "Nobody with a cough like this can be OK, for God's sake."

He drew in a breath, then exhaled audibly. "It's congestive heart failure, Marcus. I'm going to die. That's why we're having this meeting."

Marcus felt a lump swelling in his throat.

"And before you ask," Shapiro added, "yes, I'm sure, because my doctor is sure."

Shapiro squeezed Marcus's forearm. "I guess the second time's the charm, ya know?"

Marcus's eyes welled with tears. He blew out a breath. "How much time?"

Flashing the same slight, self-satisfied grin Marcus and Lonnie got used to seeing in Vietnam, Shapiro replied, "This afternoon."

Marcus wasn't amused. "What the hell kind of doctor gives you a prognosis down to the hour?"

"A specialist. Works outside the network." The grin faded. "His treatment regimen isn't covered in the agency's health plan. I pay for it out of pocket."

Marcus's eyes narrowed. "Thought you could never get away because they were watching you."

"They are, but they're arrogant. They miss things. Not a lot, but enough."

"Like this doctor…who's helping you kill yourself?"

Marcus's sarcasm was not lost on Shapiro.

"The heart failure is what's killing me, Marcus. He's just helping me adjust the time frame. That's all."

"But, whatever you're taking will show up in your autopsy. That won't be good for people you care about, and I'm not talking about Lonnie and me."

Shapiro retrieved a large manila envelope from under the yellow windbreaker lying on the bench beside him.

"Final arrangements, my friend. A certified summary of my medical history, attesting to the seriousness of my condition. As far as an autopsy, all outward signs will point to heart failure. Not uncommon for a man with my health problems—ergo, no red flags. By the time they do a tox screen, what I'm taking will have metabolized.

"As far as burial arrangements, my estate, and a couple of other things—I need you to take care of that."

Shaking his head to clear it, Marcus mumbled, "Of course."

"Now, regarding the op"—Shapiro tapped the envelope—"there's additional information on a flash drive. Don't worry about it 'til you complete the op."

"OK," Marcus said, realizing that very soon, he would never hear that self-assured voice again.

"One more thing. I need you to stick around 'til the paramedics get here, please. I don't want to wind up another old guy who dies in a park and gets stripped naked before the ambulance shows up. You can shove off once they get me on the gurney, OK?"

"No, I can't." Marcus was almost indignant.

"Why not?"

"Sorry, old buddy," Marcus's voice broke. "Grunt's Law, chapter one, verse one."

Shapiro smiled appreciatively.

"We don't leave guys in the field, brother," Marcus continued. "We didn't do it then…I won't…do it…now. Neither would Lonnie. I'll follow the ambulance to the hospital. And I won't leave until I'm sure everything is OK."

Shapiro couldn't speak.

Suddenly, Marcus felt anger rising up. "These guys you work for are through, Brian."

"I know, Marcus." Shapiro's voice—his whole demeanor—was that of a man at peace.

Abruptly, Marcus Pentangelo was struck by a kind of lightning his father always sarcastically referred to as a BFO—Blinding Flash of the Obvious.

"I'll be damned. You…you set this up." Marcus whispered.

Shapiro gave him his best Cheshire-cat grin.

Marcus exhaled deeply. "That first time, in '89…that was… that was you."

"Hell, yeah." Shapiro's grin became a chuckle. "And thank God you said no. It would have been a disaster. These guys would have wound up ten times stronger and more dangerous than they are now."

Tapping the envelope again, "Flash drives, Marcus," Shapiro proclaimed. "They're a beautiful thing. Don't forget it.

"Now…if you would, please…call 911."

Four minutes later, the ambulance pulled up to the curb.

A distinguished-looking black man, crying silently, was cradling an elderly white man in his arms.

One look at the old man told the paramedics there was no need to hurry.

"You know this guy?" one of them asked.

Marcus couldn't speak, so he nodded.

"Could you give us his name, sir…please?" the other medic asked gently.

Marcus looked down at his friend and took the old Dodgers cap off his head.

"His name is Brian Shapiro. He's a Vietnam veteran—a Marine. He gave his life for our country."

87

IN FRONT OF LINDA PATINO'S HOUSE
LATE AFTERNOON

He'd sat in the car for five minutes after he switched off the engine. He didn't want to have this conversation.

The smile that lit up her face when she opened the door made him question even having the conversation.

"Well, well." Linda leaned out and kissed him. He kissed back in spite of himself. She tasted delicious.

Linda felt the tension. Folding her arms across her chest and leaning against the door frame, she said, "You want to tell me something."

"No, I don't…I mean, I do, but…"

She dipped her chin and gave him the "mom" look.

"But what?"

He exhaled and looked down at his feet. "I don't know what to say."

Lonnie's artistry with words had been his career. Knowing what to say and how to say it had persuaded millions of people to spend hundreds of millions of dollars, had won awards. And now—.

"I, ah…I don't know what to do."

She waited for him to elaborate, but he couldn't.

"About?" she asked gently.

"Us," he blurted out. "I don't want the ugliness"—he heard his voice catch— "that's filled my life…to get into yours." He shook his head. "Any more than it already has."

Having an inner sense of what the Lonnie who thought with his head was trying to say, she grinned.

"Do you remember what I told you before you and Connie went out of town?" She wasn't going to wait for a response. "I told you that nothing you've done will diminish my respect for you—"

"Yeah, I know"—he cut in— "but if something were to happen to you—"

"You'd live," she countered, equally abrupt. "It's part of who you are."

"It's what I do," he shot back angrily. "But this time…if that happened…"

Wiping a tear from his eye with her fingertips, she said, "You almost sound like you resent me."

"I resent the confusion—the emotion," Lonnie confessed. "Not you."

He hung his head. "Ah, hell…I don't know what to think."

He felt her studying him.

"You wanna know what I think?" she asked.

"I guess."

"I think you should come in and help me fix dinner."

He looked up and saw Linda's *gotcha* smile.

"C'mon, Lonnie," her smiled widened as she took his hand. "Make yourself useful."

PART III

88

Everything Pentangelo Group had put together—the computers, weapons, and explosives—had been delivered to the two-dozen designated locations in the Middle East—and one in the United States.

Miami, Florida
4:30 a.m. edt

"All is in readiness," Walid Abdul Walid proclaimed aloud to himself. "The beginning of the end of what the infidels so arrogantly call the developed world will commence immediately after morning prayers."

Words of an inspired leader, Walid told himself.

Words that would have sounded far more inspiring, had it not been for the Texas drawl.

His real name was Orville Dwayne Bartlett, born and raised in Paris, Texas. A homegrown psychopath who left the KKK to become an Islamic extremist—the leader of the small Soldiers of the Caliphate cell based in Miami.

He would text a fellow homegrown psychopath in the Miami cell. That would be the command for his brother jihadist to hit the "Power" icon on the new computers. As soon as all were online, a second keystroke would open a program that would spread chaos throughout the world's financial networks and energy infrastructures.

A second text from Walid would prompt a third keystroke.

Transportation systems worldwide would begin to disintegrate right in front of their operators' and administrators' eyes.

"And then," Walid shouted, "we…the Soldiers of the Caliphate, will march across the globe, bringing the order the world has so badly needed for so many centuries!"

Orville had no idea that Russell Branco had made sure that the instant those computers came online—it would be the beginning of the end of the Soldiers of Caliphate.

89

The Apartment
Pentangelo Group Headquarters
1:30 A.M. PDT

Built some thirty feet underneath the house, the design and construction were the work of Doyle Stackhouse.

Originally intended to be a panic room, Stackhouse had expanded the design in case it became necessary to live and work in it for a prolonged period of time.

The end result: an eighteen-hundred-square-foot apartment. Three bedrooms, two bathrooms, laundry room, state-of-the-art kitchen with spacious pantry, dining area, and an operations-control suite (OCS) that would be the envy of the NSA.

The brainchild of Russell Branco, the OCS housed a supercomputer and two servers.

Six flat-screen monitors displayed and regulated everything from room temperature and above-ground interior and exterior security cameras, to satellite access and repositioning, drone access and deployment, ongoing weapons movement, and all encrypted video and audio communications with any client.

Voicing a designated codeword that changed on a daily basis triggered the opening of a four-by-eight-foot section of the floor in the individual offices and the conference room.

Taking security one step further, Branco had developed voice-recognition software that would respond only to their seven voices and the voice of Mary Pentangelo. The software could also distinguish the difference between a live and recorded voice—and would not respond to a recording.

It was on the largest monitor—the seventy-two-inch master monitor displaying live satellite images of the world's seven continents—that Branco and the rest of Pentangelo Group would watch the result of his being ordered to "Do your best work."

Hearing the timer bell on one of three microwave ovens sitting on the kitchen counter, Branco retrieved the fifth bag of popcorn he had nuked. He wanted to make sure there was enough for everybody.

Popping a sixth bag into the microwave, he heard Marcus growl from behind him, "You got some coffee going, right, Russell?"

"Fresh pot sittin' right here next to me, boss," Branco shouted back pleasantly. "Mornin'."

Wearing sweatpants, running shoes, and a short-sleeve sweatshirt with "UCLA" printed on it, a bleary-eyed Marcus walked in looking like he wanted to go back to sleep.

"Russell?" Marcus queried. "You're never this friendly in the light of day, let alone at"—forgetting he was wearing a watch, Marcus looked over at the computer monitor to check the time— "one thirty-five in the morning."

Ignoring the barb, Branco asked, "The others are coming, right?" sounding like a kid asking his mother if everybody he invited to his birthday party was really coming.

"Are you kidding?" said Doyle Stackhouse as he strolled in. "You were so damn…human…on the phone, I didn't know who you were at first. I came over here to make sure you weren't having an episode of some sort. Where's the coffee?"

Branco handed Marcus and Stackhouse each a steaming mug of coffee.

"Two sugars, Doyle," Branco said excitedly, "just like you like it." Looking at Marcus, he said, "Straight black for you, boss."

Marcus did a take to Stackhouse. "Who the hell is that guy?

Stackhouse shook his head. "Yeah. And what did he do with Russell?"

90

Patino appeared and saw the popcorn, and Branco.

"So that's what you look like when you smile, Russell. Did you remember my cocoa?"

Handing her a mug, Branco said, "The lady asks, and the lady shall receive." He gave her a slight bow.

She returned his bow with a half curtsy. "Thank you, Russell." Glancing over at Marcus and Stackhouse she mouthed, *What's wrong with him?*

Branco gave Patino an admiring look. "Your configuring of the tracking devices so that they act as trigger mechanisms for the explosives planted in every crate and container was, in and of itself, the equal of what Picasso did with a brush." Branco proclaimed. "Thanks to your genius and mine, Mademoiselle Patino"—he was euphoric— "the SOC's ice cream is about to turn to fertilizer."

Seeing Watanabe, Lonnie, and Darcy walk in, Branco filled three more mugs with coffee. Placing the mugs on a serving tray and walking over to them, he announced, "The game is on."

Miami, Florida
4:38 a.m. EDT

Ten seconds after Walid sent the first text, he received an unexpected text from the psychopath monitoring the computers.

"PROBLEMS!"

Seven seconds later, another.

"VIRUS!"

"FILES CORRUPTED!"

Eight seconds later…

"CAN'T OVERRIDE!"

The last text the other psychopath would ever send in his life came five seconds after that.

"SYSTEMS CRASH!"

Being ten miles away from the computer lab his fellow psychopath had built in the basement of his home, Walid couldn't know that the house was now in flames.

It was an old house, run-down, in an even more run-down section of Miami's Little Havana.

Miami Fire-Rescue was quick to respond. Even so, containing the fire took priority over saving the house.

Pentangelo Group Headquarters
1:38 a.m. PDT

Marcus, Stackhouse, Lonnie, Cy, Darcy, and Patino were transfixed on the master monitor as it displayed a frighteningly realistic flaring of bright-red flames in the area of the continental United States where "Miami, FL" flashed on and off.

Popping a kernel of popcorn in her mouth, Patino exclaimed, "Holy crap, Russell."

"Boot up six high-powered computers all at one time, in an old house in that part of Miami?" Branco responded. "Sure bet you'll overload the electrical circuitry in the whole place. Electrical fires burn hot and fast." The smile on his face bordered on creepy.

91

MIAMI, FLORIDA
4:38 A.M. EDT

Walid was livid.

"*SYSTEMS CRASH?*"

And confused.

"*VIRUS? CAN'T OVERRIDE?*"

"*WHAT THE HELL'S GOING ON?*"

His comrade in Little Havana wasn't responding to his texts.

Walid didn't know that when his fellow psychopath began typing in the four-digit override code—the code that was supposed to shut down all six computers if something went wrong—that code activated and sent out a virus.

A virus Branco created and buried in the code. It searched out, located, and attacked all computers used by other SOC cells—as well as the computers of every individual business and organization that had ever lent any degree of support to the SOC.

As in Miami, all SOC computers around the world would be destroyed—the processors getting so hot that their hard drives would literally melt—which would cause circuitry overloads—which would spark electrical fires in the structures where they were housed.

Attacking the computers of those organizations that supported the SOC, the virus acted differently. It emptied bank accounts, corrupted all files, then crashed the computers, but left four lines of code on the computer monitors. That code was the cyber trail leading back to the origin of the virus. The computer of Walid-Orville.

PENTANGELO GROUP HEADQUARTERS
1:45 A.M. PDT

The master monitor came alive with bright flashes of explosions occurring in Aden, Yemen; Aqaba, Jordan; Beirut, Lebanon; and twenty-one other seaport cities throughout the Middle East.

These were the locations of warehouses storing the weapons and explosives provided by Pentangelo Group, as well as barracks built adjacent to the warehouses that housed the Soldiers of the Caliphate.

The five smaller monitors sitting underneath the master monitor displayed infrared images of dozens of structures exploding and soldiers already dead or still burning to death.

"Gotcha now, assholes," Darcy McManus said, taking a slow sip of her coffee.

With her index finger, Patino tapped out the timing of the explosions, her way of running a real-time double-check of the blast triggers she had configured.

She felt no remorse for the death and chaos she had helped cause. She valued life and looked at all people, even bin Laden and those as misguided as he, as children of God. But inwardly she had to laugh. On the one hand, if it were not for those misguided children of God like the SOC, bin Laden, al-Qaeda, et al., she would still have both her legs and be teaching fourth grade in an elementary school somewhere in Orange County, California. On the other hand, she'd be bored sick.

As Stackhouse watched a barracks housing Caliphate soldiers blow up on the monitor that flashed "Yemen," he was even more appreciative of the small network of people—some of them from his racing days—he had brought together.

Granted, working with Doyle for as long as they had had made all of them very wealthy. But none of them lived the kind of lifestyle that demanded they keep working for him. And God knows if they were ever caught, all of them together wouldn't be able to come up with enough money to keep from, at worst, being killed or, at best, being locked away in some CIA black site in some third-world country where sunlight had to be piped in.

So why did they take the risk? Stackhouse made a mental note to ask them in a couple of months when they all got together at his quaint little seven-thousand-square-foot "bungalow" in the Caymans.

Cy's and Lonnie's attention was drawn to the infrared imaging of three Caliphate soldiers going airborne, blown out of an exploding truck parked next to a burning warehouse.

"Not like the old days," Cy mused to Lonnie.

"Yeah," Lonnie replied, "in the old days the bad guys were smarter. They never would have gotten in the truck."

Branco enjoyed watching the fruits of his labors, because like Patino, he considered the Soldiers of the Caliphate, and everybody like them, the enemy.

"Ding dong," he proclaimed with a distinct lack of compassion, "the witch is definitely dead."

"Job well done, Russell," Marcus said.

The two men looked at each other, recalling the hard words they had thrown at one another over the whys and wherefores of what was happening now.

"Thanks, Boss. Sorry it took me a while to figure out what you meant. I'm not a good listener sometimes…well, most of the time, actually."

Darcy smiled. "You're a pain in the ass, Russell. But you're our pain in the ass."

Watanabe and Lonnie shook their heads and chuckled.

"Ms. Patino…Connie?" Marcus said.

Her head snapped up. Never had he called her by her first name.

He gave her a parental smile. "You know how brilliant you are.
Let me also say that I am very glad you are on our side."

Looking around the room, Marcus announced, "Debrief is at
ten a.m. If you want to save yourself a drive home and back, you
know where the beds and showers are. BUDS will be bringing in
brunch. Get some sleep. Job well done, everybody."

92

EIGHTH AND FIGUEROA STREETS OFFICE
LOS ANGELES, CALIFORNIA
THREE WEEKS LATER

The receptionist made no attempt to be cordial as she led Marcus, Lonnie, and Darcy to the conference room.

Marcus took the seat at the far end of the table, with Lonnie and Darcy taking the seats flanking him.

Several seconds later, the Coordinator walked in. He paused when he saw where they were sitting, Marcus in particular.

Poker-faced, Marcus knew he was sitting in the Coordinator's chair. Darcy pursed her lips. Lonnie tipped his head back and smiled. He didn't want to miss seeing that split second when the man would fight saying, *Hey, that's my chair!*

The Coordinator didn't disappoint.

Darcy found him to be an easy read, the kind of man who divided everyone into two categories: assets and those who might one day become assets.

Marcus noticed his suit was expensive, but not well-tailored. *His wife probably buys his clothes.*

Lonnie saw him as the generic "No Man." Average height, average build, average looks. The guy no one would notice, even if he was the only one in the room.

"Well played, Marcus," the Coordinator said in a flat tone.

Elbows on the table, fingers steepled, Marcus leaned forward, rested his chin on his fingertips, glanced down for just a moment, then put his hands on the table, palms down.

"Your agency is going to leave me, my family, my associates, my friends, and all their friends and families alone," he ordered. "No more school-bus accidents. No more date-rape drugs and disgusting photos. No more threats to my wife for things done in the service of her country."

The Coordinator shook his head and chuckled.

"Marcus…you should have brought your wife in for this dramatic presentation. She's the actor, not you."

"I'm not acting," Marcus replied. "I'm terminating our business dealings." He leaned back in the chair.

"We will do nothing more for your agency. And if we are targeted again, we will demonstrate, as we recently did, that my organization's capabilities extend far beyond supplying specialized equipment."

The Coordinator put his elbows on the arms of the chair and rubbed his hands together as his smile widened.

"Your people are talented amateurs, Marcus. They're like these suckers"—he gestured toward the windows— "who drive up to Vegas a couple of times a month to play poker. They win a few thousand dollars and think they're world-class card players. But their tells are obvious, and the professional players just humor them. Your little crew's tells are more subtle, I'll grant you, but nothing a professional wouldn't notice."

Marcus glanced at Darcy and then at Lonnie. "Does it occur to you," he countered as he looked back at the Coordinator, "that those tells are noticeable because our people want them noticed? So other things will be missed?"

The Coordinator's eyes narrowed; his smirk momentarily disappeared.

"Nice play, Marcus. But we both know it was only a play…with nothing to back it up."

Marcus raised his eyebrows and shrugged, then nodded to Darcy and Lonnie. All three stood up and made their way to the conference-room door.

At the door, Marcus paused and turned to the Coordinator. "Suit yourself," he said. Closing the door, he gave the receptionist a polite nod.

93

No one said anything as Darcy pulled onto the Hollywood Freeway.

"We need to make a stop," she announced.

Lonnie glanced at Darcy, bushy eyebrows knitted in a question, then turned to look at Marcus seated in the back. Marcus shook his head. *I have no idea.*

The drive from the building at Eighth and Figueroa to the stately Jewish cemetery took less than twenty minutes. Darcy had called earlier for the location so she could drive straight to the gravesite. The setting surprised her and Marcus. Rather than being in one of the newer sections, Brian Shapiro's grave was in an older area, surrounded by other graves.

The gold lettering on the simple black tablet read:

Brian Isaac Shapiro
Brother Friend
April 6, 1947–September 26, 2014

Lonnie looked up and down the long row of tablets, nodding. Marcus and Darcy looked at him, puzzled.

"You guys don't get it?" They shook their heads. Lonnie was surprised.

"Shap spent the last two-thirds of his life separated from real people. This is perfect. He isn't isolated anymore. You see that, don't you, Marcus?"

Lonnie looked down at the tablet on Shapiro's grave. Taking off his glasses and putting them in his jacket pocket, silent tears rolled down his cheeks. Then, from deep inside, he began to sob.

Darcy gently touched Marcus's shoulder and nodded. Marcus stepped over to Lonnie and wrapped his arms around his oldest and closest friend. They stood together for a long time.

94

Eighth and Figueroa Streets
Los Angeles, California
Two weeks later

Just before the coordinator left for the day—he never told anyone when he planned to leave—an administrative aide brought him an iPad showing an email with a long attachment. It came to the email address of a dummy company that served as one of the unit's nondescript public faces.

"Read and reply with response for publication," it read, above the signature of a prolific far-left British blogger. He had no credibility because he posted nothing but breathless, unsourced, anti-government screeds. On *Meet the Press*, a respected editor once said, "He makes WikiLeaks look like *The Christian Science Monitor*."

However, the attached article, which the Coordinator read quickly and closely, contained five facts about the unit's operations that were completely accurate.

Fortunately for him, the facts were so obscure that no one outside the unit, and only a few inside, would know what they described. And they were surrounded by so much fabricated, over-the-top ranting that no more than three or four readers, including the Coordinator, would notice the accurate details.

The blogger wanted a response within fifteen minutes, or he

would post the article with the line, "The government agency in question refused to respond to repeated requests for comment." Of course the Coordinator wouldn't respond.

He had his IT director hack the email, which had come from the blogger's site. The IT people would track the reporter's emails until they found the source of those five facts.

"Shouldn't take long to find," the IT director assured him. Five minutes later, the Coordinator left for the weekend.

He arrived at his tastefully expensive but understated home in Calabasas around three o'clock. He and his wife weren't due at their daughter's place in Simi Valley until six. He could get in two more hours of work.

He wasn't surprised when he saw the IT director's message in his inbox. *Good work*, he said to himself. He opened what he knew would be detailed information on the blogger's source.

"Pls call secure," the email read.

That made sense. Keep the electronic footprint on this as small as possible. The Coordinator picked up his secure line and called the IT director, who answered immediately.

"Hello, sir."

"You found the source."

"Yes, sir." His voice was shaky.

"And?" It was as much an accusation as a question.

There was a long pause on the IT director's end.

"Sir," he said, "there's something really weird here."

"Define 'weird,'" the Coordinator demanded. He heard the IT director draw a breath, hold it, and exhale more loudly than he'd intended.

"Sir, it tracks to your personal email account."

"What?" the Coordinator roared. It was for times like this that his home office was totally soundproof and protected by a low-level white-noise emitter.

"How could you incompetents possibly track top-secret information from my personal, secure account to that...anarchist?"

"I know, sir." The IT director was talking fast. "It doesn't make any sense to us either. We're still on it, and whoever this guy's been talking to, we'll find out how he did it. You can count on it."

"I am," the Coordinator said coldly. "Contact me as soon as you have correct information to report." He hung up.

95

Five minutes later, the Coordinator's incoming email notification sounded.

The subject line read, "Questions." The return path was blank. The Coordinator's hands felt cold. The unit's email system was programmed to always show the return path: the actual one, not some made-up address.

He opened the message, and his breathing got shallow.

"Following your meeting two weeks ago, you asked your associate, 'Who the hell do they think they are?' Of course, it was a rhetorical question. But it wasn't the relevant question.

The relevant question is, 'Who do you think you are?' Here is the answer, and some other pertinent information."

When he read the incoming message, the room seemed to spin. The more he read, the faster it spun.

Filling the screen was all his personal information: full name (his real name), date and place of birth, Social Security number, driver's license number, his job title and duties, government ID number, all his secure phone numbers and email accounts, home address, home phone number, cell-phone numbers, every top-secret and public reference about him, information about his family, every job he'd held going back to high school, all his girlfriends—before and during his marriage.

This data was followed by a scan of an email, with his personal account in the return path, detailing the article with the five facts contained in the blog that had been posted less than an hour ago. He felt a pounding in his chest.

There was more.

A detailed summary of the unit's history. Its inception, major players and activities, and some of its most unsavory operations. One operation in particular was highlighted in an essay entitled: "The Long, Slow Death of Brian Shapiro."

The report was a crisply written, exhaustive, compelling narrative of Shapiro's involuntary induction into the unit and his work on operations over more than forty years.

The report also included links supporting the facts of those operations. The Coordinator read things he'd never known but sensed, as he read them, that they were true: names, dates, places, outcomes. All carefully and—he had been sure—completely buried from scrutiny by anyone outside the unit he'd worked to expand over the past twelve years.

The Coordinator felt a tightening in his chest as he read the "cc:" line.

Listed were the names and email addresses of the world's leading news organizations and most influential correspondents, columnists, and bloggers, and the names of the chairs and ranking members of the of the House and Senate Intelligence and Foreign Relations Committees.

His heart was pounding in his ears. The more he read, the louder the pounding got—until he read the last name on the list. POTUS.

Then, the pounding stopped.

If you enjoyed
The Redemption of Lonnie Tate,
please keep reading for an exciting preview
of the next
Lonnie Tate thriller

Coming later this year

Available in print and ebook
from Golden Alley Press

OFFICE OF HOWARD DADE, DIRECTOR
CENTRAL INTELLIGENCE AGENCY
LANGLEY, VIRGINIA
LATE AUGUST 1968

Standing five feet, nine inches tall, Cyrus Watanabe had a face that revealed a life that had taken him around *more* than a couple of blocks, *more* than a couple of times. For CIA Director Howard Dade, Watanabe was a "Fixer Extraordinaire."

"You did good, Tate. The Director didn't want to lose you, but he knew you were right. That's why he agreed to let you go back to the Corps. That's why I'm here."

Lonnie Tate slumped in his chair. "So... just exactly where am I going?"

Watanabe gave Lonnie's shoulder a squeeze. "First things first, Sergeant. You have to know where you've been before you can go back to where you're going."

The fixer picked up two brown folders, the SRBs (service record books) Dade had left sitting on his desk.

The one in his right hand was almost four inches thick. It detailed everything about Lonnie's service in the Marine Corps: Boot camp. Graduating first in his class in language school. Three combat meritorious field promotions in Vietnam that took him from PFC to Sergeant after only eleven months in country. It detailed the circumstances surrounding Lonnie's two Purple Hearts, Bronze Star with combat V for valor, and Silver Star. The remaining 197 pages were redacted.

"*This* you?" Watanabe shook his head, "*Never* existed. Ain't nobody *ever* gonna see it…not even you."

Stuffing it in a briefcase, Cyrus handed Lonnie the much thinner SRB.

"*This*…is you now."

Walking to the door, Watanabe stopped and turned back to Lonnie. "Memorize it. Know it inside out, but *never* quote it," he warned. "You start talking like your SRB, somebody smart is going to know you and your SRB are bullshit.

"You got three hours, Slick."

Feeling like his brain had just gone run through the "extra dry" cycle in a clothes dryer, Lonnie sat down and opened the folder. A manila envelope lay on top of the first page. A note was attached.

You won't need this until you get out, but you need to see it – CW

Opening it, Lonnie discovered his DD-214, his Separation-Discharge papers. The official government document attesting to his service in the United States military. Regardless of the branch of service one served, *everybody* had one. It was postdated to the date he would get out of the Marine Corps: 15 March 1969.

Not surprisingly, the *only* similarity between the LONNIE TATE on the DD-214 in the SRB, and Lonnie, himself…was the name, Lonnie Tate.

1

The Oval Office
1600 Pennsylvania Avenue
Autumn 2014

The President gave the nation's chief spy a hard look. "You've been with CIA for, what…25 years? Don't tell me you haven't known, or at least heard, about this?"

The Director had been with the agency for twenty-three years, the past 18 months as DCI. Right now, it felt like it had been an eternity.

"As a young agent, you always heard rumors." He chuckled silently. "An 'agency within the agency.' No official name, but veteran agency officers referred to it as Room 319. One day I got up the guts to ask one of them about it. He looked at me for about a minute then said, 'Don't believe all the crap you hear in the hallways, kid.'"

POTUS leaned on the arm of the couch. "So, besides the guy who was directing this little shop of horrors—the guy who had the conveniently fatal heart attack—how long before we know who these people are?"

The Director took his time before answering. He was measuring how little he could say and still give the President enough assurance that this mess would go away quietly.

"Sir," he spoke softly, but his concern was evident by his hooded brow. "All that information about Room 319 that you, the committee chairs, and the media received *isn't* everything the source sent."

The President leaned forward. "Go on."

"I'm phasing out all Black units that blur the line in the agency's charter—immediately."

The President looked at him skeptically.

Knowing POTUS was about to ask him a question he could not and would not answer, the Director of Central Intelligence continued.

"With all due respect, sir. Delving into this eliminates any plausible deniability on the part of the Oval Office." He paused. "Sir, that email that got such wide circulation? It's compromised a lot already."

Over the next month, the DCI did what he had wanted to do ever since his appointment. Using what was known as the "FEE-PRO Closing Protocols" established decades earlier by legendary DCI Howard Dade, he terminated all operations related to the Black Ops unit informally called Room 319. It required the retirement or reassignment of all the unit's staff and assets. But it was a godsend.

Finding the source of the emails was another matter.

The "best of the best" of the agency's IT wizards would spend thousands of hours chasing down millions of digital blind alleys; which, after 20 months, led to a name. No face, driver's license, birth certificate, or passport—just a name: Walid Abdul Walid.

Nacogdoches, Texas
Autumn 2014

No longer going by the name Walid Abdul Walid, Texas born and bred Orville Dwayne Bartlett's days as an Islamic extremist were over.

It seemed being the sole survivor of the brutal attack and annihilation of a jihadist organization known as the SOC, the Soldiers of the Caliphate, was proving to be an unlucky thing.

All the anti-American business entities that had set up shell companies to funnel billions of dollars to the SOC—all the private banks and money laundering agents employed—were now bankrupt. And blaming Walid Abdul Walid.

The bad news: Orville had a price—a *huge* price—on his head. The really bad news: a few people had already tried to collect. Over the past few weeks, running for his life had taken Orville Dwayne Bartlett from Miami to Italy, to Greece, to Syria, and back to Texas. And he'd be moving again in another week, leaving him no time to find out who had set him up.

2

PENTANGELO GROUP HEADQUARTERS
ENCINO, CALIFORNIA
OCTOBER 2014

Darcy McManus, chief adviser and organizational gatekeeper for Pentangelo Group, sat across from Marcus Pentangelo's desk, arms folded in a pose that said *Absolutely not*. "Marcus, that's the most ridiculous thing you've said in the 40 years we've known each other."

Marcus Pentangelo wasn't surprised by her reaction. It was her vehemence that caught him a little off-guard.

"Darcy," Marcus began in his college professor tone, "it's the most logical step to take. You know how and what we do better than anyone." He raised his hand when she started to object. "*Anyone*," he emphasized, "including me.

3

On final approach to
Owen Roberts International Airport
George Town, Cayman Islands
Late October 2014

Buckling his seatbelt, Lonnie Tate took in the luxuriously appointed cabin of Marcus Pentangelo's private jet—a Gulfstream G280.

"Gotta tell ya, Marcus. *This*...is one nice ride. Should you decide to trade it in?" Lonnie chuckled, "Don't. Sell it to me."

Marcus looked up from the magazine he was reading. "Can't do that. She was a gift from the Prime Minister of Israel. Bibi would be insulted."

Lonnie gave Marcus a *yeah, right* glance. No doubt Marcus and Benjamin Netanyahu had sat in a few clandestine meetings together. After all, Pentangelo Group was the exclusive supplier of sophisticated weaponry to the IDF and Mossad. However, implying that the arms dealer and Israel's Prime Minister were BFFs by using the PM's nickname, "Bibi"—something reserved only for those closest to him—that was stretching Marcus's pranking skills way beyond their limits.

"*Bibi... gave* you this aircraft," Lonnie waived his hand around the cabin, "as a *gift*."

"Yes. A token of his appreciation. We'll be going to Tel Aviv to meet with him as soon as we've finished our business with Julian. Be nice, and Bibi might let you back in his country without an escort."

As the G280 touched down, its two Honeywell HTF7000 engines automatically throttled down and the auto brake system engaged. Using another 1800 feet of runway to slow down, the sleek, twin-engine jet made a ninety-degree turn to its port side and taxied another 50 yards, coming to a stop inside the Pentangelo Group's private hangar.

After unbuckling their seat belts and retrieving their briefcases, Marcus stood up and turned to Lonnie, "Ya know," he paused and gestured around the cabin, "there's a possibility that one day this nice ride will be yours."

Lonnie sighed. "Keep your day job, Marcus. You make a far better gun runner than you do a comic."

Marcus turned to make his way to the door to exit the aircraft. "We're death merchants, not gun runners, Lonnie. There's a difference. And I'm not trying to be funny. Because like your ol' buddy, Bob Dylan says"—Marcus knew Lonnie hated Dylan— "the times, they are a changin'."

4

Julian Zacharias was 47 years old when he was accepted into the School of Law at the University of California at Los Angeles. It was a journey that came by way of four years, 1957-1961, in the United States Marine Corps. Then two and a half years, stretched out over ten, of night classes at a junior college, all the while putting in 20 years with the Los Angeles Police Department.

Working all the overtime he could get, taking odd jobs on his days off, along with school, made dating opportunities scarce and any long-term relationships impossible.

Being smart with his paychecks and saving his G.I. Bill for when he transferred to UCLA was financially challenging, but tolerable.

Julian turned 50 the summer before his third and final year of law school.

Despite his exceptional GPA, he wasn't surprised when most law firms were underwhelmed at taking a 50-year old intern seriously. Especially an intern who was a former cop with seven years on the street, five as a motor officer, and the last eight as a decorated vice and homicide detective.

One law firm was intrigued, however: Seca & Marsh, a law firm that dealt exclusively in international shipping, trade, and wealth and estate management law.

Malcolm Seca and Travis Marsh worked out of their sprawling, ranch style homes in what Julian called "the rich-white-folk section" of the far west end of the San Fernando Valley, Woodland Hills.

Impressed with Julian's transcripts and GPA, and what they called his "*former* legal career," the partners were even more impressed when they interviewed him. They brought him in and taught him everything they knew.

The end result: Julian Zacharias was to the world of international shipping, trade, and wealth/estate management law, what Pentangelo Group was to international arms dealing—with the exception of three things: Everybody in Julian's world knew *who* he was, *where* he was located, and those who were foolish enough to go against him in a courtroom never wanted to do it again.

In the spring of 1997, Pentangelo Group's logistics director, Doyle Stackhouse, decided it was time for Marcus to meet the man who was key in Doyle being able to do what he did when Stackhouse was working his logistical magic for NASCAR and various Formula1 racing teams.

That was the beginning of the Pentangelo family and Pentangelo Group's personal and professional relationship with Julian. It also led to Julian meeting a subtly sassy lady his same age, in the summer of 1998. Her name was Madeline Del Vecchio.

In meeting Madeline, Julian Zacharias discovered there was more to life than a having a successful law career. In October of 1998, Julian and Madeline were married.

Now, 16 years later, Julian and Madeline decided it was time to have a life that centered on just the two of them. Hence, Julian's call to Marcus to come to the Caymans for a meeting. Julian's timing was perfect. Marcus had decided some things as well.

"We'll be there in two days," Marcus cheerfully told Julian

"Good. You're bringing Mary?"

"No. Bringing an old Marine buddy of mine. I told you about him."

Julian chuckled. "You're bringing Tate, huh? Marcus…this

meeting is a future plans kind of thing. No one needs to be maimed or killed. You sure he won't get bored?"

Ironically, Julian and Lonnie's paths had crossed several years previously, when Julian was a police officer. Neither man remembered meeting, but both had never forgotten the incident.

A WORD FROM THE AUTHORS

Thank you for reading *The Redemption of Lonnie Tate.*
We hope you enjoyed it.

Want the backstory? Read *NECK DEEP.* In this look into Lonnie Tate's time in Vietnam, we learn the origins of his enduring friendship with Marcus Pentangelo and Brian Shapiro and why they have each other's backs whenever they're in trouble, neck deep.

NECK DEEP is $.99 on Amazon.com or FREE if you sign up for our occasional newsletter. We include details of new releases, special offers, and other bits of news relating to our characters. No sharing of your info, no spam.

To sign up for our mailing list and get your free PDF of *NECK DEEP*, go to:

www.marstersandkoernig.com *or*
www.goldenalleypress.com/lonnie-tate-thrillers

You can make a difference . . .
Reviews are the most powerful weapon we have when it comes to getting our books noticed by other readers. If you've enjoyed this book, please consider leaving a review on Amazon.com.
— Loren and Gus

ABOUT THE AUTHORS

Loren Marsters and Gus Koernig became a writing team in 2013 when Loren sent Gus 28 pages of a spy novel he'd been trying to write for the last thirty years. That quickly turned into a labor of love (and occasional head-butting) they both call the most fun they've ever had writing.

From Simi Valley, California, Loren Marsters joined the Marine Corps in 1966 and did a tour in Vietnam before going back to college and parlaying his degree in communications into a career in advertising. Other than that, he leaves it up to the reader to figure out which aspects of Lonnie Tate, his protagonist, are autobiographical.

Loren and his wife, Kristina, live in Mesa, Arizona. Between them they have six children.

Gus Koernig, an award-winning journalist from San Francisco, reported from Russia during the first months after the collapse of the Soviet Union. In his 30-year career in TV news, he has been a reporter and anchor for a number of network-affiliated stations. Gus has ghost-written five books on five different topics.

The father of nine children, he and his wife, Glenda, live in Mesa, Arizona, where they enjoy traveling and hiking.

www.marstersandkoernig.com

www.facebook.com/MarstersandKoernig

fanmail: marstersandkoernig@goldenalleypress.com

ACKNOWLEDGEMENTS

Loren: It's not cliché to say that this book never would have been written were it not for my wife Kristina's never-ending love, encouragement, harassment, and all the things that go into getting a writer out of their own way.

Thank you also to author Doc Ephraim Bates for reading our work and liking it enough to refer us to his publisher; to playwright and screenwriter Chuck Evered; and to a certain Ventura County Superior Court judge who did me the biggest favor of my life. To Gus Koernig, my co-author, for being a great friend as well as great writer; and Nancy and Michael Sayre, our publishers at Golden Alley Press. To Brian Perry of Brian Perry Publishing, whose first cover design inspired the creation of the new cover and whose book trailers are the best I've seen, anywhere. And I can't leave out a whole bunch of Facebook friends (you know who you are) that cheered us on and bought the first version of our book.

Gus: Like Loren, I had the good fortune to marry up, and the editing, inspiration, encouragement, and love my wife Glenda provides are beyond my ability as a writer to describe.

I also want to thank all my friends, family, and people who've filled special places in my life for reading the manuscript and coming up with questions and guidance that helped more than you can imagine.

Special thanks to my Mesa Community College classmate Brandon Rollins for steering me right on contemporary Marine jargon, and my grandson, Zac Farr, for help with Aussie slang and dialect. Let me say "me too" to the folks on Loren's list who gave us direction and opened doors we didn't even know about.

And finally, I can't thank Loren enough for inviting me to join him in something I've always dreamed of doing and, after a lifetime of false starts, has finally come true. Thank you for being my friend.

CPSIA information can be obtained
at www.ICGtesting.com
Printed in the USA
LVHW01s0057080618
579983LV00011B/26/P